THE

TALISMAN

Also by Brenda Pandos

◆

The Sapphire Talisman-Book Two

THE
Emerald
TALISMAN
THE TALISMAN SERIES - BOOK ONE

BRENDA PANDOS

OBSIDIAN MOUNTAIN PUBLISHING

PRAISE FOR THE EMERALD TALISMAN

"The action started immediately and pulled me in. The author also described the scenes very well, and they were easy to picture in my mind. The author's writing style flowed fairly effortlessly."

- Amazon.com

". . . offers suspense, edge of your seat action, danger at every turn, and a swoon worthy bad boy- the perfect recipe for a great read! I was turning the pages of this book late into the night because I HAD to see what was going to happen next!"

-Jennifer, Extreme Reader Book Reviews

"When I first began reading this book, I truly lost track of time. The excitement I felt in the first few moments of this book carries throughout. Her characters are well developed and concise, emitting a feeling of true connection to the author herself."

-Abra Ebner, Author of Feather Series and Knights Angels

". . . was an enchanting, stimulating, and eloquently written book. Brenda introduced a promising vampire series that would interest fans of Twilight and The Vampire Diaries."

- Eleni, La Femme Readers

". . . in the story, vampires are more of a force than a constant. Second, the singular characteristics that Pandos grants her vampires are interesting and could define it as a crossover between Twilight and Buffy The Vampire Slayer."

- Michelle, book reviewer, windowpane-memoirs.com

". . . was a fantastic vampire novel. I don't usually like a lot of vampire stories but this one was nowhere near as typical as some. I was entertained by it and the book kept me interested until the last page."

– Katie, Katie's Book Blog

Pandos, Brenda, 1972 –
The Emerald Talisman: A novel/by Brenda Pandos

Cover design and layout by the author herself.
www.theemeraldtalisman.com

Published by Obsidian Mountain Publishing
www.obsidianmtpublishing.com
P.O. Box 601901
Sacramento, CA 95860

Summary: When Julia Parker, a sixteen-year-old with the paranormal ability to read people's emotions, accidentally falls prey to a vampire, she becomes aware that sometimes animals and people aren't who they seem. To survive, she must rely on her psychic abilities to help her decide who to trust and who to love.

Printed in the United States of America
ISBN: 978-0-578-05339-4
LCCN - 2010910609

5 6 7 8 9 10

To Corinne – Friends like you are one in a million.

To Dori – You found this needle in a haystack and I'm forever grateful. May our stories bring happiness to many.

LATER THAT DAY

*W*as it my fate to die at sixteen? I didn't want to, but I couldn't see any other way out of this nightmare, unless I was dreaming. My situation seemed too surreal to be true. The pain told me otherwise. I was wide awake and about to take my last breath.

In the dead of night, I hung precariously from a tree root that slowly unraveled out of the cliff face, hands bloody and raw. Above me, an animal waited to rip me to shreds. Below, the jagged rocks of the riverbed threatened to smash my body to pieces. I was trapped in between with aching arms, waiting for a miracle as dirt continued to rain down on my head. My lifeline was slipping further down the rock face, taking me closer toward my doom.

My pleas for help echoed throughout the ravine, but were greeted with silence.

It was over unless . . .

1 - DECISIONS

*W*hat kind of secret superpower would you want, Julia?"

Startled out of my usual daydream I shifted my focus to Katie's chestnut-colored eyes, concerned about her choice of subject.

"Why?" I asked, trying to act natural.

"You know that TV show about heroes with superpowers? I've been thinking about how cool it'd be to have one," she answered innocently.

"Oh," I said, relieved she didn't mean anything by her question. My brain froze though, unable to find a legitimate power. "Flying, I guess."

"That's so cliché," she said with a raised pierced eyebrow. "Everybody wants that. Pick something more obscure."

I wanted to laugh at her for using such 'big"words and tell her to mind her own business, but didn't want to look obvious. Super powers weren't all that glamorous like they portrayed on TV; they always came with a price.

"Ummm ..."

I scanned the table looking for help when I sensed Cameron's confidence. He should've been offended that Katie interrupted his riveting discussion about Calculus, but he had something he was dying to tell us though the expression on his fair, freckle covered face didn't show it.

"I don't know. What about you, Cam?" I asked hoping to deflect the question.

"That's easy; shape shifting ability." His blue eyes twinkled beneath his mop of wild red hair.

A question like that wouldn't have bothered me, if I were normal. But I did have a secret power, or gift as people might call it and I wanted to keep it that way—a secret.

"Shape shifting?" Dena asked. "What's that?"

Cameron straightened his shoulders and amusement played across his face because the conversation shifted back to his in-depth knowledge.

"To turn into anything I wanted. An animal, another person, an inanimate object, whatever suits me."

"That's cheating. You can only shape shift into one thing," Katie said, feeling annoyed but kept an aloof disposition.

I smiled. Cameron wasn't playing the game by her rules.

"Hey, it's my power, I wield it as I see fit."

Katie made a face before moving to her next victim, Dena, who now had an air of confidence as well.

The first time I was aware I was different was the last time I saw my mother. We were happy, together, laughing and holding hands when I was suddenly consumed with fear and pain no five-year-old should have to experience. The feelings seared into my conscience forever. I've never been sure if I'd always had this sixth sense of reading other's emotions, or if somehow the ill-fated event of my mother's disappearance caused the change, but I've been aware of it ever since.

To look at me, you'd never know. I'm just an average teenager with a slight build, dishwater-blonde hair and hazel eyes trying my hardest to blend in. People say I'm shy, which is fine. I'd rather have that label than "freak" any day. I do seem to wander off topic in conversations, frequently appearing ADD, but that's because it's become increasingly difficult to concentrate among my overly hormonal peers. And today was no exception; Katie's boredom screamed so loudly, I shouldn't be able to concentrate. Luckily for me, I've learned how to ignore her.

At the moment, I sat at our usual table in the quad on a chilly Fall day with Samantha, Dena, Morgan, Cameron and Katie waiting for fifth period to start. Most of us had been friends since elementary school and met for lunch almost every day.

Cameron had been rambling about Ms. Smith's lecture in Calculus, a class none of us are in, before Katie so rudely changed the subject. Even though he bored everyone, I appreciated his enthusiasm for math. He just didn't realize we didn't share the same affinity for the subject, which wasn't his fault. Gifted with smarts, he lacked social graces. I was willing to overlook that flaw, because he was a genuinely nice guy with a huge heart.

"Seriously, Dena? Only *you* would pick a super power that would help people," Katie said in contempt.

Katie's comment snapped me back into the conversation. Mentally, I'd drifted away again. Knowing Dena, I'm sure she picked something to save the world.

"Well isn't that the point? To use it for good?" Dena said, furrowing her brow. "What's wrong with wanting to heal people?"

"I think it's a very good super power. I wish I'd have thought of it," Samantha chimed in.

"I agree," I said.

"Of course you can use your power to do good, but that's not the point," Katie said pretentiously.

"I agree with Dena," Morgan said quickly. "That's better than the one I thought of."

Morgan, somewhat attractive with his dark hair and smoldering auburn eyes, was a newer addition to our little clique. Even though he didn't let on to anyone, I knew he had a crush on Dena. Daily, I felt his internal struggles. His yearning was very subtle on the outside, but not to me; the chemistry was so strong sometimes it felt like I could cut it with a knife.

"Well, what did you pick?" Dena asked.

"Oh it's stupid," he said and turned away, averting her stare.

Katie laughed. "I bet its x-ray vision," she said, flipping her short raven-colored hair, currently tinged with magenta highlights.

Morgan's cheeks flushed. "Shut-up."

Dena put her hand on his shoulder and his elation erupted,

subduing his anger.

"Well, since the rest of you won't answer . . ." Katie said, glaring at Morgan. "I'll share mine. I want mind reading abilities."

I wanted to laugh and say *oh no you don't*, but then I'd have to explain why. Of all people, that gift might be the medicine she needed to be humbled. People didn't like her total disregard of people's feelings when she verbally marched right over them.

The problem was, unlike Dena, Katie knew she was attractive. Her conceit caused her to be pretty shallow most of the time. But since I knew she was just as insecure as the rest of us, I'd encouraged everyone to give her some leeway, hoping we'd rub off on her in time. Today I didn't feel so inclined.

"I don't think I could handle knowing what people are thinking of me," Dena said softly, tilting her head down, hiding under her long white-blond hair.

I wondered if she'd feel the same way knowing people envied her.

Morgan grew nervous. I sensed he definitely didn't want her to read his mind, especially at this moment.

Currently, Katie's crush was on a very popular Senior, Tyler Kennedy, who had a serious girlfriend and wouldn't give Katie the time of day. Since Katie felt she was far prettier than his girlfriend, she saw it as a competition and tried to gain his attention any chance she got. I really wanted to tell her Tyler picked his girlfriend, Mandy, because she was pretty *and* one of the kindest girls in school, but I knew she wouldn't believe me.

I watched her glance wistfully in Tyler's direction. Mind reading definitely would've helped her formulate her next "accidental" interaction, but then she'd really know what Tyler thought.

"Well, I'd like to control the weather," Sam said.

Samantha or Sam as we called her, with her impeccable style and long brown locks was my very best friend. She was the most genuine and happiest person I've ever known—someone I called *safe*.

I've always struggled with making new friends. It's difficult to give people a real chance when you're able to size someone up as soon as you meet them. Most people are untrustworthy, so I prefer to stick with my short list of safe friends. And if Katie didn't watch it, it might grow shorter soon.

"That would be cool. Why don't you make a hurricane or something, so we don't have to go to 5th period," I said.

Sam closed her green eyes and threw out her hands, acting as if she was summoning some powerful force of nature and then peeked out to see if anything happened, which it didn't.

"Crap, I need to figure out how to use it."

A sly smile crossed her face. Everyone laughed except Katie. I'm sure she thought we were making fun of her.

"So anyone ask you to homecoming yet?" Katie asked in my direction.

What's with the questions today?

"Oh . . . um . . . no. I think I have to work that day."

"Work?" She turned her nose up in disgust. "But it's homecoming! Don't you want to go?"

"Not really?" I said, not meaning it to sound like a question.

If I really wanted to go, Cameron would take me. We'd been each other's date, as friends, for quite a few dances. But homecoming didn't appeal to me for some reason. Not only did I dislike the feelings of the crowd at dances, but I currently didn't have any prospects. It seemed the short list of guys I liked didn't know I was alive.

"I wish Tyler would ask me," Katie murmured to herself, glancing over her shoulder again.

"I'm not going either," Cameron said trying to sound like he didn't care.

"Why not?" Dena asked, sounding a little disappointed.

"Dances are lame," he said, with a detached disposition.

I knew his lack of self-confidence was the real reason, but didn't know how I could help. I had just as much trouble with guys as he had with girls.

"I don't know if I'm going either. I don't have a date yet," Dena said while looking down at her tray, playing with her uneaten pudding.

"Didn't Brady ask you?" Sam asked.

"Yeah, he did. I didn't accept yet. I don't know—" Dena's eyes drifted in Morgan's direction. "I was waiting for someone else to ask me."

I casually glanced at Morgan, who suddenly was interested in flicking the peeling paint off the table. I wanted to kick him so he'd wake up and pay attention. It was crazy they both wanted to go with each other, but neither would make the first move. Maybe letting Morgan know she wanted him to ask her was exactly what he needed since he wasn't picking up on Dena's body language.

"I've decided to go with Todd after all," Sam said.

"Oh, that's cool," I said.

I had noticed Todd McMullan, a Senior, showed a little interest in Sam and hoped he would ask her to the dance. Sam already mentioned privately she had a crush on him, but didn't want to say anything to the group because Katie had a bad habit of teasing. But Sam hadn't told me he'd asked her yet.

"Come on Cam, I'll go with you," I finally offered feeling a tiny bit of peer pressure and sorry for Cam.

"Naw, that's cool. It's no big deal," Cameron said with a waning smile. I think he was tired of the pretenses too.

I didn't want to spend money on something like Homecoming anyway. Besides, Cam had two left feet, so we never actually *danced*. All we really did was go as two singles and spent the rest of the night with friends. I didn't feel up to it this time. I actually would rather work.

I was trying hard to save money for a newer car. Currently, I drove my older brother Luke's 1984 Volkswagen Quantum. He bought it to turn into some sort of veggie oil driving automobile to save money on gas, but never got around to it. He offered to let me drive it until I could get something of my own. It was old but it got me where I needed to go.

I tried to think of something insightful to say to alleviate Cam's discomfort, but was saved by the bell. We sighed in sync as we got up and headed for our respective fifth period classes. Sam and I were the only ones who had Algebra, which was not my favorite class.

"Todd asks you and you don't tell me?" I asked as soon as we were alone, headed down the hall towards our class.

"Well, I was going to. It literally happened right before lunch. He pulled me aside after class, but I had no idea that's what he wanted to talk to me about. He seemed pretty nervous when he asked but so adorable," she said with a grin.

Sam's giddiness was like sun breaking through stormy clouds and I couldn't stay upset at her. Somehow I missed her elation all through lunch. It must have been because I was consumed with dodging Katie's question.

"That's so great," I said.

"You should try to go. Isn't there anyone you want to go with?"

Deep down inside, a part of me wanted to attend, but there wasn't anyone I felt safe to go with. It was hard to try to explain that to Sam. I'd given up on boys, for now anyway. They were all the same to me—immature and focused on *one thing*.

"Really, it's okay. I'm going to skip it this time."

She sighed. I think she wanted to double with me and I felt bad for bailing on her. Maybe I'd try to get Dena and Morgan to go with her and Todd, once I orchestrated Morgan to ask her.

We walked into the classroom and found our seats. A knot

formed in my stomach. Ms. Smith was an incredible teacher, possibly the best at our school, but I was so horrible at math it didn't matter.

"I'm never going to get it," I moaned while we worked in small groups.

"Just double check your work as you go, like this." Her pencil darted across the page, leaving organized sets of numbers meaning something to her, but nothing to me.

I chuckled. "Can't you just do my homework for me?"

Sam rolled her eyes. "With practice, you'll get it, I promise."

"Yeah, right."

A hopeful expression formed on her face. She wasn't going to let me quit. It gave me some confidence I'd actually have a fighting chance to get through this class without flunking. Frankly, I didn't know what I would do without her.

I was the first to get up when the bell rang.

As always, sixth period Spanish flew by and I became anxious to get home. I had a few things to do before leaving for work.

"Do you want me to come over tonight and help you with your Algebra?" Sam asked as we walked to our lockers.

I'd completely forgotten about Algebra and at her mention of it, I groaned. I imaged myself sitting at my desk tempted to snap my pencil in half from the frustration. What do we need Algebra for anyway?

"I think I'll manage. I'm working, but I'll call if I get stuck."

Of course the *managing* part of my comment was an exaggeration. I'd probably just put it off until lunch the next day so she could help me then.

My pocket vibrated with a text message and I took out my phone. It was from Luke.

- Jo is coming for dinner. John is out of town. You working?
Dang it!

I didn't want to miss dinner with Aunt Josephine, or Auntie Jo as we affectionately called her.

- Yeah. What time is she coming over?

Aunt Jo was the closest thing I had to a mother. After our mother's mysterious disappearance, our father moved us from Los Angeles to Scotts Valley. Josephine was his only sister and took care of us while he traveled during our younger years.

- She's coming at five.

I sighed. My shift started at four-thirty.

- I have to work. Why don't you come to the deli for dinner so I can see her?

Even though Aunt Jo lived right around the corner from us, I never wanted to miss an opportunity to spend time with her—without John, her new husband. I tried not to be jealous of him, after all she'd sacrificed everything while we were growing up; she deserved a life of her own. But things didn't feel the same anymore and I didn't feel like I could just drop by now that she was married. And thinking about it reopened a wound I'd tried to forget.

- I'll ask and see. We were planning on having Mexican.

Disappointment flooded me. Not only was I missing out being around the people I loved, I was missing out on my favorite food too.

I worked at Erik's, the best sandwich deli in town. For an emotion reader, it was a job I felt comfortable doing. Something about people being hungry didn't bother me. In all reality though, I didn't need to work. My dad, Russell Parker, made pretty good money as a computer consultant. Since he traveled on business frequently, he wanted everyone available to do things together when he was in town. My job encroached on that time, so he asked me multiple times to quit. It was tempting, but when he was gone, I would get so bored alone at the house since Luke was rarely there. Plus, I liked having my own money to spend as I wanted. But, today I wished I'd taken him up on his offer.

The crowded hallway was already buzzing with weekend plans, even though it was only Tuesday. I had plans. I was scheduled to work.

I shoved my books into my locker and slammed it shut.

"Where'd you park?" I asked Sam as she did the same; her locker just a few down from mine.

"I got a spot in the front today," she said in a teasing tone.

"Oh? Well, I'm in the back today, so I guess I'll see ya tomorrow?"

I was a tad jealous because she'd be home by the time I left the back parking lot, but that's my fault for getting to school at the last minute.

"Yeah. See ya," she called from behind me and we headed in separate directions.

We lived close to my school in a quaint three bedroom, two-story, Cape Cod home, the cutest house on the block. It had a lot of character with navy blue shutters, a large front porch and white picket fence covered in fuchsia-colored climbing roses.

I parked at my usual spot on the street and walked up the cobble stone path to the front door. Luke and Dad were already home, hanging out in the kitchen catching up after Dad's weeklong business trip.

"Welcome home, Dad," I said giving him a big hug.

My dad, a very handsome man in his early fifties, was tall and trim and slightly balding with salt and pepper hair. At the moment, he was still wearing his 'monkey suit', as he liked to call it and appeared tired.

"Thanks. Good to be home, Jules," he said affectionately while he flipped through a huge stack of mail.

"You guys still going to Mexican food for dinner?" I asked, slumping down at the kitchen table already knowing the answer.

"We were talking about it," Dad said.

"Oh, I wish I wasn't working."

"Just call in sick," Luke said as he leaned against the counter, his mouth full of food.

He wore his favorite torn jeans and faded black tee-shirt, eating a bowl of cereal. Every time he leaned over to take a bite, his black hair fell into his eyes and he had to brush it aside.

Luke was four years older than me and still lived at home. He was taking a few courses at the local junior college unsure of what he wanted to do "*when he grew up*" and currently unemployed. So, for him to give me "work" advice was a bit ludicrous.

"I can't do that," I said annoyed he'd even suggested it. "They are depending on me to be there tonight."

"There's a simple solution to this," Dad said, looking at me with kind but weathered eyes. He could give me his full attention now that he'd pulled out all the bills and tossed the rest.

"Dad, we've talked about this before."

"It's just that you're only young once in your life and you'll have plenty of time in your life to work," he said matter-of-factly. "Actually, there's only one person in this room that should be working but isn't, but I'm not pressing the matter since he's still in school."

My dad's eyes stayed glued to me, but Luke instantly got interested in rinsing out his bowl, humming to himself. I chuckled. It seemed comical for a second, until I took to heart what my dad said.

"I know," I mumbled, biting my lip. "Maybe I should quit."

My dad walked over and hugged me again. His disappointment mixed with mine and I found it difficult to stick to my decision, until another idea came to mind.

"Maybe I can get off early."

"I'd like that," he said as he let go of me and took his bags upstairs.

If I left early, at least I wouldn't miss the whole evening and work wouldn't be upset with me. I sat for a few minutes mulling it over while Luke changed the conversation to the most recent car he was dismantling. But I tuned him out as soon as he mentioned distributor caps.

Aladdin, our cat, rubbed up against my leg, begging for some attention. We called her Aladdin, even though it was a boy's name, because one day, she magically showed up and put a spell on us.

I reached down to scratch her ears, but then felt the weight of my procrastination. I couldn't prolong getting ready for work any longer.

"I need to go," I finally said. "Tell Jo I'm sorry, okay?"

I headed upstairs to my room situated in the back of the house and peeled off my school clothes. The sofa burgeoned with my entire wardrobe, making it difficult to find my work polo shirt and khakis.

My Dad was kind enough to give me the master bedroom a few years back. He thought I'd appreciate having my own bathroom, being the only girl in the house. But the best part of this sanctuary wasn't the view out the windows of the redwoods surrounding the patio and creek below. My favorite part was the fact the distance separated me from the rest of the family and allowed me freedom from their emotions—huge bonus.

I touched up my make-up, started some laundry before saying my goodbyes, and ran out the door. I really hoped my idea would work and the deli wouldn't be crowded tonight.

As I started my car and drove down my street, I fought a foreboding feeling I was making a mistake. Unsure, I glanced back at my house through my rearview mirror wondering if I should turn around. But, my sense of responsibility took over and I kept driving unaware my decision to go to work tonight would forever change the course of my destiny.

2 – FALLING

I rushed into the deli, glanced at the clock and breathed a sigh of relief—right on time.

My shift should've started without a hitch except I was starving and the aroma of baking bread hit my stomach like a jackhammer. I would've been snagging a piece if it weren't for Kelly's impatient glare behind a long line of customers. So reluctantly, I deposited my things in the back and tied an apron on instead. My hunger would have to wait until my break.

The deli's interior resembled an old fashioned café, very homey in its decor. An old wooden fence stood, separating where customers ordered and where they sat. Lanterns, wooden wagon wheels, and camping paraphernalia littered the walls along with a potbellied stove in the corner.

I took over the cash register and Kelly left without saying a word. I shrugged it off and greeted my first customer. The quicker I got rid of the line, the sooner I could get out of there. But hope of leaving early turned into disappointment as more and more people came into the deli and I couldn't help them fast enough. I did my best to keep a good attitude, but felt it slipping as I saw my window of opportunity close.

After three grueling hours of serving what seemed like thousands of hungry, demanding customers, the deli was suddenly empty. I was shocked when the manager asked if anyone wanted to go home early and I jumped at the chance.

"Thanks," I called out as I exited the store.

Once outside, I ripped off my apron and ran over to my car, threw it onto the back seat and checked the clock on the dash—7:46. Knowing my family, I suspected they'd eaten already and were home by now. I wondered if I should let them know I was on my way, but decided to surprise them instead.

I flew down the road and imagined their faces, especially Jo's, when I walked in the door. They couldn't continue the ongoing card game *Nertz* without me and I felt tonight that I would be taking the crown from Luke. I smiled and pressed the gas pedal harder.

My car hugged the winding road that flanked the forest surrounding my housing development. I had to drive the long way around, the back entrance still buried by a quarter mile of rock deposited by a mudslide years ago.

It didn't matter—there was only a mile to go and I'd be home in five minutes, but I felt my car jerk. I eased up on the gas, but it jerked again, this time losing power. I panicked and imagined my car dying in the middle of the road so I pulled the car onto the shoulder. To my dismay, the engine sputtered and quit.

"You've got to be kidding me," I muttered.

I tried the starter again. Dread spread throughout my body as I turned the key, listening to it moan over and over without catching. I gave up and rested my head on the steering wheel. There was no use in trying anymore—I was pretty sure I'd run out of gas, again.

Sometime ago, my car decided to permanently display it had a ¼ tank of gas. To keep track of the mileage, I pressed the odometer counter each time I filled up the tank, so I would know when to refill. But the last time I got gas, a really cute guy in a BMW distracted me and I forgot to press the button. After I realized my mistake, I decided to keep track mentally. I should've known the flaw in my plan, since math and I didn't get along.

Luke kept making excuses when I asked him to fix the stupid thing. And for me to spend my hard earned money on someone else's car when I was trying to save money for my own was counterproductive. Shame on me.

I dug in my purse and found my cell phone.

Dad is going to kill me.

This wasn't the first time I'd run out of gas and I'd promised it would never happen again. This would be the third time I'd broken that promise.

The phone was off.

Oh no . . .

I pressed the "on" switch and it flashed "low battery".

My battery is dead too?

I dialed my home number.

Please have enough power for just one phone call.

Before it started ringing, the phone died.

"No way," I muttered under my breath.

I flipped the phone shut and tossed it onto the passenger seat. Through the front windshield I watched the headlights of approaching cars and suddenly felt vulnerable. Between each passing car, the road became dark—scary dark.

I had two choices. Either take the main road home or the short cut through the woods.

The woods? Was I that desperate?

I shivered. I loved hiking through the woods during the day, but at night the trees took on a life of their own and creeped me out.

Then I imagined the alternative. The road, dark and curvy, led to Ernie's Pizza where I could call my dad. But then I feared some weirdo would pull over and offer me a ride so he could kidnap me. I shivered again.

Slumping back into my seat, I sighed and made a mental note: after I survived this, I was going to buy a cell phone charger for my car.

Waiting in my car was definitely out, so I let fate decide. Heads I walk on the road and tails—the woods. As the coin spun in the air, I held my breath and waited with my palm open to catch it. But like a sick joke, the coin bounced out of my outstretched hand and fell onto the dark floor.

Terrified, I decided it would be safer to cut through the woods. I didn't have much with me besides my coat and purse. I pilfered through my purse, removed the necessary items—my wallet, keys and cell phone and tucked them into my coat pockets. I didn't want to be hampered by carrying anything extra, so I locked the empty purse in the trunk.

I looked both ways, took a deep breath and crossed the road towards the tree line, praying I'd make it home safe and sound.

As soon as I entered the path beneath the huge redwoods, I could no longer hear the traffic up on the road. My heart beat a little irregularly as my eyes adjusted to the dimly-lit trail before me.

Silvery patches of moonlight filtered through the vast expanse of branches overhead and splashed light onto the trail. It was actually a nice evening for a stroll. The cool air smelled of dew as the tree leaves rustled in the evening breeze.

Darkness enveloped me as I forged deeper into the woods. I tried to keep my thoughts light and happy as my heart pumped a little faster. The setting could have been a scene right out of a horror movie, a genre which I faithfully avoided. I knew one day I'd be in a similar harmless scenario that would only terrify me by fueling my over-active imagination.

On the other hand, walking with someone, like a cute boy, would make this whole scary ordeal into a romantic dream. I shifted my focus to imagine myself walking hand in hand with him. Maybe he'd stop, look into my eyes and I'd get my first kiss.

The rustle of a fern next to me broke my happy thoughts. I froze, stopping in the middle of the trail. With wide eyes, I searched for the source. I held my breath, straining to listen for what seemed like an eternity, as the noise of pounding blood filled my ears. I was ready to run if something jumped out at me.

Nothing happened, so I took a little step sideways. Still nothing, so I tried another step. Something launched itself out of the bush towards me. I shrieked and shielded my eyes as it flew by my face.

My legs folded underneath me and I balled my arms around

my head. The last thing I wanted was a bat or some flying insect to nest in my hair. The air couldn't come into my lungs fast enough as I tried calming myself down, suspecting every second I remained in this panicked state, precious years were coming off the end of my life. I listened and heard nothing further.

Mentally, I encouraged my legs to straighten, but they were still frozen and starting to shake. My effort to soothe myself wasn't working. I took a few more deep breaths.

You're just being paranoid. You're alone and you know it. Nothing in this forest can harm you. Just get home.

My thoughts comforted me; my heartbeats subsided to a normal rhythm in response. I opened my eyes to focus on my surroundings. The cricket's soft chirping encouraged me to stand up and keep going. The walk home was really no big deal. I knew this path by heart. Ahead was the suspended foot bridge that spanned the creek and I'd be home.

Courage replaced fear as I stood up, dusted myself off and spotted the bridge's lantern through the trees gently swaying in the breeze. It softly beckoned to me, welcoming me in the darkness.

Over time, the creek's erosion created a large ravine that wrapped around the great redwoods of the forest. The cliff sides were covered with ferns, ivy and moss, making perfect homes for little birds and other animals—the same animals that were scaring the living daylights out of me.

"If you don't bother me, I won't bother you," I whispered.

I gently stepped onto the time-weathered bridge, causing it to shudder and creak. The last thing I needed was my presence alerted. I tried my hardest to keep my shoes quiet as I walked across, but it still moaned in protest.

Between the wood slats, I could see the moon brightly reflecting off the water's edge, rippling brilliantly in the current. The gentle flow of the stream echoed in the caverns, softening the noises I made. But when the wind picked up and ruffled the ferns, it swayed the massive bridge.

My heart began to beat faster as the bridge loudly groaned under the wind's strain. Fear took over as I bolted the rest of the way across, panting for air on the other side. An animal, startled by my sudden wild movements, scurried into the brush. I jumped.

It's just another animal, Julia—don't freak out!

I took a deep breath and held it, listening. Whatever it was seemed to be gone now. Annoyed with my constant overreaction to every noise, I turned to face the last part of the trail, determined to stop wasting time.

On this side of the bridge, the redwood trees grew thicker making the trail harder to see in the moonlight. My eyes adjusted as I looked down the cold and uninviting path.

I mustered up my courage and began to move forward focused on my destination, ignoring the menacing shadows and spooky dark caverns. Something brushed my face.

"AHHH!" I yelled, as a spider's web clung to my cheek.

Hyperventilating, I swatted at the sticky, gossamer wisps imagining a large, hairy spider crawling on me. But as if the forest responded to my scream, suddenly everything became quiet—eerily quiet. I stopped, afraid to make any noise whatsoever and waited. Then an invisible wave of blood-lust washed through me. I froze. I was no longer alone.

I held my breath and fought the panic, looking around for where the feelings came from. I didn't hear or see anything, but I knew they came from someone dangerous and close. My neck prickled as I sensed him staring at me with a lecherous appetite, calculating his next move, like a hunter watching its prey.

My heart raced harder. I needed to make a run for it, but my legs wouldn't obey. The crack of a branch sent me sprinting down the trail, but the predator followed. Terrified, I ran with all my strength as I felt the lustful desire grow into mocking pleasure as he closed in on me.

I might have escaped, if it weren't for a protruding tree root that foiled my plans, tripping me. Amazed, I landed on the soft dirt with a thud. But the momentum propelled my body forward and I tumbled over a ledge. Feverishly, I grasped for something, anything, to keep me from plummeting off the mountainside. I felt a branch and grabbed it forcefully, holding on for dear life, and suddenly found myself hanging from the cliff.

Worried the branch would break, I searched for a ridge to climb onto, my shoes slipping off the sheer rocks. Looking up, I expected to see my attacker gawking at me, but found no one. I searched with my senses to probe for their presence. They were still there—the pleasure now a furious anger. I hoped it was because my location kept me from their grasp.

My eyes were drawn to look into the shadowy blackness below me when I heard the sound of shattering plastic. My heart dropped when I realized my cell phone must have slipped out of my pocket. I couldn't decide what was worse, crashing down on the rocks that destroyed my phone, or getting attacked by the dangerous person above. Either way, without help, I was a goner.

"Help!" I screamed into the night air.

The sound of my voice echoed through the caverns followed by silence. I closed my eyes and reached out, feeling for a kind soul to help and realized I was alone again.

Where did he go? "Help!" I screamed again.

I waited in desperation and prayed someone heard my cries—someone strong enough to pull me off the mountainside before the psycho came back.

Please, Dear God. Would this be it? Would I only live to sixteen? My arms trembled, growing weaker with each passing second, along with my determination. Was I going to die here? I thought of my mother and wondered how my father would survive if he lost me too. I kicked myself for not fixing my gas gauge.

"Please help me," I called out, this time with less enthusiasm.

I began to give up. There was no use. No one would hear me or be able to save me now.

"Hold on," I heard a man's voice reply.

I blinked, astounded. Hope flooded my body along with an outpouring of joyful tears while I clung to the branch tighter, knowing my rescue would be soon. I blocked out the fiery burn in my muscles and concentrated my attention on the new person above; my hero.

"Oh thank God," I whispered.

He radiated courage and resolve which bolstered my faith. I waited for an offer of a rope, or a branch, or something to pull me off the cliff when I heard a growl. Fear consumed me. *It* was back.

I felt helpless as I sensed the two square off—both confident—both ready for the kill. The cliff muffled obscenities I thought I heard, before a large thunder clapping crash shook the cliff face. Dirt rained down on my head and I tucked my body into a ball, resting my foot on another little branch protruding below me. I didn't want to get in the way if a body flew off the edge. I worked to sort out the intermixing feelings, frustrated I couldn't see anything. They were fighting harder than I'd ever believed possible. I closed off the noises and focused my energy to try to predict who was ahead—good or evil.

A crack of a tree limb and falling foliage forced me to open my eyes. A tree fell right above my head, frightened birds flew out of the leaves, and a cackle of laughter echoed across the ravine—extreme happiness mingled with the loathing hate. Selfishly, I prayed the fight would end in my favor and quickly.

But then suddenly I heard something that sounded like sizzling fireworks and felt someone's surprise turn into fear . . . then nothing. The evil vanished. I breathed a sigh of relief too soon as the branch shifted in the earth next to me.

"Hurry!" I cried, but it was too late.

I screamed as I fell, knowing I was about to die.

3 – ALIVE

*T*he last thing I expected was to have someone catch me. I opened my eyes in utter dismay to find I was cradled in the arms of the most handsome man I'd ever seen. He had to be an angel; there was no other way to explain it.

"You okay?" he whispered worried.

Shocked, I blinked. Never in my wildest dreams could I have imagined such a rescue. He plucked me effortlessly out of the night's sky with such precision. I wasn't sure how I felt.

I stared up into his eyes. They were oddly familiar, but I certainly would've remembered if we had met before. I grasped to find something articulate to say.

"You, you caught me," I finally stuttered out. "How did you . . ."

He put me down onto my feet.

"Oh," I moaned.

Pain shot up my leg, starting from my ankle. I grabbed his arm for support when all of a sudden the fear and emotion bubbled to the surface. Before I knew it, I'd thrown my arms around his neck and sobbed shamelessly into his chest. He gently put both arms around me, pulling me close. With his hand, he caressed the back of my hair and sighed.

"It's going to be okay. It's over. You're safe now," he said.

I couldn't stop crying as I hugged him tightly and began to feel weak as the adrenaline dissipated from my veins. How close had I just come to possibly falling to my death or worse, being attacked, or even murdered tonight?

I'm so stupid!

Patiently, he held me not seeming to mind as I broke down. All of his feelings revealed concern and tenderness. It broke his heart to hear me cry.

I felt the need to gain my composure and pushed back from him, wiping the tears from my eyes. My mind buzzed, trying to piece it all together. Everything happened so quickly.

"I . . . I ran and tripped and slid right off the side of the cliff," I said with a sniffle.

"Well, it's over now," he said in a soft, soothing voice.

I looked up at the looming cliff face. I could see what remained of the branch I clung to, twenty feet up. It was even further to the top of the ledge where I initially heard his voice coming from.

I wanted to ask him how he got down to the bottom of the cliff in time to save me, but felt too overwhelmed to question him.

"Are you hurt?" he whispered.

I sniffled again. "I'm not sure."

My left palm began to sting. I opened my hand to find a dirty, bright red scrape that ran the length of my arm, past my elbow. The burning ache continued down the side of my body. Lifting up the bottom corner of my shirt confirmed the injury ran the length of my body. The wounds began to throb, along with my ankle and I contemplated what to tell him.

"Well?"

I decided to be brave and not complain, until I put weight on the other foot.

"Oh, ouch."

"What's wrong?"

"My ankle . . ." I pointed to show him which one.

He bent down, pulled up my pant leg and gently inspected it. I winced.

"It's starting to swell. Best if you stay off of it. Can you climb on my back?" he asked.

"Yeah?"

My heart fluttered. I couldn't believe I actually intended to climb on his back. The whole thing seemed completely surreal. How could this really be happening? I would've thought this was a dream, but then I couldn't deny the presence of the stalker.

"But what about . . ." I gulped and pointed towards the cliff.

"I wouldn't worry. It's gone."

"*It?*"

His comment sounded as if the stalker wasn't human.

"Yes, I chased *the animal* away," he insisted in a growl. "Now climb on. I need to get you home."

The animal?

I hesitated for a minute, contemplating his comment. Could it really have just been an animal? The thought boggled my mind but at the moment, I didn't care. All I really wanted was to get home where it was safe. I would ask him about it later.

With his help, I climbed onto his back. I could feel his large muscles under his jacket and admired his nice physique.

"Ready?" he said.

"Yes," I said and hugged his neck.

Nimbly, he charged his way down the ravine along the mountain side. A path leading back up to the trail was about 100 yards ahead of us. Keeping a tight grip on his neck, I closed my eyes, enjoying the calming peace exuding from his body and realized I was no longer worried. It was as if he'd wrapped me in a warm comforting blanket and nothing in the world mattered. I wanted to stay there forever.

But suddenly he changed course and barreled up the side of the cliff on a path unknown to me. I snapped out of my new found utopia and squeezed tightly, feeling like a butterfly hanging on for dear life, afraid I'd fall off. When I looked up, we were level again and on the original trail.

"Which way?" he spoke, barely out of breath.

I glanced behind us, but it was too dark to see the path that led from the ravine to the trail. Furrowing my brow, I wondered where this mysterious path lay hidden, as I knew the trails by heart. Maybe we weren't where I thought we were?

"It's that way," I motioned, pointing him in the general direction of my home.

With ease, he carried me swiftly through the dark. I clung to his back, but sensed his worry and inner struggle, like he fought to control his feelings. I wondered why.

Soon enough, we exited the woods and we were on the road leading to my house. He relaxed and continued on quietly, carrying me as if I were as light as a feather.

The road was deserted, lit only by street lights. The mudslide made the street into a dead end, so no one drove down it unless they lived in the area. I was secretly grateful. I could imagine what my neighbors would think seeing me ride piggy-back on some guy's back.

Who was he anyway? And what was he doing in the woods at this time of night? And what happened to the person he fought on the trail?

It seemed odd for him to be at the right place at the right time to save me from my demise. That kind of stuff only happened in movies. I felt the urge to ask him my questions until I caught a whiff of his scent. I knew it wasn't cologne, but his natural masculine smell that made me secretly swoon. I buried my nose close to his collar and inhaled. With my eyes closed and my mind in pure bliss, I almost fell off when he spoke.

"What were you doing wandering around the woods alone at night?" he asked.

My eyes flew open and I froze for a minute, trying to be inconspicuous when turning my face away from his neck.

"I was just going to ask you the same thing," I blurted out.

"I asked first," he said with a smile in his voice.

"I ran out of gas and I was sorta taking a short cut home."

When I uttered the words, I felt like a complete moron.

"I see," he said softly.

I could tell he wasn't impressed and I wanted to crawl into a hole. I desperately tried to think of something clever to say, but nothing came to mind.

"And you?"

"I heard you calling for help, so I came."

"Do you live near by?"

"No . . . not really."

Tension slinked into the air and I felt my questions weren't welcome—like he didn't want to tell me why he was in the woods. This time my curiosity got the better of me and I couldn't let it go.

"So what were you doing?" I asked, gauging the atmosphere carefully.

Ever so slightly, he breathed a twinge of panic, followed by frustration. "Like I said, I was in the area, heard you scream and then call for help. Did you not want me to help you?"

"Well, yes . . . of course." I bit my lip. "I heard a lot of noises before you were able to get to me. What were you doing?"

He chuckled and I felt unnerved, thinking I asked a stupid question.

"*It* put up a fight. I almost didn't get to you in time."

I hesitated before asking him what I really wanted to know. If he insisted my attacker to be an animal, then I'd sense his deception. And if he chose to lie to me, then no matter how much I enjoyed his company, this would be our final meeting. I didn't make friends with liars, especially compulsive ones.

"I was going to ask you about that . . .you said it was an animal?"

I felt his disdain and then his curiosity.

"Didn't you see it?"

"No . . .. actually, I didn't."

My mind raced as the tables turned. He was very happy about the fact I didn't see anything and I hoped he wouldn't ask anymore details. If I had to make up a story on the spot about why I ran, I would surely botch it up. Without revealing my insight, it would be hard to explain how I could know to run from an unknown, unseen predator and then *I'd* be the liar.

He flowed out a huge sense of relief.

"Well, it's gone now. So you don't need to worry about it anymore."

I clamped my lips closed to stop my gasp. I knew for a fact he fought a person because my powers didn't cross over to animals. But why couldn't I sense he was lying?

"I need to warn my neighbors," I blurted out.

"You do?" he said in alarm. "Why?"

"Because that dangerous animal is still out there."

He stopped, slid me off his back and turned to face me, his hands holding my shoulders. I suddenly felt self-conscious not knowing if mascara or dirt covered my face, electrified by his touch. I peered into his emerald eyes. My breath caught in my throat. He squinted and looked deeply into mine.

"I promise it's nothing to worry about, okay? I'd rather no one knew about it."

My throat constricted in anger. I was tired of this charade and frustrated my powers couldn't reveal the lies he told. And now, he wanted me to cover it up too? I actually didn't want my dad to know anything about the stalker part of my evening, but I needed to know what actually happened first.

"You can tell me," I pleaded.

He let out a large sigh while he stood there, lips pursed, still looking directly at me with an expression that conveyed the message I should just trust him. But I wanted to know. No, needed to know. The thing he defended me from stalked *me* after all. I held his gaze determined not to back down.

"Fine, if you must know," he said coolly. "It was a small mountain lion and I had to kill it before it hurt you."

This time I felt it for sure. Something in his story was not true—his feelings definitely betrayed him. My powers weren't broken after all. Problem was I didn't know which parts were the lies.

He said it was an animal earlier and I sensed that to be true. But now, when he said it was a mountain lion, he lied? Or maybe he didn't actually kill it, but scared it away. I had no clue and the story was getting more and more convoluted with each attempted clarification.

Were my powers shorting out, or worse—crossing over into the animal kingdom? I never saw anyone, so I couldn't know for sure. It would explain a lot if a bloodthirsty animal stalked me. I couldn't imagine anyone who'd have feelings like *it* did—totally unnatural and animalistic, but even still, I couldn't confront him without revealing my secret.

"Okay," I said, giving up.

I looked away. Lying or not, his eyes were the most exquisite green imaginable and I couldn't handle them looking into the depths of my soul any longer. I felt powerless against them.

Then we had an awkward pause. I stood there, with all my weight on one foot, not sure of what to say. Luckily, he broke the silence.

"Do you want me to continue carrying you?" he asked.

I looked up. He smiled and his eyes were kind again. It made it hard to stay frustrated with him.

"Yes," I murmured, annoyed he wouldn't trust me.

Again, he helped me onto his back and slowly walked down the road carrying me. I noticed the soothing warmth return again—something about being close to him, made all the confusion drift away. I fought to stay centered, still remembering I needed to figure out a way to get him to honestly answer my questions when a vision of a bloodied dead cat came into focus.

"Someone's going to find it."

"Find what?" he said, sounding confused.

"The dead mountain lion?"

"I said I'd take care of it," he said in an irritated tone.

"When?" I bit my lip, purposely pressing my luck.

"Julia, please. Just let me worry about it," he snapped.

Julia? My heart skipped a beat.

"How do you know my name?"

He tensed his back.

"I know your name because we've met before."

This caught me off guard.

"We have? When?"

"It was a while back."

I searched through my memories looking for his face and came up blank. Yet his eyes, they seemed so familiar. There was something that sparked inside me every time he looked at me, but I couldn't place what it was exactly.

"Well, I feel bad. I don't remember meeting you—or your name."

"Nicholas."

Nicholas. I sighed. As I repeated his name in my mind, it instantly became the most beautiful word in the English language.

"Well, it's very nice to meet you, *again.*"

I was happy he couldn't see me blushing but then I chastised myself. What in the heck was I doing? I couldn't let myself get emotionally attached when he wasn't being completely honest with me. Where was my better judgment?

It probably flew out the window the same time you decided to trek through the forest.

My desire for him showed plainly on my face, so I was thankful he couldn't see me. I'd never understood the attraction some girls felt for "bad boys" and prided myself in staying away from them. Of course my gift usually tipped me off. But Nicholas was different.

I never felt so drawn to someone before. His pull felt almost magnetic and every moment we stayed close to each other, the connection grew stronger. It frightened and electrified me at the same time.

Maybe I judged him too soon and he wasn't a "bad boy" although he definitely wasn't like the other "nice boys" at my school. He radiated a maturity I craved but never found before. And there was something more—a feeling of déjà vu.

'*You can trust him,*'my heart said while my head screamed "no".

It was a relief when we neared the corner where I lived and approached my house, because I needed this turmoil to stop—to think rationally about things. Nicholas carried me up the stairs to my front porch and sat me on the swing that hung there. I breathed a sigh of relief.

"Is anyone home?" he asked.

As he stepped away, I felt the serenity of his aura leave and I wanted to catch his hand and bring him back to me. Like a moth to a flame, I craved his touch even though that meant the risk of being burned.

"You okay?"

My heart dropped as concern spread across his beautiful face. I'd been too late to cover up my struggle. I gave him the first excuse that came to mind.

"I'm just . . . dizzy," I choked out.

He pursed his lips; the concern still there, I could feel it right under the surface.

I put my hand up to my forehead to try to get my bearings. Why was this happening to me?

"Is anyone home, Julia?" His worry now expressed in the tone of his voice.

"My brother or my dad should be," I squeaked out.

He walked over and knocked on the door keeping one eye on me. I gave a weak smile, trying to reassure him I was all right, but I was still confused as to how we had this mysterious electric connection.

"My dad's going to freak when he sees me like this. How bad do I look?"

A smile appeared on his face. "You're a little banged up, but I think you'll survive."

As he stood on the porch waiting for an answer to his knock, I took the first real opportunity I had to look at him. His chiseled face with dark brown hair and olive-toned skin perfectly framed his dazzling green eyes. He wore a long, brown floor-length leather trench coat over a dark-colored, button-up shirt, faded blue jeans and some mean-looking boots. His face had a certain youthful, yet rugged appearance. A shimmering emerald green stone peeked out from under his shirt hanging from a gold chain around his neck.

Nicholas noticed the focus of my gaze and tucked the medallion back under his shirt, out of view.

Looking up at his beautiful face made all the pain fade away and I blushed as the butterflies flew around in my stomach. I knew my eyes must be red from crying and dirt covered me from head to toe, not to mention my clothes were torn, but he acted as if he didn't see any of that.

Nicholas bent forward and looked directly at me. Seriousness crossed his face. "Promise me you won't wander alone in the woods again. Promise me," he quietly demanded.

"I promise."

"And no mention of the mountain lion, okay?"

"Okay, but . . ."

Luke opened the door. His eyes went from Nicholas then to me. When he saw my disheveled appearance, he gaped in horror.

"What the hell?" Luke said.

I clenched my teeth preparing for a barrage of questions. I must've looked pretty bad.

Luke rushed to me.

"What happened?" he demanded, glaring at Nicholas.

"I fell and twisted my ankle and Nicholas kindly helped me home," I said calmly, trying to reassure him that Nicholas was indeed a friend and not a foe.

"You what?" Luke snapped, his eyes squinting into slits. "Where?"

"The trail," I cringed, choosing my words carefully. "I ran out of gas and my cell phone died. I thought taking a shortcut through the woods would be better than walking around."

"You took the trail?" His faced screwed up like he'd just smelled something rotten. "In the woods? In the dark? Alone!"

Luke acted angry, but I felt a wave of frustration and powerlessness come over him; I instantly felt guilty.

He took a deep breath and swore. "Julia!" he growled.

"It's okay Luke. I'll be fine. I just twisted my ankle."

"And how did that happen?"

"I tripped and fell." I forced a smile.

"I think she needs medical attention," Nicholas interjected, shifting the subject.

"I think you're right. I'll get the Blazer. Wait here."

I blinked and became horrified when the words *medical attention* registered in my mind.

"No," I bellowed.

My sudden insistence startled them.

"Why not?" Luke asked.

I would rather eat shards of glass than go to a hospital. They had no idea the personal hell it would cause me, forced to feel everyone's pain and angst—especially in the emergency room.

"I'm fine, really. I'll heal. Nothing's broken, see?" I tried to stand up and then almost toppled over, wincing in pain. Nicholas prevented me from falling.

"You're NOT fine and you're going!" Luke insisted.

I stared them both down and clenched my jaw. I knew neither would budge and I couldn't get myself into the house without help, so like it or not I'd be forced to go.

"Fine." I snapped, surrendering.

Luke left the porch and headed in the direction of his Blazer. Alone with Nicholas, I didn't want to waste my last chance to avoid a trip to the ER.

"I'm really not that hurt."

"I think it would be best for a doctor to check you out, just in case."

Why did he have to be so sensible? This maddened me. It was my body. I should be able to decide when and if I needed medical attention. I let out a determined huff. They could try to make me go, but I wouldn't be forced.

Luke pulled around front and got out, opening the passenger side, turning to head in our direction. Nicholas, two steps ahead of him, swept me up and carried me to the Blazer effortlessly. My mouth fell open as he carried me off the porch. This wasn't how I imagined them getting me to the car. It was hard to be an uncooperative hostage when I didn't have legs to run away.

I looked into his eyes and my anger subsided as I felt his tenderness again. Losing myself in his intoxicating aura, I forgot where he was carrying me as we headed to the Blazer. Feeling all giddy inside, I wrapped my arms around his neck secretly glad he didn't have the power to read emotions like I did.

"Will I see you again?" I said in a slip.

My cheeks flushed in embarrassment for being so forward.

"Well, if falling off cliffs and such is going to be your favorite past-time, then I imagine yes," he joked.

I gave him a dirty look relieved he thought nothing of my comment. We were almost to the car and I wished I could hold onto his neck forever. I pouted as he put me down gently on the front seat. I felt the same ache return with the absence of his touch.

"Drive carefully Luke. I didn't go through all this trouble just to have you crash on the way to the hospital," Nicholas said.

My heart fluttered listening to his concern for my safety. I thought I saw him wink at me.

Luke finally relaxed. "Thanks man," he told Nicholas. "Hey, you need a ride?"

"I'm good. My car is down the way," he said as he motioned down the road.

I followed his motion with my eyes, confused as I didn't see a car. Then Nicholas closed the door and I quickly rolled down the window. I wasn't ready to say goodbye.

"I'll check on you later," he said as he reached out and squeezed my hand resting on the windows ledge.

My heart leapt. There couldn't have been a better ending to a perfectly horrible day.

"Okay," I said softly.

I watched him, hoping the moment wouldn't end. He smiled at me, but his emotions changed again as he stepped back away from the Blazer. The sadness and guilt had resurfaced, even though his face didn't show it.

I wonder what's wrong?

Whatever it was, I wanted to help. I secretly hoped he'd let me. Hoped he would answer the questions that nagged me about our evening.

Luke pulled away from the curb and I took a deep breath, sinking back into the seat, already missing Nicholas' arms around me. But I felt a searing pull. Something cried out inside me, warning not to let him go.

I bit my lip and felt my eyes grow wet, unsure if I should make Luke stop the car. The further we drove, the more agony I felt. I finally turned around to get one final glimpse of him. But no one was there.

"Are you in pain?" Luke said after looking at me, noticing my tears.

I was, but not from my fall. I didn't know how to explain it to him without sounding boy-crazy. And frankly, it confused me how my body reacted after the separation from Nicholas. This had never happened before.

"A little," I fibbed.

"I'm glad I was the one who was home and not Dad. He just left to take Jo home because he didn't want her to walk. If he saw you . . . with what happened with mom . . . "

He let out a loud gust of air and became silent.

I imagined the scene and shuddered.

"When Dad found me on the doorstep, I wasn't injured and I was *five*. It's nothing like before." I defended rather gruffly.

Luke glanced over at me and tilted his head, pursing his lips. I knew I grasped at straws speaking of technicalities. The scene would have been close enough to bring back the bitter memories. I turned to look out the window and wished I could open the door and jump out. His unspoken guilt-trip started to bother me.

"I should call him and let him know," Luke said in a low murmur after a few moments of silence.

"Wait," I said hoping he'd help me fabricate a story first. There had to be a way to cushion the blow for Dad and for me.

"Wait? Are you kidding? We can't lie our way outta this one, Julia. Your car is out of gas somewhere on the road and you've probably got a broken foot. We are going to be at the emergency room all night. We have to tell him."

Why couldn't he be away on business?

"Don't get mad at me," I said with a huff. "It was an accident."

He just glared and snapped his mouth shut while his anger flared.

"Could you just wait until we get there?" I asked softly. "I don't want to hear your conversation. Okay?"

He glanced over at me with surly eyes for a second.

"Whatever," he said, while he shrugged.

Maybe if I wasn't around, Luke would be more inclined to smooth things over. One could hope.

We came around the corner and the red emergency signs came into view. I braced myself. There was no way to avoid this dreadful place now.

To our surprise, the waiting room was deserted. The doctor pronounced I only sprained my ankle and the rest of my bumps and bruises weren't serious

As we drove home, I prepared myself for the lecture ahead. After seeing Luke's reaction, I could imagine Dad's. Luke called Dad, like I asked, once we arrived at the waiting room, but I hadn't asked the details yet.

"What did you say?" I said, while studying my purple toes peaking out from under the ace-bandage neatly wrapped around my ankle.

"I told him what happened."

"Is he mad?"

"What do you think, Julia?"

I looked out the window and bit my lip. It was a stupid question. Whether I wanted it or not, I was going to get a verbal beating in the next few minutes and I totally deserved it.

"What should I say?"

"Just say you're sorry and don't make any excuses. He hates excuses."

I took a deep breath. Luke specialized at staying out of trouble, but I never got away with anything. Maybe that was a good thing. It certainly kept me honest.

We pulled into the driveway and I saw the silhouette of my father standing at the doorway with his arms folded across his chest. I'd hoped the wait would help calm him down, but I hoped in vain. I crawled out of the cab of the Blazer, with Luke helping me. He handed me my brand new crutches and I hobbled the walk of shame slowly past glaring eyes into the house. I went directly to the couch and awaited my punishment.

His infuriation bowled me over and all I wanted to do was go to my room. The intensity told me I was going to be grounded for life. I looked down at the dingy carpet and waited, in deafening silence, as he paced back and forth.

"Say something, Dad," I finally said.

"I'm just so upset with you, Julia. I'm afraid of what I would say."

I hung my head lower and waited. In all actuality, he really didn't need to say anything. But I knew if he could just talk to me, it would help his frustration go away sooner.

"I just don't know what you were thinking, walking alone in the woods. In the dark," he said slowly, controlling his anger. "I can't believe you'd be so careless."

"I know, Dad. I'm sorry," I whispered as I glanced up at him through my bangs.

"Nobody knew you were out there."

I looked down again as I felt wave after wave of frustration and horror. I cringed. This was the one time I wished to be normal. Feeling my dad's disappointment with me was by far worse than any other real punishment I could have experienced.

"If that boy wasn't there . . ." he exhaled sharply and stopped.

I gulped back my tears and glanced up at him with his arms folded, towering in front of me, his body tense.

"Julia, I could have lost you tonight, do you understand?" he said just above a whisper.

The cushions squeaked when he sat down next to me. All I

wanted was for him to put his arm over my shoulder, but the lecture wasn't over.

He struggled to keep his emotions under control, but I caught the twinge in his eye. He was reliving the distress again. The same distress I remembered eleven years ago when they found my mother's waterlogged car in the river with no sign of her whereabouts. I wanted to sink into the couch and never come out.

"Yes," I whispered, feeling a prick of pain in my own eyes as they started to get watery also. "I'm really sorry, Dad."

From my peripheral vision, I watched him nervously turn his wedding band on his ring finger. I fought to remain calm as the silence droned on, but I didn't dare say anything further. No matter how much I fought to fill the void, I would follow Luke's advice.

"I guess I need to go get your car now," he grunted after several agonizing quiet minutes.

I shook my head just a tiny bit, but still looked down.

"Fine! Let's go Luke," he barked. "Where are your keys?"

I took them out of my pocket and held them out for him without making eye contact. He snatched them out of my hand and stormed towards the door. I breathed a sigh of relief as I read his real feelings. He loved me; overwhelmingly so.

"I hope you've learned your lesson!" my father said over his shoulder just before slamming the front door closed behind him.

Full of guilt, I hobbled up the stairs to my room, anxious to shower away the grime and guilt from the fall. The warm water felt good over my sore muscles but stung the large raspberry covering most of my left side. I knew tomorrow I'd be feeling a lot worse.

I winced while examining the new cut on my left cheekbone in the mirror, wondering how I could have been so stupid; a possible permanent token symbolizing my lapse of judgment. A scar might be just what I needed to wise up.

A flash of his shimmering eyes gazing down at me the first time we made eye contact stole into my thoughts. Butterflies tickled my stomach and threatened to rage out of control as I stifled a giggle. I pressed my eyes shut and sobered myself up, disgusted I could so easily let the circumstances amuse me, remembering my dad's grief instead.

Downstairs, I heard the door slam followed by muffled voices. On one foot, I hopped to my bedroom door and quietly closed it. Keeping out of sight seemed prudent at the moment. I dug around on my floor and found my favorite loose-fitting jammies and gingerly put them on before crawling into bed.

My tattered shirt sat on the edge of my comforter. Picking it up, I felt the fabric in my hands. A memory of Nicholas carrying me down the trail surged through my mind. Who was he really? I bit my lip and thought through what happened, replaying every gory detail. I brought the shirt to my nose and inhaled. It still smelled like him.

I turned off the light and looked out the window. The stars twinkled softly in the night's sky. It didn't matter which way I lay on my bed though, every direction I tried hurt something someplace. I picked the least painful position and snuggled my face against the shirt feeling closer to Nicholas with each inhale.

Was he looking at the same stars thinking of what happened too? I hoped so.

I felt someone approach before I heard the gentle tapping on my door.

"Yes?" I said as I frantically stuffed the shirt under my pillow. I knew it was my dad, who seemed to be a lot calmer. But I didn't want to be caught sniffing my dirty shirt.

"I wanted to say goodnight," he said while cracking open the door.

He walked over to my bedside and sat down. His soft expression comforted me.

"I'm sorry I got so angry," he said while reaching out and squeezing my hand. "I just don't want anything bad to happen to you."

A tear came to my eye.

"Oh, Dad; I'm so sorry." I sat up and threw my arms around his neck. He hugged me tightly while gently patting my back.

"Just promise you'll be more careful next time," he said.

Too choked up to speak, I nodded in agreement. He kissed me on the forehead, smiled, and left my room.

I wiped away my tears and rolled over, vowing to never hurt my dad like that again. I sighed as I reclaimed the shirt, holding it to my face, and closed my eyes.

Since my dad and I made up, I didn't feel so guilty anymore allowing the memories of the night to run wild in my head, and let the more confusing aspects of it come to light. There were just too many things that didn't make sense. And the nagging "lie" bothered me too.

What was he hiding? What was he doing there?

Maybe it was illegal to kill mountain lions and he feared he'd get in trouble.

I rolled to the other side and felt the throbbing ache from my hip grow worse. Utterly exhausted, all I really wanted to do was sleep, but my mind wouldn't let me, as the scary "what ifs" played mercilessly when I closed my eyes. I reached over to look at my pain pill bottle thinking it might be time to take one.

'May cause drowsiness"it read.

Good.

Within minutes of taking two pills, my brain began to grow hazy and visions of wild animals became rainbows in fluffy clouds, as my eyes closed sleepily and I drifted off to dream land.

I tried to run but my legs were stuck as if in quicksand and I didn't have the strength to move them. I fearfully pulled with all my might to make them move forward. Everywhere I looked, the blurry forest seemed to close in on me. I could hear the footfalls of something coming closer in the distance. At its snarl, I turned and gasped. A very large cat lay crouched down in the mist. Its yellow menacing eyes studied me, lips snarled up to reveal large meat eating teeth glistening in the moonlight. It sprung.

"Ahh," I screamed sitting up, flailing my arms trying to prevent the cat from attacking.

I blinked and caught my breath. My head was covered in sweat but I safely sat in my bed. The clock read 2:20 in the morning. I slumped back and thought about what I saw, my heart still pounding against my chest. I felt my eyes grow heavy and sleep took hold of me once again.

I woke up the next morning feeling like I'd been run over by a Mac truck. Everything involved in getting ready for the day was a challenge and took twice as long as normal to accomplish. I hadn't realized how much I'd taken my ankle for granted until it wasn't a functioning part of my body anymore. I barely made it downstairs in time for Luke to drive me to school.

Earlier, I'd called Sam and asked her to meet me in front of the school where Luke would drop me off. I knew I'd need help with my books, but I didn't tell her anything about what happened, except that I hurt my ankle. I wanted to tell her all about Nicholas in person.

"Oh my gosh; what happened?" she asked as soon as I tried getting out of the Blazer. Both she and Luke had to help me get out.

"You'll never guess," I said with a wry smile.

I explained the whole story to her as she helped me get to our first period P.E. class.

"You're kidding!" she said wide-eyed as I got to the part where he caught me.

I'd conveniently left out the "mountain lion" part. I just changed the story slightly saying that the spider caused me to lose my balance and then I toppled off the side of the cliff. It didn't sound as good, but a mountain lion sighting could cause some to panic. If that information got back to my brother or my dad, I would surely get it. It would be Nicholas' and my secret.

By third period, news spread like wild fire around school about how I'd almost fallen to my death and some stranger rescued me. Girls I barely knew stopped me in the hall to ask me what happened. Each time I told the story, the reaction was the same—mouths open, then comments of how lucky I was. Every one of them were astounded and a tiny bit jealous, and I could only assume it was because they wanted to have the same thing happen to them. I would gladly trade my injuries and the attention with any one of them, as long as I knew for certain I'd meet Nicholas another way. But then, I'd be willing to fall again, just to feel the warmth of his arms.

The endless questions grew annoying as the day dragged on. I just wanted to get home and wait for Nicholas to come see me. Plus, my armpits were sore from hobbling around on crutches all day.

"What does he look like?" Dena asked me, while Sam and Katie listened in during lunch in the cafeteria; the boys talking about something else.

"Well, he's probably six feet tall with dark brown hair, green eyes, medium build and I think he's my age. Oh and he's really strong. I couldn't believe he carried me up the side of the trail and then all the way home. He acted as if it was effortless. And the weird thing was he knew me."

"You don't remember meeting him?" Sam asked.

"No, I think I'd remember meeting *him*."

Again, I tried to place when we could have met. I wasn't one for going to parties and we had a relatively small student body. I'd also grown up in this town and knew a lot of faces from the deli. I made a mental note to ask him when we had met. Yet another question he needed to answer.

"Maybe he's a peeping Tom and he was stalking you," Katie said with a smirk.

I shot her a look.

"He's not like that." *I would know being stalked, for real.*

"Do you think he's in high school still? Or maybe he's in

college," Sam suggested.

Dena and Katie giggled. I hadn't thought of that. What if he was in college? Would he think I was too young?

"Now you have a date for the homecoming," Dena said in a sing-song sort of way, eyes beaming.

"Oh, I don't know about that. We just met," I said quickly.

I wonder if he'd want to take me.

The bell rang and we all groaned.

I tried to concentrate in Algebra, but I kept daydreaming about what happened, and the entire class faded into a blur. I didn't snap out of it until I saw our homework assignment and panicked. I hadn't paid attention one bit and now was behind in two lessons. I'd forgotten to do my homework the night before. But it wasn't due until the end of the week.

But when sixth period Spanish finally came to a close and I was free to go, I started to get nervous. And seeing Luke's Blazer come into the parking lot to pick me up made me break out in a sweat. The wait would soon be over. He got out and helped me into the cab, putting my crutches in the backseat.

"How was it today?" he asked after pulling away from the curb.

"It was actually a good day. Everyone wanted to know what happened. It was crazy! I had girls I didn't know wanting to hear the story. I couldn't believe it!" I gushed.

"No one had the guts to tell you you were stupid for going out on that trail alone last night?" he said with a smirk.

"No," I chided back, sticking my tongue out. He did have a point. "I think my school is just desperate for some good gossip and my mishap fit the bill."

"Uh huh."

I could tell he only half listened to me.

"I still can't believe it happened, you know?" I babbled. "I mean, here I am, hanging off the cliff and Nicholas is there to catch me just in time. If you think about it, it's so crazy."

"Yeah, you are."

"Shut up!" I said as I jabbed him in the side, deciding it would be better to remain silent the rest of the ride home.

At home, I quickly changed and put on a light pink shirt I always received compliments on. I also touched up my makeup and fixed my hair a little bit, still trying to look natural.

I decided that I would sit on the couch close to the front window, with my leg propped up and work on homework until he showed up. This would give me a perfect view of the street and still look casual.

But I got nothing done. Every car that drove by, or walker on the sidewalk, drew my attention and my head bobbed up in anticipation. This constant back and forth made it impossible for me to concentrate, so I gave up trying to do anything and just stared out of the window instead.

I tried to imagine what he might be doing at the moment. Did he have a job? And did he live close by? And how old was he really? Maybe he would take me to homecoming. Visions of me and him dancing on the floor with the "popular" guys looking on made me smile. I would have a real date for once.

I also couldn't wait to get a little better so I could return to the place where we'd met. The thought of going back to the cliff made my insides knot up, in a good way. Maybe I could find some answers to my questions too.

"Don't even think about milking this injury," Luke joked as he walked past the living room. "You're still going to have to do your chores."

"Whatever! I'd trade this sprained ankle with you in a second to do chores!" I yelled after watching him disappear upstairs.

I hoped he wasn't watching me a few seconds ago when a goofy grin covered my face.

Dad cooked salmon for dinner and it made the house smell like a seafood restaurant. I moved from my choice location into the kitchen to watch him work. I needed another distraction to help me in my quest for patience.

"How was your day?" Dad asked, turning for a brief second.

"Okay I guess. I'm pretty popular all of a sudden. Everyone was curious about what happened."

"Oh?" he said, as he chopped up veggies to stir fry.

I'd always felt like my dad was different than other dads. For one, he loved to cook. So did Luke for that matter. Most other kids' dads that I knew enjoyed sports or news on TV in their spare time, but not mine. When he wasn't traveling on business or in the kitchen, you could find him in his office, on his computer doing research or reading a book.

If I wanted any of his attention at all, this would have to be the time.

"I think the kids at school are just bored for something to talk about."

"Uh-huh."

"The good news is my ankle feels a lot better. I can move around the house without crutches, so I think I won't need them for a week like the doctor said."

"I see."

"I also think now is a good time to get my gas gauge fixed since I won't be driving until I do get rid of my crutches. I was hoping you and Luke would take it in for me."

"Okay."

"Oh and when I woke up this morning, I had a weird incision on my left temple. I think alien's abducted me in the night, and returned me in the morning, because I don't remember having to get stitches yesterday."

"Uh huh . . . Wait?" He spun around, his face contorted. "What did you say?"

I laughed. "Just checking to see if you're listening, Dad."

Normally, Dad or Luke would make dinner and I'd clean up. It became an unspoken rule since all I could cook was cookies out of a pre-made package and scrambled eggs. But tonight, someone else would need to do the dishes because of my injury. That made me kind of happy.

"How was dinner last night? Is there anything new going on with Auntie Jo or *John*?" I tried to hide my disdain while saying his name.

"Dinner was nice. John got a new job and likes it. But Jo said she misses you and would like you to come over soon. Says you're always so busy. Are you avoiding her for some reason?"

I knew eventually someone would notice that I'd completely stopped spending time with Aunt Jo and John. The reason I avoided them happened to be that I couldn't stand to be around John. If I had an *unsafe* list, John would be the first one on it. He made it impossible to spend quality *alone* time with her.

The last time I tried, he inadvertently invited himself along and turned it into a "let's analyze Julia" nightmare. I secretly hoped his new job insisted that he travel like my dad.

"No. I'm not," I half fibbed. "I just don't want to intrude since she's married now."

"I don't think John minds if you come over every once in a while and spend time with them. He understood when he married her you and your brother are practically her children."

"I mind," I muttered under my breath so he couldn't hear me.

After the *let's analyze Julia* session, I refused to let John know anything further about my life. But what bothered me the most was Jo seemed oblivious to the intrusiveness of John's inappropriate questions. On top of that, it hurt that she hadn't come to find out why I'd distanced myself, or even seemed to miss me. It felt good to know she actually did.

"Okay. I'll try to make it over there this weekend," I said, figuring it was time to at least make an appearance.

Dinner came and went and I'd completely lost track of time

until I noticed it was a little after eight. My heart sank when I realized Nicholas was unlikely to show up tonight. Where was he? Did I misunderstand? Maybe he was running late?

I needed to find something to do. There was a slim possibility he might come within the next few minutes but I couldn't wait and watch the clock.

I limped into Dad's office and sat behind his large desk, moving the mouse to activate the screen. From the desktop, I opened the browser and typed in 'mountain lion"and clicked 'search'. A few menacing images of lions popped up with over a million links to choose from.

I scanned the list and then clicked "*mountain lion attacks on people in the US and Canada.*" On that page, I clicked, "*statistics of attacks,*". The new page loaded and I looked for the details in California. To my surprise, there had only been one attack last year and no deaths.

Interesting.

I clicked another link and jumped as the sound of a cougar cry came through the speakers.

"Geez!" I exclaimed.

"What's that?" Dad asked, calling from the other room.

"Oh, nothing. I'm just researching something for school," I said and quickly turned down the sound.

On the screen was a list of Do's and Don'ts.

Do's and Don'ts . . . Never turn your back on a lion. Never ever run from a lion. Do look at them in the eyes. Don't go out in lion territory alone. Don't go out from dusk to dawn. Act aggressively towards the lion. Make menacing noises. Smile and show your teeth. Use a stick and thrust it towards its face . . ..

Then I scrolled to the bottom and my eye caught a peculiar sentence.

It's important to keep in mind that lion attacks are still extremely rare in California and nationally.

Rare?

I clicked to read some first hand stories and noticed a common thread. All of the attacks happened during the day and most of the victims survived. Still the stories were creepy and I shivered.

Maybe it was another cat? I looked up "bobcat".

Though the Bobcat prefers rabbits and hares, it will hunt anything from insects and small rodents to deer.

Nope, it wasn't that.

Extremely rare?

Something just didn't fit.

Suddenly Aladdin jumped up onto my lap and startled me. She looked right up at me and meowed loudly, begging for some affection.

"Laudie, you brat," I said as I gave her my meanest glare.

It didn't faze her as she rubbed her head against my outstretched arm, meowing repeatedly. Reluctantly, I scratched her neck.

She gently purred and started kneading my leg as if it were dough. I continued to pet her when it donned on me; she belonged to the cat family.

I mentally reached out to see if I could sense her emotions. I would think I'd be able to feel her happiness and contentment as she purred softly on my lap, but I felt nothing.

So, it had to be something other than an animal or was it only extreme emotions I felt.

I thought about startling her to be mean, but decided against it as I casually glanced at the time. It was 9:32 p.m.

Where did the time go?

I felt all hope drain from my body like a deflated balloon as the reality sank in. He hadn't come and I would have to start the wait all over again tomorrow. I sulked as I limped upstairs and got ready for bed, fighting my disappointment.

Why did I make such a big deal about it at school today? If it wasn't for Luke actually meeting him, I would be sure people would think I'd made the whole story up. I started to think that I had, but my healing cuts and aching bruises were a constant reminder that it had really happened.

Oh, this is so embarrassing.

I climbed into bed and turned off the light. I looked out the window again at the night sky, wanting the stars to guide me, maybe give me answers.

But what could have kept him? I didn't know his last name, where he lived, or anything about him to find him. I worried my earlier gut reaction was right and I'd never see him again.

The letdown was overwhelming. I had such hopes that maybe he was different. That he cared. Not knowing made me furious. I started to wish he'd just left me there. I'm sure I would have survived the fall. At least being laid up in the hospital, with pain medication, would feel better than the complete embarrassment I felt right now.

Why would he promise to come see me and not come? I wanted to feel sorry for myself, but my frustration overpowered me. He wasn't going to have this type of pull on me any longer.

I refuse to get upset over some boy I just met! Get ahold of yourself, Julia!

Angrily, I grabbed the dirty shirt I slept with the night before and threw it in the corner. His scent had no business lingering on my bed, even though it had faded to just a whisper. I balled up my pillows before throwing my head down on them and shut my eyes tight. I was going to go to sleep if it killed me.

It didn't matter though. As soon as I closed my eyes, I saw his face; his beautiful eyes shining radiantly down at me, and felt the pull that melted my heart. I knew, no matter what I did, he was going to haunt me forever.

5 — FRUSTRATION

My eyes slowly opened and I strained to focus on the blurry surroundings. I recognized the place at once—I stood alone in the dark forest. What was I doing here again? I knew the creature was going to return and eat me like it wanted to and I had to get out of there, but my legs wouldn't move. I turned before I heard the angry snarl. The noise came from just beyond the trees. Frozen in fear, I waited and watched. Evil green eyes appeared and stared out at me, with lips curled up to reveal teeth ready to rip me to shreds. I shied away but knew I couldn't defend myself. I gasped when I recognized the face that bore daggers into me. It was Nicholas.

I found myself sitting up in bed, drenched in sweat and screaming. I looked around the dimly lit room for the thing I feared, but the dark images floated away like a fine mist, and suddenly I couldn't remember what it was I searched for. I flopped back onto my pillows and I rolled over shivering, afraid to close my eyes. The clock read 2:20 a.m. like it did the night before.

The soft light of the full moon gently shone into my room and helped bring me to reality. My heart finally slowed as sleepiness clouded my mind.

I'll just close my eyes for a second.

Something made a horrible buzzing noise. Feeling groggy, I opened my eyes to find the sun's happy rays glaring throughout my room. Annoyed, I reached over, hit my alarm, and groaned. My body ached all over.

Keeping very still, I wondered how I would make it to school today. Staying home seemed like a more logical choice, but I knew I'd go stir crazy waiting around at home all day.

Once I got to school, I wished I'd gone with my first instinct. Even though only two days had passed since the accident, life at school had returned to normal. My rescue story was already yesterday's news and everyone stopped living vicariously through me. Actually, they were starting to get annoyed at my disability and so was I.

The girls played volleyball again, while I sat on the bleachers and watched during P.E. class. I tried to listen and take notes in History, but found myself daydreaming and tuned out Mr. Marshall's monotone voice. When the bell rang to let us out of Chemistry, I packed up my things and gasped when I looked at my notes. I'd unconsciously doodled Nicholas' name all over my paper. Quickly, I crumpled the evidence into a ball before Sam could see it.

There goes turning over a new leaf.

We waited until the crowd subsided before leaving the room—less people for me to accidentally run into. She took one look at my pathetic heavyhearted expression and furrowed her brow.

"You're not doing any better, are you?" she asked.

I pouted up my lips and nodded my head.

"I'm trying, but I can't stop thinking about him," I said, completely despondent.

We headed across the lawn towards the cafeteria and Sam kept a slower pace. Since the accident, my appetite diminished to practically nothing and the thought of food made my stomach lurch.

"I know, let's go do something tonight," Sam suggested cheerfully.

"I can't do much with these," I said while lifting up my crutches.

She sighed. "When do you get rid of them?"

"The doctor said, depending on how I'm healing, I could try moving around without them on Monday, but he warned me not to overdo it."

"How does your ankle feel?"

"Still tender," I said, not wanting to reveal my heart felt a hundred times worse in comparison.

"I can't wait until you can walk again. It's hard to cheer you up when you can't go anywhere."

"Tell me about it," I said with a sigh.

"Hey, I know what we can do."

A mischievous smile spread across her face.

"Oh no. What?"

"How about going to the Boardwalk?" she said while raising her right eyebrow. "We could get you a wheel chair so you don't have to wait in line."

I imagined how stupid I would look and rolled my eyes.

"No," I said, wrinkling my nose.

Everyone knew the only reason locals hung out at the Boardwalk was to show off their current infatuations, which I didn't have. And even if all the rides happened to be free, I did not want to be subjected to unbridled displays of affection.

"There's always the beach," she suggested.

"How am I going to use crutches on the sand?" I said, completely annoyed my injury prevented me from enjoying everything.

Her sudden embarrassment made me realize my harsh tone hurt her feelings.

"Sorry, I didn't mean to sound like that. I know you're just trying to help."

"It was a stupid suggestion."

"No, you know I love the beach. I'm just . . ." I searched to pinpoint my actual problem. " . . .being stupid."

Sam laughed.

"No, you're not. It's Nicholas' fault. He's the one being stupid."

"You're right. I'll stop being so difficult," I said with a smile.

We joined Cameron, Dena and Morgan at our regular table.

"Do you want anything?" Sam asked me as I sat down as lithely as I could.

"Just a Luna bar, if they have one. Thanks."

"I'll come with you," Dena said as she got up and followed Sam to the cafeteria line.

Prompted by Morgan's longing, I decided to take advantage of my window of opportunity.

"Hey, Morgan," I said.

His eyes flickered quickly to mine after realizing I'd caught him checking out Dena as she left the table. He looked away, his cheeks turning red.

"Oh, hey, Julia," he said while drinking his soda to hide his embarrassment.

"I was wondering . . .Who are you taking to homecoming?" I asked with a smile.

He took one short breath, appearing calm, his anxiety known only to me.

"No one. Why?"

His eyes darted back and forth between me and Cameron.

"I think you should ask Dena to go with you," I said softly.

I watched as panic spread across his face.

"Dena?" his voice cracked.

"Yeah."

"I think she wants to go with someone else," he said sheepishly, glancing over at her as she stood with Sam at the cash register.

"I think she wants to go with you."

His eyes came back to mine. I sensed his disbelief.

"Me?"

"Yeah and you better ask her soon, before someone else does, and she has to say yes because she doesn't want to go alone."

Cameron cleared his throat rather loudly. We looked up just in time to see Sam and Dena's return to the table.

"What are you guys talking about?" Dena asked.

Morgan stiffened.

"Just football stuff. Hey, where's Katie?" I asked.

Dena's powder blue eyes studied my expression as I feigned

innocence. She paused for a moment then glanced at the tables around us.

"Off trying to get Tyler alone I think," she finally said.

"She's persistent," I muttered followed by a chuckle.

"Yeah, it seems sorta hopeless," Sam said.

Hopeless.

That's what I was. Why was I torturing myself, hoping Nicholas would show up?

The bell rang and I got a pit in my stomach; time to endure another torture session in Algebra. My only saving grace would be going out with Sam later. I almost hoped Nicholas would show up and find I wasn't at home. I could imagine his face when he found out I was out having a glorious time without him.

It would serve him right for standing me up. I do have a life after all.

"Are you coming?" Sam asked.

I snapped out of my fog and realized she was talking to me. As we headed over to our classroom, Cameron nudged me.

"You're pretty sly, you know that?" he said.

"What?"

He nodded his head and I looked over in the direction he motioned. Morgan was sheepishly talking to Dena. I smiled.

At least someone was following their heart.

During Algebra, I decided dinner and a movie would cater to my crippled condition the best. Sam thought so too. Actually, she didn't seem to care what we did, as long as it cheered me up.

"Can we go right after school?" I whispered in class.

She nodded.

That would be my solution for avoiding home completely. The sooner my distraction started the better. I sent Luke a text under my desk letting him know my plans. His confirmation reply came a second later. I suddenly felt excited.

6 — FOREWARNING

$\mathcal{W}$e took off down the freeway, the wind in our hair, tunes blaring, without a care in the world. I finally felt liberated, keeping thoughts about Nicholas in the far recesses of my mind. He would stay locked away so I could enjoy our fun-filled girls-only evening. I totally needed it.

"Where do you want to go for dinner?" Sam asked while we waited at another long red light.

"I was hoping you'd want pizza," I said, even though we ate at Pleasure Pizza all the time.

"Ooh, that sounds good."

They had the greatest pizza ever, amazing homemade dough cooked to perfection in a stone oven. My mouth watered as I imagined my favorite, the Greek combo with feta, olives, tomatoes and artichokes.

"And then, I thought it would be fun to watch the sunset at The Point."

"Good idea."

"And then, a movie?"

"That sounds perfect," she said in a purr.

I never grew tired of hanging out with Sam, even though we mostly did the same things together. She always acted as if my ideas were something completely new. I liked that about her.

"Hey, pull in here," I said as I pointed to a little restaurant on the corner. "We need to get the movie times."

The restaurant had a kiosk that held the *News and Review* paper right by the front door. Sam zipped in, parked and jumped out to snag a copy.

Sam sped down Main Street as I flipped to the movie section. I couldn't handle a romantic movie or a tear-jerking drama and horror was completely out. Experiencing fear to the nth degree once in my life was plenty for me. I scanned the remaining short list of movies.

"Okay, we've got *Ghost Flight, Arial's Rampage, Ballad of Maria* and—" I spotted a familiar title. "How about *The Bucci Brothers' Revenge?*"

"Never heard of it, what's it about?"

"It's a comedy about two brothers who start a business venture designing a line of purses, trying to compete with Gucci. I saw a preview; it looked funny."

I bit my lip. A comedy with two gay brothers couldn't possibly have any romance I could relate too, if any.

"If that's the one you want, I'm game," she said, a chipper tone in her voice.

"Are you being agreeable just to make me happy?"

"Jules, the goal tonight is to do what you want. It's your therapy, remember?"

I huffed. "Yes, but . . ."

"I promise, so far, everything's been cool with me," she said with a grin.

I let it go. Maybe if I stopped making suggestions, she'd come up with something she'd want to do. I didn't want the evening to be all about me.

My attention was diverted when I noticed the temperature drop. The ocean view was just around the bend in the road. I could visualize the majestic crystalline water. It was like being reunited with a long lost friend. I took in a deep breath and filled my lungs with the crisp, salty air. Something about the beach always relaxed me.

"Wanna go to the cliff?" Sam suggested.

She knew me too well. I nodded, smiling.

She accelerated and I sat back, eyes closed, feeling the warm sun on my face, trying to sing along to the songs blasting out of her speakers. Even though I sounded completely stupid and grasped at the words, I felt my heart heal a little.

Within minutes, we pulled up to the familiar dirt parking lot on top of the cliff overlooking the most pristine beach, our beach.

"You seem to be feeling better," she said as she killed the engine.

"You know, I am actually. I think this is exactly what I needed."

I gave her a big reassuring smile.

"Good."

We relaxed in her car and watched the waves roll in, crashing one by one onto the barnacle laden rocks. Sam filled me in on the most recent gossip she had just heard at school. Apparently Katie asked Tyler for help with her Chemistry. He agreed to meet her in the library after school, but when she got there, Mandy came instead. He forgot he had practice and figured since Mandy was acing Chemistry, she could help Katie. Katie was furious and became the fastest pupil Mandy ever tutored.

"Wow, I wonder how she remained civil," I said with a chuckle.

"Well . . ." I sensed Sam's compassion and felt guilty for being so mean. "I've been trying to tell her to move on, find someone else, like Erik or Logan McKay. They are both cute and single at the moment."

I imagined her with another football player and sighed. She wouldn't have any trouble nabbing either of them but I felt sorry for the poor guy. She'd only use him to try to make Tyler jealous and then dump him when it didn't work. She was totally stuck on Tyler— like I was stuck on Nicholas.

I cringed at the realization that I had let thoughts of Nicholas seep around the wall I put up. Worse yet, the memories that flashed through my mind were so real I could almost smell his earthy scent.

"Oh, yeah, she should do that," I said, trying to sound perfectly normal as I stuffed the feelings back down.

I had to face it. Our relationship was over, plain and simple though it never really had begun and I had no need to reminisce any longer. Maybe another guy would help me as well.

I re-centered myself and remembered back to when Sam and I found this place. It was shortly after Sam got her car. Ever since, I dreamt of exploring the beach below, but the sheer cliff edge made it impossible to traverse, even with a working ankle. I never saw a living soul down there, ever.

So, I imaged I was a bird, swooping and flying in the wind. With wings I could get to the beach, no problem. I envied their easy life as I watched them soar, wishing I could be one for just one day, only worrying about where to find my next meal.

Suddenly, our stomachs started to make horrible music together.

"Was that you or me?" I asked.

"Me, but I think I heard yours too," she said with a giggle. "You still want pizza?"

I nodded.

"Good. Me too."

I knew we needed to eat soon, because if we didn't, Sam would turn into the Incredible Hulk and that wouldn't be a pretty sight.

The parking lot at Pleasure was full, but we luckily snagged an empty spot right in front. I hobbled to the patio and found us a table at once and Sam headed for the doors.

"Wait—" I said, as I turned and shoved a $20 into her hand. "My treat."

She tilted her head and gave me the *mom* look.

"Take it, or I'll make a scene," I whispered.

She opened her mouth as if to say something but my insistent glare stopped her. She knew I would do it too and I felt her resolve waiver.

"Okay; you win. Greek?" she asked.

"You know it," I said with a smug smile.

I tried to wait patiently as Sam disappeared to order, perusing the movies again, reading each preview making sure I'd made a good choice.

When I couldn't wait another second, Sam magically appeared and plopped the hugest piece of pizza on the planet in front of me. The smell alone launched me into the stratosphere.

"This is heaven," I said with a mouthful.

Sam just nodded.

We felt no shame as we stuffed our faces in silence.

"I hope this movie is good," I said while I sucked on my soda, patting my full tummy.

"It sounds funny."

That was the whole idea. I needed an hour or so when I could escape and experience simultaneous joy from the other movie goers around me.

The Point was right down the street from the pizza place and we parked with Sam's windshield positioned at the horizon. It would be our personal IMAX Theater when the sunset fire show began.

"This is so ro-tic," Sam said with a surly grin.

"Ro-tic?"

"Yup, romantic without the man."

I chuckled and faked a smile as Nicholas came to mind.

Argh.

Frustrated with myself, I pushed his face away again and tried to find a distraction. The glassy surf was peppered with surfers and I zoned out staring at one of them getting ready to catch an incoming wave. I cheered in my head as he paddled and popped up, riding it in gracefully. He made it look effortless.

The sun started to touch the horizon behind him and instantly turned everything a vibrant orange. The waves danced and reflected the fiery hues creating a warm glow across the water. And slowly the sun fell behind the low-lying clouds, and golden purplish rays of light pierced like knives into the sky. We both watched in silence, the light getting dimmer and dimmer until in one tiny flash, everything turned to dusk. The beauty was breathtaking and sharing it with Sam's awe and wonder made it even better.

"Wow," I said, feeling like I should break out in applause.

"Pretty amazing."

"No wonder the real estate around here is so expensive."

"No kidding."

We sat for another minute, before Sam started up her car.

"Ready, Madam?"

She gave me a mischievous look and revved her engine. I knew what she wanted to do. I smiled and I nodded my head to give her the signal. She tromped on the gas, pushing me back into my seat and I squealed lifting my arms out of the convertible's top as she jetted down the road.

We raced through town and parked on a side road nearby the theater. Sam had offered to drop me off at the front, but I didn't want the extra attention. I could hobble down the street if it wasn't far.

"Hey, I have an idea," she said with a twinkle in her eye.

Before I could object, she ushered me towards a tiny house with "Fortune Teller" glowing in the window.

"No." I dug my heels in.

"Why? How come? It'll be fun. Don't you wanna know if Nicholas is ever going to come back?"

Oh nice. Bring Nicholas into it, why don't you.

"No, actually I don't. Besides, they just lie anyway."

I would know. They couldn't deceive me. Not with my gift.

"I really want to, please?" she begged, flashing me puppy dog eyes.

It was against my better judgment to go, but since she really wanted to, I conceded. We walked to the porch and spotted a sign in the window that said "come in". Sam, now completely afraid, looked to me for support, so I turned the rusty knob and opened the door. Bells rang out to alert the owner of our presence.

"If she really could see the future, she wouldn't need those," I whispered.

Sam wrinkled up her nose and smirked.

The dimly lit room stunk of animal dander, patchouli oil and incense. Dusty plum colored scarves with gold fringes hung over the lampshades and tabletops. They matched the ugly gold and purple metallic paper on the walls. The only light in the room came from a few candles, which didn't brighten the dismal appearance. I wondered if the décor scared off potential repeat customers.

A black cat, with icy blue eyes, hissed at me from its perch on top of an armoire in the corner.

"Shhh Enigma," a voice said from the other room.

A plump old woman full of distrust and pessimism entered the room through a doorway framed by a thick curtain held back with a beaded sash. She picked up the cat and shooed it into another room.

"Come in, come in," she said, while loosening the sash, letting the curtain fall.

Her high pitched voice sounded out of breath, like she was going to croak at any minute.

We looked at each other and stepped inside. The sound of the door slamming shut behind us signaled finality. I shivered, reminded of the children in *Hansel and Gretel.*

"What can I do for you girls?" she said, her red lipstick not quite exactly on her lips.

"We'd like our fortunes read," Sam said sheepishly.

The old woman smiled revealing crooked teeth aged from time. "Fine dears, lovely, come . . .sit down . . . sit down."

She motioned for us to sit in two chairs by a table adorned with more dark tapestries. Sam patiently waited as I hobbled over and leaned my crutches against the wall. I sat down, but kept a watchful eye as the woman waited for us to get comfortable. Her black taffeta dress swished as she moved to sit directly across from us.

"That'll be $10 each," she said.

"What a rip off," I murmured.

Sam jabbed me in the ribs, before she plunked down the money. The old woman pocketed it and snatched Sam's hand, flipping it over. She paused, I'm sure for effect, before giving her answer. She told us Sam would have two children, marry the man of her dreams and live a long and prosperous life, but cautioned her to avoid making big decisions if the date happened to be the 16th and a Tuesday.

Sam asked a few specific questions about her family and Todd. The woman wanted to know their birth dates and then made up some niceties about how Todd could be the one because their birth signs were compatible.

I rolled my eyes. *What a crock!*

But before I could stop her, Sam put down another $10 and plunged my hand into the old woman's.

She latched on like a crab and her distrust overwhelmed me. I recoiled, but she didn't let go. Her feelings seemed ironic since she was the one who made a living deceiving others in the first place. I wanted to laugh, before running out of the place, but I was slightly curious at what she had to say.

"Hmmm," she said, as she studied the lines on my hand.

Her long boney finger traced along the ridges of my palm then froze. Her dark empty eyes fell into slits. She was afraid.

"You've got quite a life line here," she said quietly.

I tried to pull my hand away again, but she held on, her grip amazingly strong.

"Danger surrounds you . . . danger unknown to you." She paused and furrowed her brow. "Ah . . . and you bear the mark . . . the mark of the innocent one."

I started to feel unnerved because as far as I could tell, she told the truth.

"The innocent human . . . the one to rid us of *them*."

Sam sat next to me with her mouth gaped open.

"Them?" I asked.

"You don't know about *them* yet, do you?"

The old woman looked deep into my eyes. I had no idea what she meant; her words gave me goose bumps.

"But what about Nicholas?" Sam said.

I kicked Sam under the table. The last thing I wanted was to reveal anything private to this looney. Sam felt confused and clammed up.

The old woman's eyes shifted from Sam and then back to me. She dropped my hand.

"He's trouble. Stay away from him."

I rubbed my hand, grateful to have it back, wanting to wash it off thoroughly with antimicrobial soap.

"That's all I can see. You can leave now," she said, getting up abruptly.

I wanted out of there, so I got up too, grabbed my crutches and headed toward the door. Sam led the way.

"When you want answers, you'll be back," she said quietly behind me.

I pretended I didn't hear her.

Once outside, I hobbled quickly down her walkway and took a deep breath to cleanse my lungs. She disturbed me. Her touch unleashed a wave of toxic emotions, as if she'd poisoned me. I moved as fast as my crutches allowed, down the walkway, relieved that with each step, my feelings began to return to normal. No way would I ever return to her house again—never.

"Sorry about that," Sam said as we rounded the corner of the theater. "She was totally weird."

"Yeah—" I looked back towards her house. "She was."

I tried to process what the woman said. What did she mean by *them*? And being innocent? She sounded like I would save the world, from some unknown darkness, like a super hero.

And then her insistence to avoid Nicholas? Not that I had any choice in the matter seeing how he completely avoided me like the plague. Could she have been anymore cryptic? I looked at my palm for a special mark, but saw nothing out of the ordinary.

I wanted to tell Sam about how I believed the mountain lion incident and the old lady's rants were more than coincidental. I might have told her, if I could've done so, without disclosing my lie. I marveled at how insane my life had become, as if I was on a collision course with some crazy alter universe. I wished for normalcy.

There was a line outside the theater. We walked to the end of the line to wait our turn. I checked the time. We had ten minutes until the movie started.

"What do you think she meant by 'you bear the mark'?" Sam asked me.

"I have no clue. She's crazy."

"I thought she was okay at first, like when she said—"

Sam kept talking, but I didn't hear her. The same eerie stalking hunger-filled feelings from the forest were here. I whirled around to find the source.

I spotted a group of college-aged people walking in our direction. Something about them seemed unnatural, almost surreal, but I couldn't put my finger on it. I stiffened and felt the need to protect Sam who still prattled away about the old woman. I put my arm around her and ushered her closer to the wall, away from the middle of the walkway. I glanced back in their direction. One member of the pack looked right at me with his dark black eyes and smiled a wicked grin. Frightened, I looked away and watched their feet out of the corner of my eye as they paraded past—not wanting to cause any trouble.

I breathed a sigh of relief as they moved away from us and the hunger feelings dissipated. Sam, oblivious to what just happened, was more concerned with paying for our tickets, than fearing for our lives, but I knew it wasn't over.

Someone, who looked an awful lot like Nicholas walked hurriedly towards us. He wore the same long, brown leather trench coat and it flapped in the wind as he made his way in determination. When I spotted him, he flipped up his collar and averted his sunglass covered eyes, just before walking by.

"Nicholas?" I said as he passed.

He ignored me.

I spun around and spoke louder.

"Nicholas."

He stopped and turned towards me.

"Oh, hi," he said coolly.

"Hi," I said, nudging Sam. "This is my friend Sam. Sam this is *Nicholas.*"

I emphasized his name. He reached out and shook her hand.

"Nice to meet you," she said with a smile and wide eyes that said *'yeah, he's gorgeous'*.

"Likewise," Nicholas said, with a nod, his voice polite, but his face like stone.

He made no attempt at small talk and the pause in the conversation became awkward. His emotions were completely different than before, as if our connection never happened. I searched his aura and looked for some sort of reassurance that we were still friends, but only sensed fear and icy aloofness.

"So . . . how are you?" I asked, trying to relieve the tension.

"Julia, I can't talk right now. I have to go," he said abruptly "It was nice to meet you, Sam."

A lump formed in my throat and I blinked back the tears, feeling completely stupid as he walked away. I couldn't believe he didn't want to talk and just ditched me. Why did I call out to him? Sam, not sure how to react, tugged at my arm.

"Let's go, the movie is about to start."

My body went into autopilot and I followed her inside, unable to pay attention to where we were going. Before I knew it, she'd found us seats and I sat down, thankful for the darkness.

The movie started and so did my tears.

What was I doing insisting he notice me? I'm so stupid.

As the movie progressed, I did my best to try to follow along, but couldn't concentrate. The movie I watched was the one in my head of what just happened, not the silver screen. I slumped back into my chair and stifled my sniffles. Everyone was enjoying the movie and their laughter echoed all around me, but I'd never felt so lonely in my life.

Sam passed me a tissue.

I'm so pathetic. I can't even keep myself together.

I tried hard to stop crying; not wanting to ruin everything Sam had done to help me have a good time, but I couldn't. The damage was done.

"This movie is lame, wanna go?" she whispered after a few minutes.

Relief flooded me—I did want to leave. I wasn't sure how much longer I could endure the torture of holding back my emotions.

"Yeah," I murmured.

We pushed the double doors to exit and I felt thankful to leave the theater alone, without curious onlookers. I could image their confusion, because I'd looked like I'd just left a tragedy, instead of a comedy.

"I'm so sorry, Jules," Sam said as we walked to her car.

"It's fine. I'm fine. It's just—" I choked back a sob.

She put her arm on my shoulder and squeezed it, her care and concern soothed me.

"I guess he's not who I thought he was," I finally said. "Maybe he *is* trouble."

I wanted to say *jerk*, but my mouth wouldn't form the word. I cared about him still—too much actually. I was astonished at my willingness to be a glutton for punishment.

"Trouble? No, he was plain rude," she said, slamming her car door. "Honestly, he saves your life a few days ago, but now he doesn't have a few minutes to say hello and meet your best friend? Whatever."

She started her car and backed out of the parking spot.

I appreciated her desire to protect me and her interpretation of the situation helped me see that I wasn't crazy. Nicholas was the one with the problems. But, I still wanted to know why he didn't like me anymore?

"Yeah, you're right. I just don't get what happened."

"Guys are weird. They get all spooked for the stupidest reasons."

"I guess so." I gave a fake chuckle.

Luckily, he only met Sam and not my whole group of friends. Now, that would have been utterly embarrassing and Katie never would have let me hear the end of it.

I slumped back in my seat and watched the world move by in a blur as Sam drove. She'd found a man-hater song on the radio that seemed to match the mood. I could sense her worry, but I didn't want to talk for fear I'd burst into tears again. It was a lousy way to finish our evening.

"Sorry I ruined your movie," I said as she pulled up to my house.

"You didn't. It's understandable considering the circumstances."

"But still . . ."

"Do you want to talk about it?" she asked, her eyes kind.

"No. I think I just want to go to bed."

"You sure?"

"I'll be okay, honest." I did my best to muster up a convincing smile. She studied my face for a minute then bought my charade.

"Definitely call me tomorrow when you wake up, okay?"

I got out and peered through the open door. "I will."

I gave another weak smile and shut the door.

She waved one last time, with sympathy in her eyes, and then drove away. I watched until her car disappeared, took a deep breath and limped up the cobblestone path to the house. Disappointment flooded me when I opened the door to find it dark and empty.

It was times like this I wished I had a mom to talk to. Even if Dad were home, he would never understand and it would be awkward to try to explain it to him. I thought of Jo and sighed. If any consolation was going to be given tonight, it would have to come from me.

I walked upstairs and decided to forgo the whole "getting ready for bed" routine and just changed into my jammies. I had little energy to do anything beyond that. Aladdin jumped on my bed and wound her body into a circle resting her head on my hand.

What rotten luck. Why did he treat me like that? Was fate trying to tell me something?

I looked out the window after shutting off my light and snuggled under my covers. It was partly cloudy, so I couldn't see any stars to wish upon. I rolled over and yearned for sleep, but I couldn't shut off my brain. It hurt inside; ached actually.

I wanted to know why. Next time, if there ever was a next time, charming or not, he'd give me answers, or at least get an earful about what I thought about his wretched behavior.

I groaned and pulled the covers over my head. Any normal person would get a grip and move on. But the panicked feeling inside made me question if I just lost the best thing that ever happened to me. How stupid to hang onto the past. But the brutal reality, raw and unkind, told me he didn't want to have anything to do with me.

I wished I didn't care.

7 – FOG

*E*ven though my eyes were closed, the early light of morning pierced them like daggers. All night I longed for happy dreams to escape into so I didn't have to think about my pathetic life, but ended up with nightmares instead. Unable to sleep any longer, I rolled over to get out of bed and accidentally knocked Aladdin off in the process. She meowed loudly and sulked out of my room.

I stared at the ceiling, wondering why I kept dreaming about mountain lions and evil people with red eyes and sharp teeth hunting me down with the intent to kill me. I wanted to just grab my pillow and scream into it, but I couldn't find the strength and worried Luke would hear me.

My tummy growled as I limped down to a cold, dark kitchen— the first time without the use of my crutches—and pulled my favorite tattered robe tighter around myself, disappointed to find the room empty. Saturdays were supposed to be big breakfast mornings, but Dad was still away on a business trip. My mouth watered thinking of fluffy scrambled eggs, sausage links, cubed fried potatoes and golden pancakes drizzled with lots of syrup. Somehow, the thought of toast and cereal just didn't seem as appetizing.

While the toast cooked and the coffee finished brewing, I watched the birds out the kitchen window bathing in the fountain. Something about how they frolicked made me want to sit on the patio and watch them.

Maybe the fresh air would help me feel better.

With my toast balanced on the top of my coffee mug in one hand and a fuzzy blanket in the other, I carefully walked outside and snuggled up on the wooden lounge. I rested my head on the back of the chair, closed my eyes and focused on the peaceful sound of the creek gurgling through the ravine. Normally, the ambiance would diminish my worries, but was clearly not going to soothe away my wounds today.

I tried to think of a good reason why Nicholas had been so rude to me the night before, but drew a blank. It just didn't make sense, almost like the Nicholas I first met and the one I ran into last night were two separate people. I wanted desperately to forget all about it—the fall, his eyes, how being connected with him made me feel so alive and safe, but I couldn't make it go away.

This wasn't how I wanted to feel. I prided myself on my ability to handle my emotions better than other girls my age, being forced to feel their rollercoaster's all the time. But one interaction with one guy and I'm just like them? I felt completely crazy, irrational and wished for a switch to turn it all off.

I glared at the dying potted flowers scattered around the deck, trying to blame them for looking so needy. The last thing I wanted to do was garden, so I looked away, fighting their wilting-leaf guilt trips. But after a few minutes, unable to stand it anymore, I got up and grabbed a watering can. I figured maybe some gardening therapy would help distract my mind.

Before I knew it, an hour had passed and I'd weeded, watered and even planted some bulbs for next year feeling a tiny bit better. I was dusting off my hands and admiring my handy work when Luke walked onto the patio.

"What are you doing?"

His happy-go-lucky nature nauseated me, so I kept my back to him.

"Baking a cake," I said with a smirk he couldn't see.

"Ha-ha. Very funny."

I turned and glared at him, giving him the *don't mess with me* look which he should have been very familiar with.

"What's your problem?" he said half joking—half serious, but then he stopped chuckling after I kept scowling. The regret he felt gave me a sick satisfaction.

"Nothing," I said, my tone terse, forcefully tugging a handful of weeds.

I wanted him to pry, but didn't want to look dumb either. It was already embarrassing enough. If I admitted my feelings to Luke and he teased me, it would be more than I could bear.

"Must be that time of the month," he mumbled under his breath while turning to leave.

"What?" I gasped. "Whatever."

I pushed past him into the house and slammed the door behind me. Why did every male believe that if a woman was upset, it was because of her monthly cycle? I was particularly annoyed by his comment as it was his male species that wreaked havoc on my life at the moment, not my hormones.

"I'm not on my period!" I yelled through the closed door.

My anger welled up and I stood there, fists clenched, realizing I could no longer wait anymore for the person I really needed to talk to. So I walked directly over to the phone, picked it up and dialed, prepared to say what I needed to say to get my Jo back.

My ankle ached when pressing the gas pedal as I drove the short distance to Jo and John's. Every second that passed seemed to make my heart beat a little faster and my palms began to sweat while holding the steering wheel. In my head, I rehearsed what I would say if John was home. I should've had the courage to ask Jo if he was at home, instead of being too chicken. I decided if he was there when I arrived that I'd just be blunt and tell him he wasn't welcome then ignore his hurt feelings and pouting.

I parked in front and noticed a new "Welcome to the Ritchie's Home" sign that hung on the side of what used to be Grandma's house. My stomach churned. Yet another reminder Jo and Grandma were no longer a part of my life—I wished I wasn't jealous. I pushed the thoughts aside, walked up the walkway and knocked, prepared in case John answered the door.

"Julia!"

Jo ambushed me with a huge hug almost knocking me off my feet after opening the door. I melted into her hug and fought back my emotions as we embraced for a moment—basking in the warmth of her undying love.

"I've missed you. Come in . . . come in."

It felt really good to be genuinely missed and I realized how stupid I was—John or no John, I shouldn't have waited so long to see her. As Jo ushered me into the house I smelled cookies baking.

"I just made some chocolate chip cookies. Would you like some?" she asked as we walked towards the kitchen.

I nodded while turning the corner and stopped in my tracks. The kitchen had been totally remodeled.

"Wow," I said, overwhelmed by the ostentatious colors and furniture changes. "When did you . . . It looks so . . . different."

"Do you like it?" she said, her joy flowing all around us. "Well, now that Mom is gone, John and I felt we should make it more our home. I hope that doesn't make you feel like we are trying to erase the memory of your Grandma."

"Oh, no . . . yeah, you should," I said while heading toward a newly upholstered bar stool to sit down. I needed a moment to take it all in.

The walls were now a buttery yellow which complimented the oak cabinetry and granite countertops. The bar stool upholstery matched the draperies, a burgundy fabric with white magnolia flowers. The kitchen was completely unrecognizable from before and very modern. For as long as I could remember Grandma Mae hadn't changed anything in her home. I wondered if she'd approve of what they were doing to *her* house.

I felt like someone was staring at me and I turned. A huge wedding portrait of John and Jo hung on a now deep burgundy colored wall in the dining room. The photo perfectly captured the beauty of Jo's hazel eyes and long auburn hair that flowed ever so gently over her cream colored dress; her slender arms draped delicately around his neck. I remembered the day well and felt guilty for feeling such disdain towards the man she loved with all her heart.

"Where's John?" I asked, not feeling his actual presence but expecting him to come around the corner any minute.

"He had some things to do today and will be so disappointed he missed you, but he'll join us later for dinner, "she said, while dishing up another batch of cookies to bake in the oven. "What's new in your life?"

I stood there stunned. I couldn't believe I'd have Jo's attention all to myself for the entire afternoon and didn't have to insist on it. My mind went haywire for a second, trying to think of where I wanted to start.

"Boys," I finally said. "I—I don't understand them."

Jo suppressed a giggle and smiled appreciatively.

"Yes, I remember what boys were like when I was your age. And that's what they were—boys. What's going on?"

I looked in her eyes and sighed as she took pity on me. Her depiction of boys my age wasn't good news.

"Well . . ." I thought about Nicholas. He wasn't what I would classify as a boy, but he sure wasn't acting like a man " . . .they can be so immature."

"Ah," she said, as she put her arm around my shoulder, looking at me with a tender expression. "Have patience, they'll grow up eventually . . . just give it a few years."

"Years?"

My gift constantly reminded me girls matured faster than boys, so I didn't understand why this revelation shocked me. Maybe it was because I'd compared every guy to Luke, who was very mature for his age and hoped I'd find someone like him someday. No one ever measured up until I met Nicholas. Or at least that's what I had thought. Now I wasn't so sure.

"Well, I'm sure you heard about what happened," I began, my tone somber.

"With your accident? I've heard bits and pieces. Tell me what happened."

I smiled because she really wanted to know, and I kicked myself for not fighting harder to have the privilege of sitting in her kitchen sooner. Her kind, listening ear was always there through my toughest storms. She never judged and knew exactly when it was time for listening or time for finding solutions.

The non-mountain lion version of the story flowed easily from my lips as I'd told it so many times already, but I fought the urge to tell her everything, knowing she'd overreact and tell my dad, which meant I'd never be allowed to leave the house unchaperoned again. It hurt again to tell her how Nicholas had reacted at the theater, which was a complete flip from the week before. I studied her face and emotions to see what she thought. Her quiet concern bothered me.

"I'm not sure if he really is busy, or he's blowing me off. What do you think?" I asked sheepishly.

She took another bite of her cookie and thought for a moment.

"Well, I'm not sure Julia. I think young men have a hard time expressing how they feel about things, especially to a woman they might like. You say he seemed rushed and surprised to run into you? I don't think that's a good sign."

I bit my lip to hold back a tear. The honesty hit me like a punch in the ribs.

"Or he might just be acting tough, like men are supposed to act. They may like a girl, but then they don't show it, possibly because they are afraid they'll be rejected. You may think it's easy for them, but it takes a lot of courage to put your feelings out there. Imagine being in their shoes. Take John for example. It took him a whole year to finally ask me out," she said with a chuckle.

I sighed secretly on the inside.

"I hate to tell you this, but it seems young men don't get over this until they get some relationship experience. Maybe he was embarrassed because Sam was with you."

I knew he wasn't embarrassed. It was more like distracted. He had a legitimate reason to go. And he was afraid too, not the fear you feel when you're scared, but the one you feel when there's impending danger.

"It's hard to know exactly what's changed. I'm sorry honey. I think you need to try to move on. For some reason, he's not interested in getting to know you right now."

Listening to her words, something in my heart broke, but I knew she was right. Even though I still longed for him to stop by my house and end my agony, I knew he wasn't going to—at least not this new Nicholas anyway. I needed to face the facts. It was over. There would be no us and I needed to move on.

"Julia, these things happen. There will be a few guys in your life that you will have a huge connection with. Some will be poor timing for you; some will be poor timing for him. But one day, the timing will be right for the both of you and hopefully, that will be the one you'll spend the rest of your life with. I know you'll find someone who's as wonderful to you as John is to me; you'll see."

She smiled again and I forced a fake smile in return. Her love for him beamed like the sun reflects off new snow and I saw John in a new light—Jo's light. And I decided, for her, I'd look for the good in John even if it was probably going to kill me. After all, he did make her so happy.

She squeezed me tight and I soaked in her aura's sensation that I'd missed so much.

"My suggestion is to move on—find someone new to think about. I'm sure there's got to be another boy at school who you might be interested in perhaps?"

She lifted her eyebrow at me and waited for my reaction. No one came to mind at the moment, so I made a face and shrugged. I'd never felt like that with anyone before, so imagining myself finding another guy like him so quickly seemed preposterous.

I shook my head.

"Well then you've got it bad my dear. So give yourself some time to heal. But, if for some reason he does come back around, find out first why he took so long, before you get upset. He may have a very good reason for making you wait. John did."

"Okay," I said after a short pause, letting it all sink in.

John's big excuse was that he was a chicken. I refused to think Nicholas was like him, but hopeful it wasn't completely over just yet. Maybe he did have a good reason and it was something like he thought he was too old for me, or that I had a boyfriend already. But would I have to wait a year to find out?

Oh please dear God. That would be dreadful.

"So, let's move on, shall we? Get your purse," she said in delight. "I'm kidnapping you."

"Kidnapping me? But . . ." I pointed at my bandaged ankle.

"This won't require walking and actually might help your ankle."

I gave her a suspicious look and before I knew it, she ushered me to the car in the garage and made me get in the front seat. Her contagious excitement made me wonder what she was up to.

The entire ride I tried guessing our destination, but she remained tight-lipped, not revealing any hints about where we were going until she pulled up into the parking lot in front of a nail salon.

"We are getting pedicures," I announced in glee.

"Not just any type of pedicure," she said with a twinkle in her eye. "This one will be . . . different for sure."

I furrowed my brow. "Okay, now you're scaring me."

"You'll see, come on."

We walked into the salon and Jo went up to the counter and whispered to the receptionist. I looked around and everything seemed like a normal salon. A variety of nail polishes sat in little racks on the counter and pictures of manicured hands and feet hung on the walls. A sign with the pricing of the services was on a wall behind the receptionist. The only thing that struck me odd was the sign saying they offered Dr. Fish Treatments. I sat and waited patiently for Jo to rejoin me.

"Are you ready?" a girl with long blonde hair said as she motioned us to follow her down the corridor. "Please come this way."

Jo kept watching for my reaction as we followed the receptionist into a room with some oversized chairs. I sat down in one and Jo sat in the other, a Cheshire grin across her face. I was still trying to figure out what the big deal was.

"Okay, what are we going to be doing that's weird?" I finally asked.

"Just wait. You'll see."

Two ladies came into the room and introduced themselves, then washed our feet.

"Is this your first fish treatment?" the brunette asked me.

"I . . . guess so?" I looked to Jo for reassurance, afraid I was supposed to know something.

"Yes, this is Julia's first treatment. I've had several," Jo said.

"Fish treatment? As in real fish?" I gasped. Images of soaking my feet in fish guts filled my head and I panicked. "I'm not putting my feet in fish guts!"

Everyone giggled and I blushed.

"No, it's nothing like that," the other woman said and she smiled kindly at me. I felt my cheeks return to normal. "You'll be visiting our famous Doctor Fish tank, where our little friends are going to clean your feet for you."

Clean my feet? Ewww.

I was not crazy about fish in general, which is why swimming in lakes and streams always freaked me out. I didn't want any fish within 100 yards of me, so actually letting them bite me was absolutely insane, not to mention much worse than putting one's feet in fish guts. The only fish I knew of that ate flesh were piranhas.

"You're kidding me, right?"

"I'm not kidding. They are special fish that only eat dead skin. I promise they won't hurt you."

Ewww gross!

"Okay?" I said with trepidation. The idea of letting the fish nibble on me just seemed wrong, but the peer pressure kept me from running out of the salon screaming, to wait in Jo's car.

We stood up and followed the ladies into another room where a rounded bench seat surrounded a shallow tank. A bunch of little gold colored fish swam around in the water.

Jo sat down and plunged her feet into the water. The fish instantly swam over and covered her feet and toes. I gasped.

"Does it hurt?" I asked while squinting.

"No, it actually feels good. Are you going to try it?"

I sat on the bench and hovered my feet over the tank. Was I actually going to do this? The only reason I wasn't begging for a normal pedicure was because Jo was enjoying herself. So, I closed my eyes and before I could think, put them in the water. It surprised me that the water was warm. I opened one eye. My feet were covered in fish and it tickled. I let out a squeak.

"This is so weird," I said, trying not to wiggle.

"I know, but just wait. Your feet are going to feel so soft," Jo said.

The fish worked their way around my cuticles and heals and I fought the urge to flick them away. I didn't realize I had so much dead skin.

"How did you hear about this?" I asked.

"They suggested it here when I got a regular pedicure. I was apprehensive at first, because I hate fish. But you know me; I'm always willing to try anything one time."

"Well this is something I never would've guessed I'd do and can't believe I'm doing," I said while shaking my head, still gritting my teeth. "They seem to be finding a feast on my toes."

"You'll thank me later," she said while grinning. "How's

school?"

"Fine, I guess. Algebra is going to kill me though," I complained.

"Oh, really?"

"Well, Sam's been helping me a lot because she's really good at math. I just hope she doesn't get so frustrated with me that she pulls out all her hair."

Jo chuckled. "You're so dramatic sometimes."

"Hey, I try." I swished my feet around forgetting that the fish were doing their job and then froze thinking I might have accidentally kicked a few in the process. But they came back unafraid, nibbling hungrily again. I still couldn't get over how weird it was.

"I do have some good news," Jo said with a big smile.

I'd noticed Jo seemed happier than usual, both on the inside and outside. She had a huge smile plastered on her face the entire time we'd been together.

She pressed her lips tightly together.

"Yeah?"

"John and I are expecting a baby."

My eyes grew big and I screamed in delight.

"Oh. My. Gosh. That's wonderful!" I threw my arms around her neck and gave her a huge hug. She had tears in her eyes.

"Oh, Auntie, I'm so excited for you guys."

I had an unfair advantage when it came to babies because I knew exactly what they wanted. Mothers were amazed at my ability to get even the fussiest baby to sleep so easily. Thoughts of holding my new cousin whenever I wanted was so exciting. Their sweet emotions were up there with the blissfulness of falling in love and it had been a long time since I'd had the privilege of holding one.

"You know, I wasn't ever sure if I'd get to be a mommy, I mean I will always feel like your mom in a way, but to have a baby of my own. We are so excited."

"Yeah, this is really awesome. You feeling okay?" I asked

"So far so good. I'm a little tired, but I'm four months along already."

Jo took out ultrasound pictures from her wallet and handed them to me. I tried to find the baby in the black and white photo, but all I saw was a peanut looking thing.

"The baby is right there. See?" She pointed to the dark blob in the photo. I squinted and it came into focus. The larger part of the peanut shape suddenly looked like a head and I could see where arms and legs were forming.

"Wow. This is truly amazing." Seeing the picture brought it all to reality and I had tears in my eyes too. "Have you thought of names yet?"

"Well, a few but we want to wait until we know if it's a girl or a boy. That'll make it easier."

I instinctively reached over and felt her flat tummy.

"I think I feel a bump already."

"No, that's just the cookies from earlier. I've had the worst sweet tooth. It's horrible," she complained, but with a giggle. I saw a light in her eyes I'd never seen before.

"Then it's going to be a girl," I joked, not sure if that was how the saying went or not.

"We'll know soon enough."

After the fish pedicure, we decided to have lunch at a little café in town. We had to fulfill the baby's craving for Chinese chicken salad and no other restaurants would do. After lunch it started to rain again, so we rented a movie. It seemed fitting for the afternoon. We contemplated going to a theater, but Jo said the popcorn smell made her queasy and I didn't want to share that feeling with her, so I agreed (with much enthusiasm) to watch a movie at home.

I prayed secretly John would not come home early so we could watch it in peace. The last time, he talked over the entire movie and even ruined the ending by telling us 'who done it'.

But John didn't show up until closer to six when Jo just about had dinner ready. They invited me to stay. To my surprise, John and I got along better this time, making dinner an enjoyable experience. However, after dinner, the lack of sleep started to catch up to me and I just wanted to go home. I congratulated them again on the great news of the new baby and then drove home.

When I walked into the house, I planned to head straight for the stairs and my bed, but heard the TV going in the living room. My guilt surfaced as I felt Luke's dread. He had no idea where my moodiness had come from earlier and it wasn't fair I'd taken my frustration out on him, so I swallowed my pride and stood in the doorway. Luke faked like he didn't see me.

"Hey," I said.

He flickered his eyes to me and then back to the TV.

"Hey."

I entered the room and sat down. I didn't know exactly what to say, so I waited for a minute before speaking.

"Sorry about earlier."

He hit mute on the remote.

"It's okay," he said quietly, while studying his fingernails. He acted tough, but I knew he was more upset than he let on.

"I'm just frustrated."

"About?"

"You can't tease me," I said quickly.

Luke put his hands up, as if in an act of surrender and I smiled. It was sweet he wanted to know.

"I just don't understand guys sometimes," I said while playing with the string on my sweatshirt.

"Psscht . . . I could say the same about girls," he said, rolling his eyes, but then he smiled. He wasn't being rude. He was trying to sympathize. "So who's the guy you don't understand?"

I bit my lip and then let out a sigh, still afraid to share. Luke waited intently and raised his eyebrows, encouraging me to continue.

"It's Nicholas. He said he'd come by a week ago and he hasn't and then I ran into him last night. He was kinda rude and said "*I can't talk now*" and rushed away. I didn't expect him to be like that, so I don't get it."

"Really," he said, surprised. "Wow. I thought he was a cool guy. I wonder what happened."

"Me too."

"Well, it sounds like he's blowing you off."

"You think so?" I said disappointed.

"I don't know. It's hard to tell. I wasn't there."

"Why do you think he did that?"

"Heck if I know, but you can't just sit around here and hope he's going to come and see you. You need to move on, have fun and realize, if he's blowing you off, then he's a jerk and he doesn't deserve you."

It warmed my heart to hear Luke hold me in such high regard. I knew he was right about the moving on part. I just hated not knowing.

"Julia, there's a lot of cool guys out there; you don't need this one," he said with a convincing smile

I found his gesture sweet, but I didn't want any other "cool" guys. I wanted Nicholas.

"Yeah, I know."

I continued playing with my sweatshirt string. And after Luke realized I was finished, he turned up the TV and started watching his show again.

I sat for a few minutes, happy we'd reconciled, then headed towards my room. Flopping down on the chair at my desk, I listened to the rain coming down outside and thought about what Luke and Jo had said. There were way too many thoughts going on in my head, so I decided I needed to write them down to get closure and clarity. I pulled out my journal and began to write.

Dear Diary,

It's been a week since I've seen Nicholas. Tomorrow, I'm going to say goodbye forever.

And then I knew what I wanted to do. I pulled out another sheet of paper and began to write.

It started out . . .

Dear Nicholas,

I'm writing to say goodbye . . .

I just wrote what my heart needed to say in order to move on. As the ink spilled the words out onto the paper, my eyes welled up with tears. At the end, I signed it, then folded it up neatly. I had plans for it in the morning.

8 — FAREWELL

*T*he crisp morning air and the warm travel mug in my hands should have stopped the lump from forming in my throat, but this wasn't going to be a normal stroll. Birds sang happily to welcome the day after the night rain, but I couldn't rejoice with them. Everything inside me felt numb.

Earlier, when I got up after another disturbing, restless night, I discovered Luke had already left the house. But to my surprise, I found a pot of hot coffee waiting for me. It could only mean he'd forgiven my girlish behavior. He also left a note telling me he was at the store, which was a good idea since all we had in the fridge were a few rotten vegetables and moldy bread. I ducked out quickly, leaving a vague note next to his about my whereabouts, to avoid any unnecessary questions. I felt within my pocket to make sure I'd remembered to bring my new fully-charged cell phone just in case.

The road to the forest trail seemed lonely as I listened to the crunch of the wet gravel under my shoes. I wanted to laugh out loud at the irony. Every day since I'd met Nicholas, I wanted to return to our meeting spot—until today. Had it only been a few days since we made the trek in the opposite direction? I inhaled and refused to reminisce about the past, pulling my coat tighter around myself.

Soon, too soon in fact, I stood at the mouth of the trail and my heart beat a little faster. Stairs made of railroad ties wove their way down into the dark redwoods below. I questioned my sanity.

After a moment of waffling, I carefully limped down each step. I couldn't help but remember how nimbly Nicholas carried me up these stairs. It was going to take me an hour at least to traverse them by myself later.

Why did all this happen?

At the end of the stairs, I stepped onto the muddy trail,

thankful I wore my old sneakers. All the familiar landmarks were welcoming in the daylight and the ominous scariness seemed completely non-existent. No wonder I thought I could walk through here unafraid, even if it was dark.

Unable to help myself, I looked around for evidence of Nicholas' presence: a foot print, a possible piece of torn fabric off his shirt, maybe even fur from the mountain lion. I rounded the corner and gasped. Someone had run a tractor through the area, or at least it looked like one had. Huge holes in the ground were all that was left of the trees that once stood and the ones remaining seemed askew with fresh overturned dirt at their trunks. A huge indentation against the trail wall showed evidence something large had been pushed against it, dislodging the soil upwards, widening the fissure in the rock face.

Whoa, did this happen before or after my fall?

Confused, I wandered around and tried to piece the scene together. Nicholas and the mountain lion couldn't have possibly made all this damage. A pit formed in my stomach as I remembered the hungry feelings from "it" and then shook my head. I still didn't understand how, for that brief moment in time, I felt its feelings. Maybe it was because I was in mortal danger.

I slowly crept to the edge of the trail and looked down. A piece of the remaining branch stuck out of the earth part way and I gulped. This was the cliff I had tumbled over. My fall really did happen and it was a long way down to the creek bed below. Without Nicholas' help, I would have been a goner falling from this height. Who knows how long I would have been down there, unconscious. Suddenly I felt woozy and I backed away from the edge, drawing my arms around myself. I didn't want to think about the 'what ifs'.

I sat down on a stump to think as the weight of the past bore down on me. More questions than answers tumbled around in my brain. The closure I desperately craved wasn't going to be obtained today.

Out of the corner of my eye, I spotted the protruding tree root that started this whole mess. A broken piece of wood lay next to it on the trail. I picked it up and turned it over in my hands. One side was smooth from where people had walked on it and the underside rough, torn like my heart.

Folding my hands over the wood, I contemplated my next actions. Part of me wanted to keep it and the other, to throw it off the cliff. My goal had been to get rid of the past and leave it here in the woods with the rest of my demons, but I couldn't. Too much had happened.

I picked up a sharp rock and carved the date into the smooth side of the wood. And against my better judgment, I carved a heart around the numbers. The pressure broke the piece into two. I laughed. The break went straight down the middle of the heart.

Transfixed, I gazed off into the woods while holding the wood, and took the letter from my pocket. The wind blew the trees softly, bringing down large droplets of rain water as though the forest was crying for me. The letter felt heavy in my hand as I read it one last time. I thought I would cry, but I didn't. Instead, I gently folded the paper around one half of the wooden pieces and threw it off the cliff while tucking the other half in my pocket.

It soared through the air and disappeared out of sight. At the same time, the wind whipped up and tousled my hair. I held my breath, hoping for closure, finding disappointment instead—the whole charade suddenly feeling over-dramatic. Then I felt someone was coming down the trail so I quickly limped back home, afraid it would be someone I knew.

The next morning came and so did the sun.

For once, I actually wanted to go to school, anything to give me a mental break. I planned to take Jo's advice. There had to be at least one guy at school that I could like. I just wasn't sure who. The idea seemed insurmountable, but I was willing to try. I needed to do something.

Running late, I rinsed off my breakfast dishes and rushed towards the door, happy I was driving myself today.

"Hey," Luke said while walking past me into the kitchen sporting a bed-head hair-do. He deeply inhaled. "Is that coffee?"

I turned around and stood in the doorway. "You're up kinda early?"

Luke scratched his head and filled up his favorite coffee mug. "I have a job interview this morning," he said with a yawn.

"Really?"

"At Bic's"

I continued to look confused.

"The auto parts store?" he said with a sarcastic inflection. "I can get a discount if I work there."

I knew there had to be a catch.

"Oooh," I said and punched him in the arm before heading out. "Good luck."

He grimaced.

"Thanks."

I walked across the lawn and reached in my pocket for my cell phone to text Sam when I noticed a white piece of paper folded up on the ground near my car door. I unlocked the car, put all my junk inside, then fetched the note. My throat went dry as I stared at the words written inside.

Was this note for me?

Baffled, I closed the note and looked around even though I knew I was alone. Someone had written "I'm sorry" in scratchy masculine-looking lettering and left it unsigned. The penmanship didn't look familiar.

My mind raced and I quickly thought of who could possibly owe me an apology. My cheeks turned bright red as I imagined Nicholas gawking in the shadows while I threw the letter over the cliff—the letter that revealed all my feelings. Did he retrieve it? No. I would've felt it if someone was close by. I was sure I was alone. It had to be someone else. Who else owed me an apology? John maybe?

I got in my car and inconspicuously looked in my mirrors feeling vulnerable. Nothing seemed strange or out of place, but I was beginning to question my abilities. Someone could be watching from far away. I folded up the note, shoved it in my pocket and started my car.

The mental exercise to figure out the anonymous note writer faded after I parked and actually walked to class, free from my horrendous crutches. But I'd forgotten to tell Sam the good news and she was waiting for me at the front of the school.

"When are your crutches?" she asked when she saw me.

"Sorry I didn't tell you. I meant to text but . . ."

"Yeah, no call or text all weekend? What gives?" Sam put her hands on her hips and acted annoyed.

The guilt of neglecting my best friend hit me. All weekend, I'd spent my energy on myself and I'd not called or texted once like I promised I would.

"Sorry. I forgot. I did get your text though. Thanks."

Sam let out a sigh. "I was worried. I thought you fell into a deep depression."

"No," I said and rolled my eyes at her exaggeration. "But I did make up my mind to move on. I'm done with him, Sam. It's over."

I tried to sound convincing.

"That's good to hear. Well, it's not like I could talk anyway. I was at Aunt Patrilda's all weekend for a family reunion. They don't have cell service where she lives. I felt completely cut off from society."

We hurried to our lockers as Sam filled me in on her boring weekend with her cousins. I had to tell her about my pedicure experience. She couldn't believe I'd let fish peck away at my feet. I wanted to mention the weird apology note, but I didn't have enough time before she rushed off to change for P.E. class.

Just before I turned to walk towards the gym, I noticed

someone's ardent desires and reluctantly turned around. My gaze fell on Justin, a geeky Sophomore with greasy brown hair that rimmed the top of his glasses.

"Hi," Justin said with a stutter.

Just my luck.

I sighed on the inside. It was obvious where this awkward conversation was headed. Maybe if puberty had been kinder to his pockmarked face, or he was a little taller, I might possibly say yes to going to the dance if he asked, but his feelings left me feeling rather violated.

"Hey," I said with a straight face while shutting my locker door.

"I, um—"

A group of Junior cheerleaders walked by and giggled, whispering to each other. I sensed their insecurity, something I felt daily—more so from the popular kids than anyone. Their cruel teasing was only a cover-up of the real truth of how they viewed themselves deep inside.

"Justin." I cringed inside, but tried my hardest to protect his ego. "I'm late for class. What do you need?"

His cheeks flushed and fear hit 7.0 on the Richter scale.

"Oh, nothing."

He took off down the hall.

Relieved, I shook Justin's feelings off and walked to class, sitting alone on the bleachers as my classmates filed in one by one. Coach Hoffman split them up into teams to play volleyball. My doctor's note was good until the end of the week and I planned to milk every day of it. And lucky for me, since the fields were drenched from the rain, the guys were playing basketball indoors. I shimmied down the bench inconspicuously, hoping Coach Hoffman wouldn't catch me, so I could watch the boys play.

My eyes were drawn towards the new guy with sandy blonde hair who just started school a few days ago—someone more my type.

I wondered why I hadn't noticed his surfer physique with broad shoulders and a strong upper body before today. He also had impressive basketball skills.

His charisma was evident in his camaraderie between the other players. But the real test would be if he was as nice on the inside as he appeared on the outside; that was if we ever met.

The distraction of watching the guys worked and before I realized it, the bell rang. I took off, hoping to find a warmer classroom in History. Being the first student to arrive, I tried to act busy until Sam came and sat next to me. Mr. Marshall was writing dates on the blackboard, preparing to review for our test tomorrow. Since I'd been daydreaming in class all week, I'd not taken any notes and stared at the unfamiliar topics on the board. I thought my life was over, until I read *Open Note Test* at the bottom. With relief and after my fingers defrosted, I asked to borrow Sam's notes.

"You going to the bonfire tonight?" she whispered.

"Bonfire? I hadn't heard about it."

"Some of the Seniors on the football team are getting together and Todd invited me to go," she said, filled with anxiety and excitement.

"Oh . . . I don't know," I said with apprehension, imagining the overly amorous environment. "I . . . have a lot of homework to do."

Her sudden disappointment and fear told me she wasn't asking me to go, she *needed* me to go.

"Really? Can you work on it after school?"

Her doe-like eyes were more than I could bear.

"Okay. I'll try," I said, feeling the atmosphere change in the classroom.

Mr. Marshall had stopped lecturing and the silence was deafening. I looked up and met the source of the invisible loathing I sensed. My cheeks grew flushed and I quickly looked down and acted like I was writing, praying the silence would stop. I was relieved when he started lecturing again.

Going to a senior bonfire sounded very intimidating to me. I'd never been invited to one by that crowd before. In the past, I figured I was overlooked because I wasn't a cheerleader, rich, or good looking enough. But that was fine with me. Tonight though, I would be totally out of my element, especially if Sam left me to be alone with Todd. The more I thought about it, the more I regretted that I said I would go.

English and Chemistry were a blur and before I knew it, it was time for lunch. My appetite came back and something in the cafeteria smelled appetizing today. I scanned the room to find Sam when I noticed the new guy standing at the end of the line. My heart quickened at the thought of actually trying to start a conversation with him.

I mustered up courage and walked quickly to stand behind him before a chatty group of freshmen got there first.

"Hi," I said with a little smile.

He turned, flashing baby blue eyes at me and my heart did flip flops.

"Hi," he said, smiling back.

I noticed his perfectly straight and incredibly white teeth. Close up, he was way cuter than from a distance on the basketball court. His darling dimples, coupled with his admiration of me, made my mouth feel like it was full of cotton balls.

"Are you new here?" I asked with a squeak and then felt stupid for asking such a dumb question.

"Yeah, I'm Phil." He extended his hand to shake mine. When we touched, his free-spirited happy aura infused me deeper and calmed my nervousness.

"Nice to meet you," he said.

"I'm Julia . . . Julia Parker," I gushed. "Did you . . . just move here?"

"Yeah, from Los Angeles."

"Really? I'm from Los Angeles too. What part?"

"I'm from the Valley, but my Dad got transferred, so we had to move." His distress amplified. He must miss home. "Is the pizza any good?"

I was concentrating on his feelings and missed the question.

"Pizza?" I fumbled. "Oh, it's okay, I guess."

He grabbed a slice and winked. "I'll know soon enough."

I followed suit. I wanted to take a slice of chocolate cake, but decided I should grab a banana instead.

"We used to live in the Valley too. Well, when I was a kid. We moved to be closer to family. My Dad's a computer consultant," I said, feeling comfortable to share. "I'm not sure what that means, but he's gone a lot. What does your dad do?"

"My dad is an engineer. He builds computer chips. Wasn't too bad moving here. At least I'm still close to the beach, but this school needs to loosen up."

With his free hand, Phil leaned into me and put his arm around my shoulder.

"Take that guy over there," he whispered in my ear. "He's trying to score, but he's doing it all wrong and she's not buying it."

Brad, a sophomore, was a bit too loud and his laughter a little too forced, while talking to a pretty freshman I knew he liked.

"If he'd just loosen up, talk to her like he talks to his buddies, she'll eat it up. Trust me."

I smiled and nodded my head amazed at how at home I felt under Phil's arm. I found I didn't want him to move it away. I was disappointed when we got to the cash register and he let me go to get his wallet.

"I'm getting hers and mine," he told the lady.

I blushed. I'd never had a guy buy my lunch before.

"Thank you."

"No problem. It was really nice to meet you," he said and he turned and walked in the other direction. "I'll catch you around."

I just stood there and watched him go sit with the guys he was hanging out with in P.E. class.

"He's cute, who is he?" Katie asked as I walked up to our table at the other end of the cafeteria.

"Phil. He just moved here," I said, a little stunned, trying to make heads or tails of what just happened.

"What, no more . . . what's his name?" Katie snapped her fingers repetitively. " . . .Nicholas?"

I shot her a glare. She was the queen of being fickle when it came to boys. How dare she question me when I was just being friendly?

"I just said 'hi'. It doesn't mean anything."

"It looked a little bit more than that. It looked like he bought your lunch."

"A . . . loan. I'm paying him back," I stammered.

I finally understood why Sam kept her feelings for Todd a secret. Nothing got past Katie. Like a shark, she smelled blood and was in for all the gory details.

"Hmm . . . I wonder if Phil's got a date to homecoming," she said and glanced in his direction.

Two senior cheerleaders hovered over him flirting and it surprised me that I felt jealous.

"You have a date, why do you care?" I snapped, feeling stupid I even took the time to talk to him.

"Not for me, for you. I figured since you stopped talking about Nicholas, things didn't work out. But it looks like you've got some competition now."

I stopped staring at Phil and looked down at my pizza, which was cold. Somewhere, my appetite changed and my free lunch mocked me.

"Whatever. I just met him," I said, wanting to be anywhere but there listening to the laughter coming from the other end of the room.

"So who's going to the bonfire?" Katie asked the group.

"Me," said Sam with a gleam in her eye.

"Really?" Katie said, somewhat surprised. "That's cool with Todd?"

"Yep."

"How about you, Cam?"

"That's funny, Katie. I wasn't invited by the "in" crowd," he said while using his fingers to make quotation marks in the air. "I'm not a jock, remember?"

"Don't be silly, Cam. You don't have to be a football player to go," she said.

"It helps," he muttered under his breath.

"You know what, Sam? I really can't go either," I said quickly, hoping Katie could be my substitute so I didn't have to endure anymore awkward moments.

"What?" Sam said hurt. "Why not?"

"I have so much homework to do. You'll be there with Todd and Katie."

"No, Julia, you have to come. It'll be fun. It's not just the popular people going," she said, begging. "Please?"

I wanted to believe her, but I knew better. I felt the return of her fear. This would be a big step to be there alone with Todd, almost like a date.

"Okay . . . I'll go," I finally said.

She had no idea her feelings had twisted my arm. I could endure a little bit of humiliation so she could spend some time with Todd. If love was being gracious to her, I couldn't be cruel—even if it happened to be tormenting me.

"Cool," she said, sitting back with a relieved smile.

I smiled back and over her shoulder, I caught Phil looking in my direction. He flashed his pearly whites back and winked. I instantly looked away, hoping Katie didn't catch the exchange, my heart quivering in my chest.

9 – CHANGES

I arrived at the beach right at dusk and instantly regretted my decision to come. There was a huge bonfire as promised, along with an overly amorous group of popular kids from my school—which I totally expected. My first instinct was to leave, but my obligation to Sam kept my feet firmly planted in the sand. Where was she anyway?

I ducked to avoid a flying football and wove my way around couples making out on scattered blankets, towards a vacant log close to the fire. I sat down, thankful not to be noticed, but still feeling awkwardly alone. The heat from the blaze felt good and helped me warm up from the wind's chill. I kept my gaze glued to the flames and blocked out the lovey-dovey feelings around me. Sam had only a few minutes more to show up before I high-tailed it home.

"Julia, you made it," Sam said out of breath, dragging Todd by the hand behind her.

"Hey."

"Great bonfire, huh?" she said.

I took a deep breath and faked a smile. "Yeah . . . Just great."

She sat down next to me. Todd stood, until she pulled his hand to have him sit too. She tried to make small talk that included all of us, but their invisible longing and anxiousness made me feel like a third wheel. Maybe it would work to my advantage. After a few minutes I couldn't handle it anymore and insisted they take a walk on the beach so I could take off. Sam tried to hold back, but with Todd's encouragement she caved.

"Please don't leave," Sam whispered in my ear.

"Okay," I said and kept a smile until Sam turned.

Darn it!

Alone again, I needed a new game plan. I couldn't take the romantic atmosphere any longer. Distancing myself from the crowd was the only way I would find solace. With my blanket in hand, I walked along the beach until I found a spot far enough away from the crowd to provide relief, but still within view in case Sam needed me.

The wind had died down leaving the surf glassy and quiet except for when the waves would break, crashing perfectly from right to left. I sat at the surf's edge as it eroded the sand into a miniature cliff with each pass, making a protective barrier, keeping me dry.

The full moon shone down onto the waves, illuminating the white crests of foam as the water peaked and then splashed over. Something peculiar was happening though. After each wave, the water radiated a strange pale green color as it washed up and lapped the beach. I'd heard of a red tide before, but not one that turned the water green. The waves entranced me and I watched intently, hoping to figure it out.

"Pretty cool, huh?" a familiar voice said.

I looked up.

"Phil?" My stomach flip-flopped for the second time that day.

"This seat taken?" he asked, pointing at the spot next to me.

"No, please . . . sit down," I scooted over and gave him a corner to sit on. "I didn't know you were coming tonight."

"Well, I thought it might be a way to get to know some people, but everyone is here with their girlfriend. So . . ." I felt his longing. "It's really making me miss mine at home."

"You have a girlfriend?" I tried to keep my voice even.

The disappointment hit me a little harder than expected.

"Yeah," he sighed. "It's okay though. I only have to endure being apart for a few months. We're going to the same college next year so we'll be together soon. It's really been lame having to change schools my senior year and come here. I had to leave all my friends . . . my girlfriend . . . everything."

"I didn't know. Sorry."

"No biggie. What about you? Where's your boyfriend?"

I almost busted out in laughter, but his seriousness quickly sobered me up. His question was truly genuine.

"I . . . don't have one," I finally said.

The admission was slightly embarrassing. His laughter startled me.

"You don't? Really?"

I laughed back nervously. Like I had any control over the matter. How was he to know boys avoided me like the plague at school? I dug my toes in the sand and wriggled them around to help alleviate my anxiousness.

"I don't know. I don't think anyone likes me," I said quietly.

"Don't be silly. I'd like you if I didn't have a girlfriend."

His candor took me off guard and my cheeks flushed in response. I instinctively reached up and tried to hide them. From the corner of my eye, I could see him smiling at me.

"Honestly, I think I scare guys away," I said, surprised at my new found realization.

"What makes you think that?"

His tender concern enveloped me like a ray of sunshine. Since the threat of trying to make a good impression evaporated once I found out he had a girlfriend, I couldn't stop the words from falling out of my mouth.

"You're going to think this is corny."

"Try me."

Before I knew it, I'd proceeded to tell him the whole story about running out of gas, traipsing through the forest without a flashlight and then tripping and falling off the ledge catching a branch on my way down the cliff. I told him everything, even about the mountain lion.

"That's literally insane," he said astounded. "Did he actually kill it? That's a felony offense I think."

"Well, I'm not really sure. He said he was a hunter." I started to panic. I didn't know Phil very well. What if he told someone?

"Please don't say anything, okay? I don't want him to get in trouble. He did save my life."

"Of course," he said truthfully. "I mean, if I was in the same situation, I'd probably do the same. What did he kill it with?"

"Um . . ." I couldn't believe I didn't know this or think this part through. I never asked Nicholas if he used a weapon or not. ". . . I don't know."

Phil laughed. "I think he was showing off and just scared it away."

I remembered the hissing and snarling and the endless waiting before Nicholas came to my aid. I knew for a fact he fought something and very valiantly.

"Even still, he carried me the whole way home because I hurt my ankle and then promised to come back and check up on me. But he hasn't. That was a week ago," I said with a sigh.

"Maybe he's in jail."

I jabbed Phil in the ribs. "Very funny."

He laughed. "He could be."

"Well, I know he's not," I shook my head. "I ran into him later and he didn't want to talk to me."

"The guy sounds bipolar." Phil said flippantly.

"He does, doesn't he?" I forced a chuckle to cover my hurt. My family had been more considerate of my feelings when talking about Nicholas' behavior, unlike Phil.

"Sorry Parker. Guys can be idiots." Hearing him call me by my last name was endearing but his apology for the whole male species didn't really help me feel better. "And if I knew him, I'd tell him so. But don't worry. I'll find someone worthy of you. I think I know your type."

Again, I blushed. "Well, that's really not necessary."

"What? You don't have faith in me? I've hooked up a couple of my buddies with great girls."

I laughed nervously. This was starting to scare the tar out of me, because plain and simple, I wasn't normal and being someone's pet project made me feel more like a freak.

"For now, I think I'll pass. Thanks."

We sat in silence. Phil's carefree spirit let me know his feelings weren't hurt after I declined his matchmaking services. I marveled at how different he was from other boys and yet so similar to Nicholas—both very self-assured and confident. But why did Nicholas have to be such a jerk and Phil taken? Was I doomed to forever meet incredible yet unavailable guys? Was my gift really a curse when it came to love?

"You know why the waves glow like that?" Phil said, breaking my spiraling thoughts. "It's actually plankton. The waves break their bodies apart and they glow because of it. I've only seen it one other time before. It's pretty rare."

As we watched, I wondered if the plankton died when they were broken. It seemed really sad they were sacrificed to produce such a beautiful phenomenon.

"Thanks," he said out of the blue.

"For?"

"For letting me hang with you. I was really bummed a minute ago."

He reached over and hugged my shoulder and kept his arm around me. I melted into his side, leaned against his body and allowed his concern for me heal my wounds. I ignored my secret hope that something more than friendship could be blossoming between us.

"I can't wait to surf these waves. Look at how they're breaking. If they were a little bit bigger, I'd be out there with my board and wetsuit right now."

I chuckled. "I'd be scared to surf at night."

"Why?"

"Haven't you seen *Jaws*?"

"You can't think about that, only the thrill of the ride. I'm willing to take my chances."

I imagined a shark watching my legs dangle under the deep dark water and shivered. Phil responded by pulling me tighter to him. He made me feel safe and I found myself relaxing and leaning into the comfortable curve of his shoulder. I could've stayed that way all night, but reality intruded. The hair on my arms prickled as a feeling of ravenous primal hunger overwhelmed me. My stomach tightened and my heart began to pound. I had sensed the same feelings before; first in the forest followed by the time at the theater. Since then, they've consumed my nightmares. Panicked, I raised my head from Phil's shoulder just enough to peer down the beach trying to determine the source of these horrifying feelings.

Two groups of people were squaring off on the beach—our football players against some guys with Soquel High letterman jackets on. They'd probably walked up to talk smack about the upcoming homecoming game. It appeared to only be harmless antics full of testosterone driven angst, nothing more.

Until I spotted them.

On the fringe, three familiar faces watched the interaction; the weird, spooky group from the theater. The dark haired boy shot a look at me that sent chills up my spine. I hid behind Phil's shadow to shield my face from his view.

"You know them?" he said, as he realized I was using his body as a buffer.

"Not personally, but they aren't people I want to get to know." After I said it, I realized Phil wouldn't understand who I was referring to, or why they petrified me, so I changed the direction of my statement. "I think they are from Soquel High."

"Why do guys always have to mark their territory?" he said shaking his head. "I mean really, it's so juvenile."

Normally, I would have laughed, but I was terribly frightened. Every impulse in my body called for me to run and hide.

"I think we should go," I whispered.

Phil ignored my pleas and stood up.

"I want to see what's going on," he said, taking a step towards the feud.

"No," I grabbed onto his pant leg. "Don't."

"Why?"

"I'm not getting a good vibe. Trust me," I said. "Something very bad is going to happen."

"Back off," someone yelled.

I stood up behind Phil and held his arm firmly. He tried to free himself from my grip but I held tighter.

"Hey man, we don't want any trouble here," said Jake Callahan, our star quarterback.

"Then get off our beach!" another yelled from the opposite side.

"It's a public beach. We have every right to be here as you do!" Ali Johansson said.

A tall lanky boy in a dark colored hoody called her a derogatory name and Ali's boyfriend lunged at him. A few guys held him back.

"That wasn't cool man," I heard Tyler Kennedy say.

Phil looked at me, removed my hand and whispered "It's okay." Before I could object, he walked away from me confidently towards the crowd.

I stood and trembled in the distance.

"Hey, let's not cause any trouble," Phil said in a commanding voice. "You guys can settle this on the field on Friday." I felt the calming magic of his tone temporarily soothe the crowd a bit, until a red and blue flash came from the top of the hill.

Police.

Someone yelled "cops" and the rivals scattered. Two officers came down the hillside to the beach and I watched Phil walk over to meet them.

Sam ran over to me, grabbed my hand and pulled me over to

the group. I had a hard time remaining calm with overwhelming sea of testosterone filled anger washing over me. I overheard someone say they called 911 to report the potential fight and that the cops happened to be patrolling in the area.

"That was lucky," Sam said, relieved.

"Yeah," I forced out, feeling suffocated by the hysteria.

I spotted Katie and she ran over to greet us.

"Hey," Katie said out of breath, completely elated. "Fun night, huh?"

I shook my head. Only Katie would find danger exciting.

"Time for everyone to go home. There's a curfew in effect." A masculine voice boomed out of a loudspeaker from the top of the cliff followed by a large spotlight that flashed right into the crowd of kids. I squinted and held my hand up to block the glare.

"Curfew?" I asked. "Since when?"

"Since the serial murders'," Todd said in a condescending tone. "Where have you been?"

My cheeks flushed and I looked away. I must have been too absorbed in my own world to notice. What was happening to our safe town?

I scanned the disbursing crowd to see where Phil went, hoping he'd come back and join me, but he was nowhere to be seen.

"I came back and looked for you earlier. Where did you go?" Sam asked, drawing me back into the conversation.

"I was watching the waves," I said, pointing to the surf's edge, hoping to see Phil's sandy blond head.

"Alone? I didn't see you."

"No, Phil was with me. Have you seen him by chance?"

Sam's eyes grew big and I knew she suspected something more than what really happened, but now wasn't the time to go into details. I hadn't been able to shake the foreboding feeling that set in earlier and I just wanted all my friends to go home where it was safe, especially Phil. Where did he go? I couldn't believe he'd leave without saying goodbye. I thought our talk meant more than that.

"I didn't even know he was here," Sam said with a sing-song in her voice.

The cops started combing the beach and forcing people to leave. I didn't want them to come over and hassle us, but then I didn't want to walk back alone either.

"Can you guys walk me to my car?" I asked Sam and Todd, frustrated Phil had disappeared on me.

I gathered my things and we trudged up the hill to my car. I weakly smiled to the officer directing the kids off the beach. He didn't seem amused, so I kept my head down and we silently paraded past until we reached my car, which was parked further down the road, close to a small thicket by the lagoon.

"I'll see you tomorrow, okay?" I said as I gave Sam a hug.

Behind her, Todd began to grow impatient.

"Yeah," she said super softly. "Thanks for staying around."

"No problem."

I slid into the driver's seat and watched them walk away holding hands and sighed, trying not to be jealous. Was it really too much to want an uncomplicated relationship with someone I could trust, too? Why was that such an impossible thing? I turned the key in the ignition and my car roared to life. I was about to pull out onto the highway when I felt a sensation of pain coming from nearby.

I looked out the car windows, but I didn't see anyone. The pain intensified, so I opened my door and got out. I waited a second to see what direction the feelings were coming from, when I heard a moan behind the bushes.

My knees almost buckled when I discovered the identity of the bruised and disheveled body hidden behind the shrubs.

"Phil," I whispered as I knelt down and gently nudged him. His skin was cold and gray and his clothing torn. He had scratches, cuts and rows of crescent-shaped puncture marks on his neck and shoulder. And no matter how much I tried to wake him, he didn't respond.

Oh Phil, please be okay.

For a second, I didn't know what to do. I looked around for help, but no one was around. He needed to get to the hospital quick. I bent over and listened for a heart beat. When I heard his breath, slow and shallow, I was relieved. I tried my hardest to pick him up, but the dead weight of his body made it difficult to lift him. The only alternative was to wrap my arms around his torso and drag him to my car.

He moaned softly again.

"It's okay Phil. I'm going to take you to the hospital."

I laid him across the backseat and then covered him with my beach blanket. He started to shiver, taking in short, raspy breaths.

"Hang on Phil."

I jumped in the front seat and drove like a maniac toward the hospital, checking my rearview mirror frequently to make sure he was still breathing.

"We are almost there Phil, hang on," I kept telling him.

I rounded the corner and flew into the hospital parking lot and raced towards the emergency room entrance.

"Help me!" I yelled, as I flung open my door and sprinted around to open the back door, showing my injured passenger. A guy in scrubs ran to the car, took Phil's vitals and then another came with a stretcher. Soon a group of hospital staff surrounded my car, separating me from Phil.

"What happened?" a blonde woman with horn-rimmed glasses and pink scrubs asked me.

"I don't know," I said as they lifted him out of the car and placed him on the stretcher. "I just found him lying in the bushes like this."

"He's lost a lot of blood," I heard another say. "Looks like it's an animal attack."

"Take him to room four."

"What is your friend's name sweetie?" The blonde woman asked, stepping in front of me, blocking my view.

"Phil," I said, frantically looking over her shoulder, watching them wheel him through the double doors. I made a move to follow, but the woman stopped me.

"And what is your name, hun?"

"I'm Julia. Julia Parker."

"Okay, Julia, we'll take care of your friend, but you'll need to wait in the waiting room until he's stable," she said, putting her hand on my shoulder. Her words were sincere, but on the inside, she didn't care. She was the gatekeeper and it was her job to keep me away from the patient until they finished doing their job.

"What? I want to be with my friend."

Her eyes were sympathetic, but it was all a façade. Really, she was annoyed, but not as annoyed as the security guard who was marching towards us.

"You can't leave your car there," he grunted, a little bit louder than necessary.

I looked at the nurse and ignored the guard, hoping she'd not really make me wait in the waiting room with all the untreated patients.

"Please. Don't make me wait in there. I want to be with Phil. He has no one to support him," I begged.

"I'll come get you as soon as he can have visitors," she said while giving my hand two nice pats. Nothing was going to break this ice queen. I clamped my mouth shut, wanting to say a few choice words but instead watched helplessly as she left me standing outside the double doors. I had to figure out another way to get inside and fast.

"Ma'am, you need to move your car," the security guard snapped, his cigarette and stale coffee breath blew in my face.

"I heard you!" I snipped and spun around. "Gosh!"

I glared at him when I drove past, but he stood at attention with his smug smile.

Even before crossing the threshold of the emergency waiting room, I could feel the putrescent stench of misery inside. The electric doors opened and shut as I waffled whether or not to go in. On the other side was agonizing suffering but I had no choice. For Phil's sake, I had to endure it.

I held my breath before plunging myself into the air conditioned room and clutched my stomach for fear I'd get sick right in front of everyone. The arrangement was different than my local hospital. There was no desk inside, just a sign with a clipboard and instructions to fill out the form and put it in the slot on the door marked *Triage* which didn't apply to me.

There was a different security guard standing in the corner by the only set of double doors leading out of the waiting room. I walked towards them and hoped maybe there was someone inside that could help me.

"Can I help you Miss?" the guard said and stepped in front of me, blocking my path.

"Oh . . . my friend is in there. I need to go see him."

"Do you have a pass?" he grunted.

"No, but . . ."

"You can't come in here without a pass. You'll need to wait over there and I'll get a staff person to assist you." He pointed behind me. When I didn't move, he became irritated. "Please, ma'am. Wait over there."

I looked where he was pointing. There were already a few anxious faces waiting in a row of well-worn chairs.

"You don't understand—" I started to say.

"You need to wait over there, or you'll have to be escorted out," he said pointing more firmly.

I scowled, knowing I couldn't win this showdown. He controlled the door to this ludicrous facility and could keep me from going inside if he really wanted. With a huff, I obeyed and walked over to the wall close to the chairs. I might have moved, but I wasn't going to sit where he told me to.

I stood for five incredibly long minutes, but no one came through the doors. The guard stood straight-faced, telling the same thing to anyone who tried to come through the doors after me.

I was beginning to think I would have to torturously wait there forever, when the doors finally opened and a nurse entered the room. She was ambushed by a group of people all explaining their situations at once. She silenced them and then motioned to someone who sat patiently in the chairs I was supposed to be sitting in and took them into the back. The others began to complain loudly, but the guard silenced them.

I started to pace. The feelings in the room were putting me on edge and I needed to focus to keep from freaking out.

I am here for Phil.

I wanted to go outside and escape the slow painful suffocation, but was afraid I'd miss the heartless nurse in the pink scrubs who promised to get me. I looked around to find the source of all the discomfort I felt.

I noticed a little boy, no older than seven in a wheel chair, with his leg propped straight out and his side badly scratched. I felt the pain throbbing in his leg and was relieved to see them take him into the back room. It didn't seem fair to have him endure that kind of pain for long. A woman in her mid-forties looked like she'd cut her hand, another feverish and nauseous, an ear ache, a sore throat. I moved closer to the disheveled bruised drunk who nursed a swollen wrist. At least his inebriated state numbed me a little.

But overall, I couldn't keep straight who was feeling what and closed my eyes to block out the agony.

"Julia?"

I opened and locked eyes with the nurse in pink scrubs.

Hallelujah! "Yes?" I ran over to her.

"Come with me."

I followed her through the doors, tempted to stick my tongue out at the security guard as we passed, but I felt his disdain. He really hated his job.

"How is he?" I asked.

"He's stable now. We needed to transfuse him. He'd lost a lot of blood."

I tried my hardest to listen to what she was saying, trying to keep a straight face as I felt new and awful ailments accompanied by hopelessness and despair. It seemed to get worse the further we walked down the sterile hall of the hospital.

"Is he awake?" I asked, attempting to keep my focus on the problem at hand.

"He's awake, but not very coherent. We can't get him to tell us what happened or where his family is. Do you know who we could contact?"

"I don't know his parents."

"Okay. We have his information from his wallet, so I'm sure we'll be able to find someone soon."

She led me to his room and opened the door. Phil sat up in bed, bandaged now, with his eyes open, but his head was turned towards the window overlooking the dimly illuminated parking lot. He had an IV in his arm and a monitor recording his erratic heartbeat. He still looked gray. The nurse left us alone.

"Phil?" I said quietly

He didn't turn.

"Phil? You okay?" I walked around to the other side of his bed hoping his hearing wasn't affected too.

His eyes were empty as he looked beyond me out into the night. Inside I mentally reached out to see what he was feeling and felt nothing. He was completely numb to me.

Then he blinked and looked directly into my eyes. The happy Phil I'd met earlier was gone, replaced by this empty shell. I looked closely at his blue eyes. They weren't so blue anymore. Dark fluid was swirling around his irises. I fought back a gasp.

"Phil, what's happening?" I said and grabbed his hand, leaning in for a closer look.

At my touch he pulled his hand away.

"I'm fine. What are you doing here?" His tone was bitter.

"I brought you here, don't you remember?"

He glanced down and glared at the IV taped to his hand then back at me. He blinked slowly and shot me a deadly look. I started to feel his hostility.

"What happened?" I said softly, as I backed away, trying not to irritate him further.

"Nothing happened, and you should mind your own business. Did they send you in here to interrogate me?" he barked.

"No."

"I really just want to be left alone," he said, while loosening the tape on his hand.

"Okay, I can go. But can I call your parents and let them know you're here?"

"No. Just go. GO!"

Suddenly feeling afraid for my life, I stepped back, tripped over the chair leg and stumbled out of the room. Something was seriously wrong and I sensed he was on the verge of freaking out. I looked for the nurse to warn her, but she wasn't anywhere to be found.

In the room, the heart machine started beeping loudly. A staff person got up to investigate, but Phil, now dressed, stood in the doorway of his room. He pushed past me, not acknowledging my presence and ran down the hallway away from us.

"Sir. SIR!" the male nurse called after him.

Phil ignored him too.

Instinctively, I ran after Phil, but he disappeared in a blur. Once I reached the doors to exit the hospital, he was nowhere to be seen.

It was if he had vanished into thin air.

10 - DRAMA

*A*ll I wanted to do was escape school and and be alone. And if stubborn Mrs. Hinney, the school secretary, would've given me Phil's address, I would've ditched.

Instead, she gave me a lecture on student privacy and how she'd be breaking the law if she gave out student information without parental permission, blah, blah, blah. So, I returned to first period P.E. class, sat on the bleachers and watched the boys' locker room door, waiting for Phil to emerge.

With my jacket's hood pulled over my head, elbows on my knees and my chin resting in my hands, I suddenly started feeling very sleepy. After finally falling asleep last night, I ended up reliving the same horrible nightmares again and woke at 2:20 a.m. unable to go back to sleep. Last night's dream was particularly disturbing and involved me running from fanged creatures at the beach. I forced myself awake when one looked similar to Phil.

The locker room door flew open. I held my breath. False alarm. It was only Jordan. Where was Phil?

Out of the corner of my eye, I saw Sam staring at me with a frown. I'd been so wrapped up in waiting for Phil I didn't notice the girls' volleyball game. She took advantage of the moment when her team switched sides and ran over to talk to me.

"You okay?" she said, out of breath.

"No, actually. Something happened after you left last night," I said quietly. "... with Phil."

"Phil?"

A smile spread on her face. I could tell she got the wrong impression again.

"No, it's not like that. Something bad," I quickly said.

"Oh?"

"Come on Sam, let's go," Coach called out. "You can socialize after class."

"I have to go play," she said and made a face out of view of our teacher and moved to rejoin her team.

The class period droned on. Sam periodically exchanged worried glances with me and I knew the wait was killing her too. After the bell rang, I paced by the locker room door. Sam was the first to exit.

"So?" she asked half-worried, half-excited. "Tell me."

I took a deep breath and caught her up to speed.

"He ran off?" she asked in astonishment.

"I was hoping he'd come to school today, but he's not here."

"Oh. My. Gosh." Sam paled. "Where did he go?"

"That's just it. I don't know. But something is wrong with him. He seriously acted almost possessed."

An image of Phil's face flashed through my mind. The animalistic fire in his eyes still frightened me and it reminded me of my nightmare.

Sam stood there, mouth open but speechless. I wanted to continue, but the second bell rang and we were now late for History.

Quickly we rushed through the door and took our seats. A messenger from the office spoke privately to Mr. Marshall and prevented him from noticing we were tardy. I took advantage of the moment and I opened my notebook to write Sam a note.

"Julia," Mr. Marshall said abruptly.

I froze.

"Yes?" I said, my cheeks changing from pink to crimson.

I slowly shut my notebook and tried to look inconspicuous.

"You need to collect your things and go to the principal's office."

A low scolding murmur came from the other students.

"That's enough," he barked, dark eyes piercing over the top of his glasses.

The room grew quiet, but people still gawked at me. I glanced at Sam and she shrugged. So, I slid my books across my desk into my arm and tried to exit quietly. One of the books toppled off the stack and hit the floor with a loud thud. My cheeks flushed again. Some of the students giggled, but Mr. Marshall paid no attention and continued with his lecture. I graciously escaped.

My heart surged faster as I walked to the principal's office. What did he want and why did he want to see me? No one knew about Phil yet, or did they? I rounded the corner and took a deep breath before approaching a frosty glass door with the name Principal Lyle Brewster in gold block lettering. I turned the door handle to let myself in.

Inside, Candy Stewart, the principal's raven-haired, bombshell secretary sat at her desk in the lobby. It had been quite a while since I'd been called to this room and noticed he'd remodeled, again. She smiled when she saw me arrive.

"Hello, Julia," she said sweetly through ruby red lips. "They're waiting for you."

They?

Candy stood up and moved around her desk, dressed in a tight, low-cut blouse and matching mini skirt. I found it ironic I was the one being called to the principal's office for some sort of infraction when Candy's outfit clearly violated the school's dress code. I rolled my eyes and followed behind as her red high heels clicked against the tiled lobby floor.

My uneasiness rose the further we walked down the hall as I sensed an increasing ocean of worry and despair. I no longer felt intimidated by her beauty, only concerned for what lay on the other side of the door. Part of me wanted to run in the other direction as I watched Candy reach for the door knob and turn.

I was surprised to find my Dad staring back at me, along with two other adults I didn't know in the room. I turned in confusion towards Mr. Brewster sitting behind his large mahogany desk.

"Come in Julia," Mr. Brewster said, motioning for me to sit in an empty seat next to my Father.

"Dad?" I murmured, scared I was in huge trouble.

"It's okay Julia. Jim and Beverly D'Elia just have some questions for you," he said and patted my knee after I sat down, but he radiated an air of confusion and worry as well.

I hadn't met the D'Elia's before. They looked like Hollywood celebrities, dressed impeccably and strikingly attractive with white blonde hair and blue eyes. Their features were strangely familiar, but they both looked haggard, like they hadn't slept in a week.

I smiled weakly, hoping it would help the situation but their stony expressions didn't change.

Mr. Brewster sat back in his chair, his face grim. He put his finger tips together to form the shape of a diamond.

"Julia, as you may or may not know, Phil didn't come home last night. The D'Elia's received a call from Mercy General telling them that you brought Phil to the emergency room. When they arrived at the hospital, Phil was no longer there. The staff reported that they saw the two of you leaving the hospital together. Do you have any idea where he is?"

My eyes darted from Mr. Brewster to Phil's parents now realizing why they'd looked so familiar. Phil bore a striking resemblance. But, then I saw the precarious situation I was in. They'd assumed I was somehow responsible for his disappearance.

"Actually, we didn't leave together at all. He got upset and took off. I tried following after him, but by the time I got outside the hospital, he was gone. I don't know where he went," I said meekly.

"What happened?" Mrs. D'Elia asked with concern in her voice and tears in her eyes.

Mr. Brewster cleared his throat, possibly because he wanted to control the conversation. I couldn't believe he'd be so insensitive to her feelings, so I ignored him and told her the story.

After I finished, Mrs. D'Elia welled up and turned to be comforted by her husband. He draped his arm around her shoulders.

I felt his overwhelming blame.

"Did anything else strange happen, maybe before you found Phil. Possibly during the bonfire?" Mr. Brewster asked.

I wondered if I should mention what happened at the beach. I didn't trust Mr. Brewster. He seemed to have an air of concern for his students, but I knew differently. He was more concerned about how *his* school was going to portray *him* to the public eye and kept tight controls to make sure his students didn't embarrass him.

"No, nothing significant happened," I said cautiously.

"Do you know of anyone who would want to cause Phil harm?" Mr. Brewster asked with distrust in his voice.

What a weird question. Everyone likes Phil.

"The nurse said it might be an animal attack—"

"Just answer the questions please."

I paused, waiting for my dad to stand up for me, but he remained silent. He was angry and I didn't know why. I'm sure being dragged in here from an important business meeting, when his daughter didn't tell him she was playing ambulance in the middle of the night, would be a lot to comprehend and forgive.

"No," I finally said.

"So, you did not see anyone physically harm Phil?"

"No, like I said, I found him in the—"

"And you took him directly to the hospital? Alone?" Mr. Brewster fired back.

"Yes, but—"

"Did anyone see you put him in your car?"

I gritted my teeth. This line of questioning was getting ridiculous.

"No."

"Did he tell you who hurt him?"

While he was unconscious? Or after he wanted to rip my head off.

I forced myself to act civilly, reminding myself that they were only concerned for Phil's welfare, as I was.

"I don't think anyone hurt him," I said emphatically. "The nurse said—"

Mr. Brewster leaned forward in his chair and glared at me. "We know what the nurse said. A yes or no would suffice."

"No," I said with a sigh.

Mr. Brewster continued his volley of questions. "Did he ever mention before if his life was in danger to you?"

I suppressed a guffaw.

"Uh, no?" I said with an intentional sarcastic tone.

"And you didn't meet secretly somewhere after you left the hospital?"

I pursed my lips before answering.

"We didn't leave together and to answer your next question again, no, I don't know where he is," I said slowly enunciating each word.

Mr. Brewster's eyes grew into slits while he remained visibly calm. If it were only the two of us in this meeting, I'm sure other words would have been exchanged. Even still, I felt backed into a corner.

"Well, then, if you were so concerned about Phil, why didn't you tell anyone last night?"

The question hit me like a blow to the stomach and I suddenly felt anything I said would be used against me and wanted a lawyer. What could I say? That my Dad was unavailable and I thought he wouldn't really care. Or that I didn't know who to tell at midnight when Phil probably just went home. I barely knew him anyway.

"I don't know," I said and looked down at my shoes.

Mr. Brewster let out a long sigh.

"Okay, then. If there isn't anything else you want to tell us, then you can go back to class," he said without hiding his animosity.

Anger burned inside me. Not only was I being accused wrongly of helping Phil run away, but no one thanked me for actually saving his life. I glanced at my dad. His overwhelming disappointment matched his "we-will-talk-more-about-this-later-young-lady" face and the D'Elias plain ignored me. I was the enemy in their eyes.

"Oh and I'd like you to keep this conversation private please," Mr. Brewster slid in right before I left the room.

The words stung like lemon juice on a paper cut. I made a loud *humph* after I walked out. What happened between me and Phil was my business and I'd tell anyone I wanted.

Candy wasn't at her desk when I exited the office and I was glad. My brave outer exterior started to crumble and I would be mortified if Mr. Brewster knew he'd made me cry.

Tears fell silently down my cheeks as I ran down the hall, careful to avoid eye contact with curious onlookers. I had no intention of returning to class, but I needed somewhere to hide. I spotted the library.

Wiping away my tears, I ducked inside. The computers were located at the back wall in cubicles with desks. I slipped into the closest one, logged in and began typing into the Google search field. After a minute, I found the exact website I needed and clicked it. I scanned the page and then read through a list of symptoms.

- *irritability*
- *excessive movements or agitation*
- *confusion*
- *hallucinations*
- *aggressiveness*
- *bizarre or abnormal thoughts*
- *muscle spasms*
- *abnormal postures*
- *seizures (convulsions)*
- *weakness or paralysis (when a person cannot move some part of the body)*
- *extreme sensitivity to bright lights, sounds, or touch*

- *increased production of saliva or tears*
- *difficulty speaking*

I printed out the list, shoved it in my pocket and left the library after more students sat at the desks next to me, giving me weird looks. I realized I needed to be in a more secluded place. My emotions were difficult enough to control as it was and I didn't want to have to deal with anyone else's on top of it.

Careful to avoid being spotted, I snuck out to the parking lot and got into my car. What I really wanted to do was drive to the cliffs, but decided against it. With my luck, I'd get caught, and right now staying under the radar seemed imperative. Since I was already excused from History, skipping the rest of class seemed harmless.

The hour flew by and I got lost sorting through the facts. It concerned me that Phil's behavior closely resembled many of the symptoms from the list. The problem was I didn't know him well enough to predict his next move. I hoped wherever he ended up, a sensible person would make him go back to the hospital. But deep in my heart, I knew whatever information Mr. Brewster and his parents were keeping from me was the key to finding him.

I watched students mill around the campus on their way to their next class and decided to stay in my car. My eyes were puffy and my mascara was a mess. The last thing I wanted was a bunch of nosey questions about why I was upset.

I kicked myself for not being more assertive. I should've demanded that Mr. Brewster and the D'Elias tell me what they knew. But knowing Mr. Brewster, he had the whole thing planned and intended to make me look guilty. It must have fed his ego to prove he knew his students so well. But they were completely on the wrong trail.

My head hurt and all I wanted to do was lean back and close my eyes. Far away I could hear the waves crash and the fog horn blare as the cool salty breeze tickled my face.

"Where have you been?"

I jerked awake. Sam stood outside my car window with her hand on her hip and a frown on her face.

"Haven't you been getting my text messages? Have you been here all afternoon?"

I groggily looked over at the clock on the dash and realized I'd slept through all the rest of my classes. Sheepishly, I avoided her gaze, adjusted my reclined seat forward and rubbed my swollen eyes.

"Tell me what's going on, Julia," she demanded when I didn't respond right away. "You didn't come back to class. Then they announced that if anyone had any information about Phil's whereabouts to let the principal know. I thought you were in big trouble or something."

I opened the door and stepped outside.

"I kind of am in trouble," I said.

"In trouble? Why?"

"Because I was an accomplice in his escape from the hospital and didn't tell anyone," I said with a hint of cynical disdain.

"What? No way."

"They—" I said with air quotes "—seem to think that my silence is admission of my guilt, but whatever. They've got it totally wrong anyway. They think someone beat him up, but the nurse told me he was attacked by an animal."

"What do you mean they? Who else was in the office?"

"Phil's parents and my dad, but I couldn't get a word in edgewise."

"Oh, wow," Sam said with concern. "So he didn't go home after all."

"No." I looked down. "I couldn't come back to class. After getting ganged up on in the meeting, I needed to get away and think. But, I didn't mean to miss the rest of the day. I'm going to be so busted."

"Oh," she said, her anger melting away. "Sorry I yelled at you. I was worried when you didn't come back, so I texted you."

"I left my phone at home by accident," I said, wondering how many other messages I had missed.

"That would explain why I didn't hear back from you."

Sam was gracious to be so forgiving and I felt bad for worrying her. Her presence could've eased the blow while I processed all of this nonsense, but I didn't need to drag her into the mire with me.

"Sorry," I quickly replied. "Please don't tell anyone, or I could get in more trouble."

"You mean I can't tell Katie?" she said with a silly smirk.

I frowned back playfully and shook my head. We both let out a laugh.

"Seriously though, don't worry. They'll find him," she said with a reassuring smile.

If I could see the hope she exuded, I imagined it would look like sunlight radiating iridescently off of her skin. I wanted so badly to think so too, but there was no way to explain the change right before he vanished from the hospital. Phil's terror and anger frightened me and deep down, I wasn't sure if I actually trusted him anymore.

"I hope so," I said knowing it was an empty wish.

We hugged and Sam's compassion flooded over me, putting a temporary Band-Aid over my tattered spirit. For a brief second I wondered if I should just have her come home with me, but I knew I was in deep trouble with my dad and needed to smooth over that situation first. Begrudgingly, I got back in my car.

"I'll call you if I hear anything," I said as I shut the car door.

And as I suspected, as soon as I drove away, Sam's buffer vanished and all my grief flooded back in.

When I got home, I threw my things on the floor, rushed into my Dad's office and slammed the paper I printed out in the library on his desk.

"I know what's wrong with Phil," I said.

My Dad looked up from his computer screen and glowered

over his glasses. I internally pushed past the annoyance I felt from him and answered his glare with determination. I had to get him to understand the truth.

"Rabies. That's got to be it, he's got rabies," I blurted out. "Look at the list."

His eyes glanced down at the paper and then back up to me.

"I could also say you've got a few things on this list as well."

My mouth dropped open.

"What?"

"Let's see." He drug his finger down the list. "Irritability, yes . . . confusion, yes . . . irrational behavior, yes."

I slumped down in the chair in front of his desk. "I'm serious Dad," I said, watching my credibility crash down in flames.

"I'm serious too, Julia. Your behavior as of late has been very disappointing."

"I can explain everything."

"You've had enough time to explain; now you'll listen. You didn't go back to class like you were instructed today. You also went to a bonfire on a school night that you didn't ask permission to attend. You didn't even let your brother know you were going."

"But—"

"No buts. I cannot trust you, or your judgment. First, you decided to take a shortcut in the woods and got seriously hurt. And now you're narrowly missing gang fights. Do you not understand there's a serious gang problem right now?"

"But—"

I stopped when Dad gave me the infamous "sleeper wave" scowl—when he knit his brow together to form one ominous fold of skin that juts out over his eyes. His uni-brow resembled the scary silent wave the beach signs warned about. If it snuck up on you unaware, it would pull you out to sea. I was a goner.

"You're grounded."

My chest constricted, but I kept silent and waited, knowing

from past experience if I didn't let him finish, the punishment would get worse.

"No extra-curricular activities, no going out after dark without permission from me. I forbid you any contact with Phil. Period. And, if anything happens that's remotely out of the ordinary, you will call and tell me. Understood?"

"Yes," I said with my head hung low. This was much worse than I expected.

"Okay, then. You're free to go."

I stood up and walked towards the door. I felt his anger dissipate just a bit. I sensed he knew he'd gotten through to me, so his love and concern could flow out instead.

"Sorry, Dad," I said with a quiver in my throat.

"Come here, Julia," he said with arms stretched wide. I ran into his chest and sobbed. "It's going to be okay, honey."

This was a typical response for him. Lots of yelling and threats and after he felt his point was made all became forgiven, though the punishment stayed intact.

"Dad, I'm so sorry . . . I didn't know what to do . . . I had to take him to the hospital . . . I didn't help him run away, I promise," I said through tearful rasps. "I really think he has rabies."

Dad gently let go and gave me a tissue to wipe my snotty nose.

"The bites were human," he said gravely. "It's a sick gang initiation and Phil is somehow involved."

Human bites?

"Oh."

"And if it doesn't stop, I'm thinking of moving. I initially wanted to come here to get you away from madness like this in L.A. Now it's infecting this city as well. I was looking to move to Oklahoma."

"What?" I gasped. "No, not Oklahoma."

The thought that I'd never see Nicholas again gripped my heart from nowhere. Deep down I must have still hoped we'd work things out, but didn't know I'd suppressed the desire until this moment.

"I'm not done doing my research, but I'm going to find a place where I can feel safe leaving you and your brother while I travel. I should have done it when you were babies, maybe then . . ."

I held my breath. He was referring to Mom's disappearance. Maybe he'd finally talk about it and break the silence. More than anything I wanted to know what really happened.

"Mom's disappearance wasn't your fault, Dad."

He cleared his throat and turned to his computer monitor. I felt the familiar stone wall come back up; the one that hid all the feelings he'd stuffed down deep. Every time the subject was breeched, he shut down. I waited for years to feel his grief and felt nothing.

For a long time I felt responsible and thought if I could only remember what happened, I could solve the case. But the memories stayed locked up tight in my subconscious without any hint of a key. And Dad's response was to second guess every decision he made thereafter. We both couldn't move on.

"I have a lot to do, Julia," he finally said.

"Okay," I said as I left his office feeling rotten. I should have known better than to mention her. "Please, let's not move to Oklahoma."

"We'll see."

11 – ANSWERS

$\mathcal{T}$he next day, the school walls were covered in fliers with Phil's description, offering a reward for information leading to his safe return. Ironically, it seemed everyone suddenly knew him personally and told first hand accounts of his last words and possible whereabouts. Some said he provoked the attack while others claimed the serial murderer left him for dead, but he escaped and ran for his life. One rumor even speculated police attacked him after the bonfire because he refused to leave peaceably and Phil ran for fear of arrest. But the general atmosphere, fuelled by greed, whetted the appetites of attention seekers, anxious to get a piece of the action.

But the worst part of it was someone leaked that I was the last person to see him. So again, people I didn't know were coming up to me asking me questions, but I declined to answer. The whole charade disgusted me and I refused to be a part of it.

"What happened?" Katie asked quietly as we all sat at lunch.

"Why are you asking me?" I said, infuriated by her insensitivity. "Just ask anyone, I'm sure they'll tell you the whole story."

I looked directly at Sam.

"Julia, I promise, I didn't tell anyone anything."

I studied her feelings, thankful to find she told the truth and felt guilty for questioning her.

"Sorry. I know you wouldn't. It must have been Mr. Brewster. He probably said something when he interviewed other people."

The thought made me furious. He was the one who said not to say anything.

"Well, where do you think Phil went?" Dena asked tactfully.

I scanned everyone's eyes and studied their intent and found them loyal. Even Katie was concerned for once.

"Whatever I say stays in this circle, agreed?"

Everyone shook their head and I took a few extra seconds to get full confirmation from Katie.

"I promise," she said after feeling the weight of my stare.

"Okay," I said, and everyone leaned in so no one outside of our circle could hear what we discussed.

"Honestly, we only talked at the bonfire for a little bit so I'm not really sure where he'd go. The only thing I know is that he's got a girlfriend in L.A. and his parents made him move his senior year because his dad got a promotion. Maybe he's upset after getting beat up and needed her support. I bet that's where he went," I whispered.

"It has to be those guys from Soquel High that roughed him up. They weren't too happy when he tried to get them to leave. Maybe they figured he'd snitched on them to the police," Katie said.

"But that doesn't explain his behavior after."

"After?" Cameron asked.

Angry at Mr. Brewster, I decided to tell them everything I knew since he seemed to be doing the same.

" . . .I thought maybe he'd been bitten by a rabid animal, but my dad said his injuries were human bites," I said.

Dena gasped. "That's disgusting."

"How does your dad know all about this?" Sam asked.

"From Mr. Brewster I think," I said.

Feelings of curiosity caused me to turn my head. As I suspected, behind me was a group of nosey freshmen girls that lingered a bit too close.

"Get lost from your sandbox?" Katie yelled at them across the table.

Embarrassed, they rushed away.

Katie leaned in again with a smug smile to finish. "Well, I heard that if they don't figure out what's going on, they might cancel the homecoming game tonight," she said with one eyebrow raised.

"Really?" I said, feeling other onlookers' snooping interest swirl behind me.

"Will they cancel the dance too?" Dena asked, concern in her voice.

"No, I think they are worried that if they hold the game, there will be a riot. The football players want to avenge what happened to Phil," Katie said in hushed tones.

"Well, I'm grounded from everything right now, so I couldn't go to the game if I wanted, but if any of our guys saw what they did to Phil, they'd be kicking the crap out of them right now. "

"I don't understand how anyone could be so cruel," Sam said. "He's such a nice guy."

I felt my stomach tighten when I remembered finding Phil half-dead behind the shrubs.

"Can we change the subject? This is really starting to bother me."

"I know this must be so hard for you," Sam said, putting her hand on my shoulder.

"Did you hear about the reporters that tried to come on campus?" Katie announced, oblivious to my request.

I glared in her direction.

"No way," Dena said.

"I guess the principal made them go away, but they tried to interview some students about what happened," she continued, proud of her juicy little tidbit.

"This is getting totally out of hand," I said, meaning both the drama and Katie's continued interjections.

At the same time the bell rang and I was the first to get up. Sitting in class, even Algebra would be better than rehashing all the ugly details.

But class wasn't the escape I desired. People still gossiped behind my back and their overwhelming feelings of curiosity gnawed on me. I almost got up and left when the girls next to me wouldn't stop gawking and whispering to each other. They finally stopped when I glared at them.

In Spanish though, Mrs. Valenzuela put her foot down and wouldn't allow any extra talking unless it was in Spanish. It almost felt like a normal day until the announcement came that the homecoming game was postponed. The entire class went into a frenzy and blamed the administration for overreacting.

I was amazed they'd do something so drastic, but at this point, keeping drama to a minimum would be Mr. Brewster's modus operandi. The game, though, was the least of my worries. My only tie to homecoming would be helping Sam get ready for the dance tomorrow night.

When the bell finally rang, I ducked out before anyone could corner me. I wanted to be far away from the school drama, and the quicker the better.

Nobody was home when I arrived to change and get ready for work. I was earlier than I had expected, so I had a little bit of time to kill before heading out.

The setting sun left the sky a beautiful display of vibrant purple and pink hues so I grabbed a bowl of cereal to eat on the back porch and enjoyed the view. The quiet breeze played against the trees and the birds sang the day away. I closed my eyes and listened to the creek gurgle along.

All the weight of the events of the past week pressed heavily on my heart. I had no idea anyone's life could be so complicated. In a short time, I'd managed to meet two terrific guys and lose them both without explanation. I didn't know if I could handle any more pandemonium.

A single tear trickled down my cheek and I tried to hold back the emotions I couldn't seem to keep stuffed down. What I really needed was answers.

What did I do to have this chaos in my life? Why was this happening to me?

I feared I'd never know the truth or ever be able to get over Nicholas fully, even though I'd said my goodbyes at the cliff's edge. In time, I hoped I'd stop thinking about him so much, but something in me craved the completeness he made me feel the night of the fall and I couldn't help it. Even when I dwelled on the mean things he said outside the theater, as soon as I let my guard down, the longing would come back—almost like his presence was the missing puzzle piece to happiness I'd been looking for all my life.

I could still feel his strong body carrying me up the hill, his touch when he brushed aside my hair, his tenderness and concern when I fought going to the emergency room. He ruined all future relationships for me because no one could compare. And the sad part was, in one small lifesaving gesture, he'd managed to capture my heart and he had no idea.

I hated him for it.

And then there was Phil. I knew he was in trouble and for some reason afraid to go home. I constantly worried about him. But then, I was banned from ever being his friend. There was no escape.

I wanted to throw my cereal bowl and smash it into a million pieces. More than anything, I needed to talk to someone who would understand and give sound advice—someone who would tell me I'd survive—someone who had been through what I was going through—someone like a mom. The tears flowed down my cheeks and splashed into my bowl. I couldn't hold it in anymore and I felt so tired.

If only I could just stay home tonight.

I drug out my pity party as long as I could before I walked into the house. I washed my face with water, blew my nose and tried to cover up my red cheeks with a little make-up. The puffy eyed girl in the mirror smiled and conveyed things would work out. They had to.

When I arrived at work, everyone was happy to see me. It was my first day back since the accident. No one said anything about my red eyes, so I assumed my blotchy face had returned to normal. I wore a smile on my face but had a burden in my heart as I put on my apron and got behind the counter to take orders.

The evening was slow, which wasn't typical for a Friday night. Everyone blamed the countywide curfew. I really wanted to keep busy, so I asked if I could organize the storeroom.

Once I saw the mess, I wished I hadn't volunteered. Straws, napkins, silverware and condiments were everywhere and needed to be consolidated to make room to stock the missing items. But eager to distract myself, I got right to work. It felt good to dive into a mind-numbing project. When I was done, I gathered up the bag of trash I'd accumulated and headed for the dumpsters out back. As I neared the back door I sensed something.

Evil lurked outside in the alley. I looked out the peep hole expecting something horrific, but didn't see anything. Convinced my recent drama had me overly spooked, I slowly opened the door and peered out.

The events I witnessed unfolded like a scene from a scary movie. Three tough-looking guys in leather trench coats approached a lone guy who had his back to me. Their voices were hushed, but confrontational, full of overwhelming, confident anger. Warning bells went off in my head to shut the door and get help, but I couldn't tear my eyes away from the showdown.

The ghostlike similarity of the thugs' translucent skin struck me odd as it strangely reflected the light of the alley. And the inky blackness of their irises reminded me of those of a shark, unfeeling and cold. I watched them shift their glances from each other to the man they encircled, almost as if to communicate a secret plan. Suddenly, the rage rose, along with the tension. They were about to strike.

I yelled in my mind for the lone man to run knowing he didn't stand a chance. But instead, he reached into the folds of his jacket and pulled out a pointed stick, holding it in his hand next to his side, poised, ready to act.

The thugs began to laugh and mock him as they tightened closer around him, but the lone guy did not move from his position, fearless as ever.

I held my breath, anxious to see what would happen, when I heard a "hey" coming from my general direction.

I almost looked behind me when I realized, the sound came from my own throat. And before I knew it and against my will, I'd stepped into the alley. The big door slammed shut and locked behind me. I froze in terror.

All four men turned to look at the noisy new intruder in the alley.

I blinked my eyes and began to process in slow motion. I fearfully stared back at the shifty men, wondering if I should try to run for it. But my breath caught in my throat and my knees grew weak when I focused on the face of the lone man. It was someone I knew.

"Julia, watch out!" Nicholas called to me, but it was too late.

Suddenly, I was knocked off my feet and one of the thugs was on top of me, his hungry black eyes excited as he growled like a tiger. I tried to scream but nothing came out. He opened his mouth and licked his long, pointed, canine teeth.

"Hmmm . . . look who came for dinner," he said with a hiss and sniffed the air above my collarbone.

I forced my eyes shut and prayed the nightmare would end, when I felt him go limp and fall heavily, right on top of me. I heaved him off and watched as he twitched with a wooden stake protruding from his back.

Not sure if he was actually dead or not, I began to crawl away. He grabbed my arm.

"Where do you think you're going?" he demanded with a raspy voice.

I pulled with all my might to get away when suddenly, fire spread out from the edges of the stab wound and consumed his torso. The thug squealed as I yanked harder, ripping his arm off his body in the process. I screamed and flailed my arm, with the smoldering appendage still gripping me tightly. The fire continued to burn down like a candle's wick towards my skin. But, right before the flame reached me, his arm's flesh disintegrated into a plume of dust that flew everywhere. I looked back at the rest of the thug's body as he dissolved into a pile of ash.

I stifled a scream with my hand and watched wide-eyed while the remaining pieces continued to sizzle. All that was left was his greasy handprint on my arm. I rubbed violently until it came off, surprised to discover my skin unharmed underneath.

The sounds of fighting and destruction drew my attention from the ashes to the other end of the alley. I watched in fear for Nicholas' life as the blur of what seemed like twenty other animalistic men-creatures ambushed him. Every once in a while, one would come flying out of the pack, slam into the pavement, stand up unharmed, then jump back in. After a few seconds, I realized it was the same two guys. They were hurling themselves at him, biting and hissing, trying to get some sort of contact. But Nicholas was faster and fought them off with a graceful ease.

I sat mesmerized at how the incredible fight looked; like a planned, choreographed event. Nicholas was actually having fun, while the thugs were just getting angrier because they couldn't defeat him.

And then, after I felt Nicholas' boredom, he whipped out two more stakes and in one fluid motion, stabbed them both in the chest at the same time. And just like the first one, they squealed and burned up in smoke too.

Nicholas was at my side before the stakes hit the pavement.

"Are you okay?" he asked, cupping my elbow and helping me stand up.

"OKAY? Am I okay? He . . . they're . . ." My mind swam in confusion. I just used my hands to motion to the scorched shells of people.

"Did he hurt you?"

I blinked and shook my head, still tongue-tied and shaken.

"Just breathe. It's going to be okay."

I furrowed my brow and slowly looked around at the three piles of dust, complete with wooden stakes. My head started feeling woozy, so I grabbed the wall to steady myself. Nicholas' worry heightened.

"Julia, I know this is hard to comprehend, but I can explain what you just saw," he said slowly and deliberately.

"Yes, you need to explain," I whispered, my voice shaking uncontrollably.

I realized I was breathing again.

"I'd prefer not to do it here. Can we go someplace else?"

"Leave?" I questioned, afraid there were more of them hiding around the corner. I only felt safe next to Nicholas.

"Yes, someplace other than here?" he asked in urgency.

"But . . . there could be more . . ." my voice sounded frightened, raspy and broken.

"There are no more, Julia. But it's not safe out in the open. Let's go to my car."

I took a few small steps forward and kicked a bag of trash, the one I originally needed to throw away.

Work. I'm still on the clock.

"I need to ask to leave early," I mumbled.

Nicholas gently put his arm around my waist and directed me out of the alley to the front of the store. The short walk got the blood moving into my limbs and I started to think a little clearer.

"I'll wait out here," he suggested. I stared blankly into his green eyes, managed to gain composure, and pulled open the door.

I don't remember what I said, or how I managed to collect my things and make it out of the store without causing my manager alarm, but I did.

Nicholas escorted me over to his black Chrysler 300, opened the passenger door and helped me get in. The door shut and left me alone in the deafening quiet. I drew my feet up onto the seat and hugged my legs. My heart was still beating a mile a minute.

The word *vampire* kept ringing over and over in my head and I wanted it to stop. I started to rock back and forth. There had to be a rational explanation for what just happened. Vampires were not real.

His door opened and he slid in, checking his rearview mirrors carefully first before turning to me.

"I'd like to take you someplace so we can talk, if that's okay with you."

I nodded, trembling, feeling a little safer in his car.

"Can you please put on your seat belt?" he asked while putting on his own.

I drew in a deep breath, straightened my legs and complied with his request. Once the seat belt clicked, he started the car, pulled out of the deli parking lot and headed towards the highway.

"I owe you an apology Julia," he started off.

I turned my face towards him in disbelief. This had to be Nicholas' twin brother or an alter ego of the one at the theater. Who did he think he was anyway? One moment he played the shining hero and the next a horrible ogre. I wasn't going to fall so easily this time, even if I knew the apology to be genuine.

"The night you almost fell off the cliff, I had to lie to you about what happened. I really wanted to tell you the truth, but I couldn't, so I told you I'd killed a mountain lion." His voice was low and even, as if he chose his words wisely. "What I actually killed was a vampire."

I gulped. That was the first time the word *vampire* had been uttered out loud, confirming that they truly existed. He hesitated when I didn't respond.

"You aren't handling this very well, are you?"

"No," I hoarsely whispered, still feeling I couldn't catch my breath.

"You don't have to be afraid," he said with overwhelming confidence.

"You're kidding me, right?" I stated, wondering if he was in the same alley I was in a few minutes ago.

"I just wish you hadn't come into the alley. What were you thinking?"

He clenched his jaw and gripped hard on the steering wheel. The sudden anger both internally and externally startled me.

"I didn't mean to." I bit my lip and turned my head down. "I seem to be a magnet for trouble these days."

Nicholas' abrupt chuckle confused me; I didn't get the joke. But whatever I said eased his tension, so I didn't ask.

"So now you know why I couldn't see you," he said matter-of-factly.

"What do you mean?"

He paused and took a deep breath. I could sense his guilt.

"I couldn't tell you what really happened. You'd already found loopholes in my story. It was best to disappear from your life."

I felt a pang of dread in my heart. Nicholas' disappearing was the last thing I ever wanted. Something deep inside me needed him to be there. I needed the safety he gave me, like a guardian angel.

He checked his rearview mirror again. The lights of the cars behind us lit up his green eyes and reminded me of the surf from the night before. Their beauty stunned me.

We turned onto an abandoned dirt road that wove through the woods and ended in front of a meadow. He parked the car and shut off the motor. The sudden silence became uncomfortable.

"Why would it matter if I knew?" I asked softly.

"It's not something anyone would openly share. And trust me; you wouldn't have believed me anyway."

"Maybe," I said sheepishly, wondering if I would believe him or think he was crazy. "So, is that why you were rude in front of the theater?"

When I said the word 'rude', Nicholas felt remorseful. It made me wish I'd chosen a different word.

"It wasn't what I wanted to do. A pack of parasites had just passed you and I couldn't let them get away."

"So those were . . . *vampires* too?" I uttered, choking over the word.

"You saw them?" He frowned. "I was afraid they'd see me talking to you. If they had any idea you and I knew each other . . . it would've been bad."

"Why?"

"Because I think they've figured out who I am," he said, his voice cold. "This group is different than the others—smarter. I'm usually able to eliminate witnesses."

"Do you do that often?" I asked with concern. "Hunt them?"

"When I can, I do." His pride swelled.

I gulped hard, unsure what to say. It was one thing to realize vampires existed, but to find out he hunted them regularly was a whole different story.

"Don't get me wrong, I'm glad you *eliminated* the ones hunting me, but don't you think it's a little dangerous?"

He turned and smiled.

"Dangerous for me? No. Only when it comes to you, then it can get tricky. This was not your first run-in with a vampire. You've had others."

"I have?" I said startled. "When?" *And how did he know?*

Another chuckle and another smile.

"Do you remember the time you got lost at the fair and the Ferris wheel guy offered to help you find your dad?"

I remembered it like it was yesterday; the creepy "wanting" feelings he had for me. I may have only been ten, but I knew he was bad news.

"Yeah, but I ran."

"Vampire," Nicholas said nonchalantly.

Suddenly it clicked and all the confusion made sense. The feeling I had felt at the fair, in the forest, on the beach and at the theater were all the same. The thirst, a cross between lust and hunger, was the vampire craving what they crave.

"Wait—you were there?"

He hesitated for a minute, like he'd accidentally revealed something he didn't want me to know.

"I've always been there."

My heart raced.

"Whoa, what do you mean always?"

Sadness swept over Nicholas' face. I looked into his kind emerald eyes but the starry night sky behind him faded in a shimmery mist. Where I was transported only happened in my mind, but it felt real. I was no longer sixteen. We sat together in the front bench seat of my parent's old Plymouth that smelled of aged leather and vanilla scented air freshener. He held my hand. I was shivering and tears fell down my cheeks. Something bad had happened. My blue pinafore dress was torn. Had blood on it. Not my blood.

"No!" I exclaimed, as the blocked memory surfaced.

I clutched my chest. I couldn't breath. I needed air.

Somehow, I found the door and tugged it open. Tears blinded me as my feet splashed through the wet grass. I needed to get away— far, far away. My mouth became dry like cotton and my muscles burned, but I ran on until a cyclone fence stopped me. I grabbed it and screamed, beating against it until my hands were torn and raw.

Then I felt his hand on my shoulder. He pulled me off the fence and into his arms. I sobbed.

"Why?" I screamed into his chest. "Why?"

It was all there—the fear, the dark evil eyes and the sickening cackle echoing in my mind. We were trapped. She shielded me from him. He clamped down on her neck, but watched me over her shoulder. I cried and stood in fear, feeling all her pain and then her empty silence. He dropped her lifeless body onto the ground. He wanted me next.

"He killed her—" I choked out of my tears as my body heaved.

Nicholas held me tight and I sunk into his body. The flood of emotion and anger cut so deeply I wanted to vomit. How could I have forgotten? This whole time, the past was locked in my subconscious. She was gone and never coming home.

"But how?" I asked in a whimper. "You were there?"

"I was," he said. "But too late. I'm sorry."

I felt his grief mix with mine and it tore my heart in two. All I knew of my mother's disappearance was somehow I ended up on my parent's front porch the morning after we were missing. Later my mother's car was found at the bottom of the river. It wasn't known if she dropped me off and left again, or if someone else brought me home, but her body was never found and no one saw what happened.

The case baffled the investigators. My dad took a lie detector test to prove his innocence. No one else had a motive to hurt her. She disappeared into thin air. It didn't help that I couldn't remember what happened, even with counseling. But, I believed my Dad never wanted to know what I'd blocked out, for fear of what I'd say happened.

"You took me home?"

"I did."

I leaned my head into Nicholas' chest and sobbed. The fact she was really gone hit me hard and I thought my heart would stop right there. I'd always believed she was alive somewhere and remained hopeful, like my father, that one day she'd come home.

As Nicholas stroked the back of my hair, his comfort infused me like I'd just crawled under a pile of warm laundry fresh from the dryer. He was the only person I could imagine being with when I finally remembered.

12 – REVELATIONS

*A*fter I somewhat recovered, Nicholas helped me walk back to his car. The distance seemed longer than I remembered now that I was clear-headed and aware of my surroundings. By the time we reached his car on the other side of the meadow, I felt drained, wanting to curl up into a ball. Nicholas' guilt made it worse, but I didn't want to be away from him.

"It's all my fault," he said, after we got settled inside.

I looked at him, confused and bewildered.

"Why would you think that?"

"I could have stopped him if I was sooner. I was only in time to save you. She'd been bitten and . . . it was too late to save her."

I closed my eyes. The scene was still alive, replaying like a bad movie in my head and the tears began again. The urge to run stiffened the muscles in my legs, but the adrenaline rush had zapped all my energy.

"How could you know?" I said to ease his guilt. "It's the animal-who-took-her-life's fault. He should get the blame."

Nicholas hung his head. I sensed his hesitation to agree.

"He didn't get away, did he?" I asked with gritted teeth, ready to become a vampire hunter too if the filthy beast still roamed the planet.

Nicholas's eyes tightened into a scowl.

"I gave him what he deserved."

"Good," I said, with a hard edge to my voice.

Finding out Nicholas avenged my mother's murder strangely comforted me and made the pain soften for a bit. But after my anger subsided, I found myself even more worn out. In the last two hours I had discovered vampires were real, the truth of my mother's disappearance, why Nicholas avoided me and why he was there in the first place. My head felt like it was going to implode.

"But wait a minute," I blurted out. "How could that be? You'd be only, what—" I counted on my fingers. "Like eight-years-old?"

He paused and looked like he didn't want to answer.

"I wasn't eight," he said sheepishly, "I was eighteen."

"But how is that possible?" I said slowly.

"It's because I'm not what you think I am."

My stomach dropped and I leaned away to study his face. Could he be a vampire and just learned to control his bloodlust? He did have unexplainable super human strength and amazing agility.

"Are you one of them?" I whispered.

I cringed in anticipation of the answer. If for some reason he was, there had to be an explanation. He waited before answering and nervously shifted in his seat.

"I'm half actually," he finally muttered out, his stern face avoiding my eyes.

"Half?"

"It's a long story," he said with a sigh. "I was born this way."

"You don't have to tell me if you don't want to," I said, afraid to pry.

"I don't see any reason not to tell you, now that you know the truth." He took a deep breath and the pain came close to the surface.

"My father is a vampire and my mother, a human. Most of the time, when a vampire falls in love with a human, the human wants to become immortal so they can be together forever, but my dad refused to turn my mom and insisted they try to have a normal relationship.

"Vampires don't procreate by having babies, so when my mom found out she was pregnant with me, my dad assumed she cheated and left her. When she went into labor, she refused to go to a hospital and had complications, so—my dad raised me."

"Oh," I said, feeling insensitive for dredging up his past. "That's horrible. I'm really sorry."

"Yeah ... so, to answer your question, I age slowly."

"That's good, right?" I said, in an attempt to recover my blunder.

"Well, until you show people your driver's license," he said, joking to cover the hurt. His mouth curled up at the corner. "You don't know how many times I've had it confiscated as a fake."

"And you're super strong and fast."

"I do have all the vampire abilities, plus I can walk in the daylight—a very nice bonus."

He flashed his white teeth and the next question slipped out of my mouth.

"Do you drink blood?"

Nicholas turned with an inquisitive smile and I became horrified at myself.

"Questions, questions," he said teasingly, "No. I don't. My father believes if I ever did, the vampire side of me would take over and I'd lose the ability to control my thirst. I don't care to find out."

I was relieved Nicholas' vampire traits were more of a blessing than a curse and that he indulged my silly questions.

But Nicholas emanated a new found freedom and the guilt melted. I couldn't imagine how difficult it must have been the last ten years—to be near me, but stay anonymous and invisible, unable to share the truth or the grief. I felt more connected to him than ever.

"So, you followed me after my family moved?" I asked.

"I did," he said. "She didn't deserve the fate she received, so I've protected you ever since."

Tears welled up in my eyes again. I was grateful; not only for his valiant effort in trying to save her life, but for killing her murderer and breaking down the wall in me that held her memory. I could see her in my mind now. Smell her sweet dewy fragrance. Feel her warmth. The healing could begin.

"Thank you," I said as I blushed. I hated the circumstances

surrounding our friendship, but I couldn't have earned a more amazing guardian.

I wanted to ask him more about his special vampire abilities but glanced at the clock on the dashboard and almost had a heart attack.

"Is that the real time?"

"I believe it is."

"I'm going to be so dead. I need to get home."

Before I could finish the statement, Nicholas spun out of his parking spot and took off down the gravel road.

"What are you doing?" I yelled and grabbed panic-filled onto the arm rail with one hand and fastened the seat beat with the other.

"Speeding," he said, completely at ease. " . . .so you won't get in trouble."

"Without your headlights?" I yelled louder. "Are you crazy?"

Nicholas laughed.

"I do this all the time. I have natural night vision," he said, amused. "But I can slow down and put my lights on if it makes you feel better."

The thought of my irate Dad standing in the doorway tapping his watch changed my mind.

"No, that's okay. I do need to get home."

My breath slowed back to normal when I realized he was in complete control of the car, even when he blindly turned onto the highway and wove with precision through the traffic.

I relaxed and trusted his instincts. We sped through the streets, and the dark night blurred past me outside. As soon as we turned off the freeway, he flipped the headlights on.

"This is insane," I said as I shook my head.

"Welcome to my life."

We pulled into the deli parking lot and I noticed my car was one of the last ones parked there. The thought of driving home alone made me nervous. I couldn't stop the flashes of the hungry eyes of the vampire that attacked me, and I pictured others waiting in the dark at home. This was worse than the imaginary boogey man I used to be afraid of. Vampires were real and quite possibly everywhere.

"Do you think you can drive?" he asked, as he parked next to my car.

"I think so. I'm feeling a little better now," I lied.

"I'll follow you home if you want."

"Please?" I asked, grateful he sensed my hesitation.

Once I got into my car, I immediately locked the doors behind me, even though I knew there were no vampires around. With a turn of the key, the engine revved to life and I waited for it to warm up while I blew hot air into my hands. My Quantum paled in comparison to Nicholas' Chrysler.

I pulled out a compact mirror from my purse and added powder to my eyes. I didn't have a clue how I was going to get past my dad without being noticed. Maybe they'd be in bed already.

After a few minutes, I looked in my rearview mirror to back out and noticed Nicholas' concerned face in the reflection. My heart warmed at the revelation of the truth. All along, when I thought he'd ditched me, he was still there, agonizing over our separation too.

I cranked the heater and drove. Nicholas followed closely behind and his headlights shone through the back window. He couldn't drive stealth following me and it made me grin.

Quickly, I formulated an excuse in my head for why I was late, just in case. Nicholas' superb driving did shave off precious minutes and instead of being an hour past curfew, I was only about a half-an-hour late. But with all the drama, I knew he'd be counting every minute and exponentially adding them.

I figured out a decent story when I noticed we passed the spot it all happened and my car lurched a little, almost as if it recognized it. I couldn't believe my late-night mishap was just days ago, when it felt like ages—back when I was still naïve.

I turned down my quiet street and felt my tension release

when I found my house dark and my family sleeping peacefully inside. Nicholas was at my door just as I shut the engine off. It was as if he'd read my mind.

"Thank you," I said as he helped me out of my car.

"I can't imagine what you must be going through," he said his face full of concern.

"I'm glad I know," I said, trying to sound brave. I looked up at him in the moonlight; his beautiful face and amazing eyes sparkled down at me.

He reached out, pulled me gently toward him and hugged me. I melted into his strong chest and inhaled the sweet aroma of his skin. His arms were warm and comforting. He rested his chin on the top of my head and took a deep breath.

"It's going to be okay, I promise," he said, as he held me tighter.

I vowed not to cry anymore in front of him, but I couldn't help it this time. A little tear trickled down my cheek.

"So, now what happens? I mean, I know I'm not supposed to be seen with you, but how can I contact you?" I asked softly, not wanting him to let me go. "What if there's an emergency?"

He held on for a second longer before pulling away to look down at me.

"You can call me," he stated simply.

"You have a cell phone?"

I didn't know why I assumed he didn't and scolded myself.

"I don't get many calls, but I do have a phone," he said with a snicker.

My cheeks grew hot and I felt sorry I doubted he'd be part of the 21st Century like everyone else. He ignored my faux pas and quietly told me his number and I told him mine.

"Memorize it. Don't store it in your phone. Call me only in an emergency. I don't want anyone to find out we are connected in any way."

He scanned the forest line again and then ushered me closer to the house. I reached out with my own powers too. As far as I could tell, we were alone.

"Do you think we were followed?" I asked once we reached the porch, wondering if he sensed something I didn't.

"Not tonight. But you can never be too careful."

He looked at me wistfully and put a stray hair of mine back into place. My heart erupted in a flutter when his hand brushed my cheek and I tried to control my breath, which came out a little quicker than normal.

"But one thing I forgot to tell you. Never invite a vampire into your house. They cannot cross your threshold uninvited. Understood?"

"Really?" I said with a snort. "Like I'd do that."

"It's just a precaution, and during the evening, stay in heavy-populated areas, just in case."

"I will."

"Try to get some sleep," he said as he gathered me to his chest once more and kissed the top of my head. His feelings were paternal at the moment. I took in a deep breath and hugged him back, hoping we could stay like this forever.

"I need to go," he whispered and loosened his arms.

I looked up at his chiseled face and frowned.

"I'll see you soon, I promise," he said in response.

His tender eyes made my stomach burst into a nervous flutter once again.

"Okay," I choked out, unsure how he was going to keep that promise, but knew he meant to.

"Bye," I nervously said and let myself into the house. I shut the door quickly, hoping it would lessen the sting this time.

In the hallway I stood with my eyes closed and felt the bitter separation. The tremendous sense of loss flooded my senses like it did the first time and I ached. Luckily, this time I didn't get the warning Nicholas was never coming back.

I tried to analyze why it physically hurt so much to leave his presence. Maybe it was because he helped me survive the nightmare of my mother's death that connected us, or some other weird nuance of my secret power. Whatever it was, I knew I would always need to be a part of Nicholas' life.

"Julia, is that you?"

My insides jumped at the sound of my dad's gruff and half-awake voice.

"Yes. Did I wake you?"

I walked over to the foot of the stairs and fearfully looked up.

He stood at the top in his pajamas and a frown on his face.

"Julia, you're late. Where were you?"

"I was talking with my manager. I know, I'm sorry," I said, my rehearsed speech rolling easily off my tongue.

"You promised to call."

"I didn't realize the time, Dad. Sorry."

He turned, mumbled something and shuffled back to his room. I heard the door shut.

I stood in the dark and realized I hadn't heard Nicholas pull away. When I went to the window to look out, the only car that remained on the street now was mine.

Exhausted, I drug myself up the stairs and got ready for bed. I knew I'd have issues falling sleep. My raw hands ached and my body felt fatigued, but my mind was alert, racing with new information.

I decided I'd try to fall asleep on my own before taking a Tylenol PM. I pulled the covers up to my neck and turned off the light. The moonlight shone into my room and I turned towards the night sky.

My phone buzzed with a message on my nightstand. It was from the number I'd just tucked into my memory bank.

- **Goodnight and don't worry. I'll stay close by tonight.**

I blinked in astonishment and instantly felt better. I sent a message back.

- Thank you. Goodnight to you, too.

I wanted to look out the window but didn't want Nicholas to see me. If anything was ever to happen between us, I didn't want to appear too eager.

Happy with the new tidbit of information, I snuggled up in my covers, reenacting his arms wrapped tenderly around me, and to my surprise, quickly drifted off to sleep.

13 – YEARNING

$\mathscr{I}$ woke up to a beautiful Saturday morning and found I'd slept soundly the whole night through. The sweet aroma of freshly brewed coffee drifted under my door and I heard pots clanging in the kitchen.

The light of the bathroom hurt my eyes as I examined the puffy marshmallows that were my eyelids. I slathered them with special cream and hoped Dad wouldn't notice.

I threw on my favorite tattered robe and bunny slippers and scuffed down the stairs to the kitchen.

"Good morning sleepyhead," Dad said with a quick glance over his shoulder. "Want some coffee?"

"Yes," I mumbled, and made my way to the pot.

With my mug in hand, I slid onto a seat at the kitchen table and put my lips to the rim to take a long slow swig. I felt the warm liquid go the length of my throat, all the way to my stomach, and let out a sigh.

"That good," Dad said as he continued voraciously dicing zucchini, onions and broccoli into slivers.

Within seconds, the veggies hit the wok with a sizzle and filled the room with a mouthwatering garlic aroma. I waited for a lecture about coming in late the night before, but he said nothing about it.

"Things going better with you?" he finally asked.

"Yeah, I guess so."

I wanted to share what I remembered about Mom, but knew this wasn't the right time. He seemed happy today, like everything between us was patched up. Why would I want to ruin it?

"Has Phil come back yet?"

"No," I said quietly. "Not yet."

"I'm sorry to hear that," he said with a twinge of worry. I

guessed it wasn't for Phil's welfare, but my own.

"They cancelled the homecoming game because of it."

"Really? That's a shame," he said sounding surprised, but I knew he wasn't. Probably something else Mr. Brewster revealed after I left the meeting.

"Yeah, I wasn't planning to go anyway."

"And you *are* still grounded," he said in a fatherly tone.

I sulked down in my seat, hoping he'd forgotten.

Before I could pout, he slid a steaming hot gourmet plate of scrambled eggs with sautéed vegetables and seasoned potatoes to die for in front of me.

"Looks really good, Dad," I said.

The skin around his eyes crinkled up when he grinned. He was unsure about his parenting skills, except when it came to cooking. It was one area he could be successful at every time.

"What's cooking?" Luke said as he sauntered into the kitchen.

"Sorry, it's all gone," I said with a mouthful of food.

Luke made a face at me before dishing himself up a plate.

We sat and enjoyed our breakfast quietly. It had been a while since we'd all been together for a meal and I treasured the moment.

"So what are your plans for today, Jules?" Dad finally said, after taking his last few mouthfuls.

"The homecoming dance is tonight and I'm going to help Sam get ready, if that's okay with you, Dad."

"Aren't you going?" Luke asked innocently.

"No," I said with a tiny hint of disdain. "I'm grounded, remember?"

"Oh, yeah," Luke said, hiding his smirk while keeping his eyes on his plate.

"Did you want to go?" Dad asked.

I sensed the dance, unlike the game, might have been something negotiable if I really wanted to go, but I didn't, at least not with anyone from my school. And Nicholas was a little busy hunting down the vampires of the world.

"I don't have a date." *That's entirely human, half-vampire actually, but he doesn't drink blood or anything gross like that.*

"You don't seem too upset about it," Dad said catching my mysterious smile.

"I hate dances, Dad. You know that."

"Ah, hey that reminds me. Whatever happened to that boy that helped you home last week?" Dad asked while picking up the newspaper off the table.

I froze. *Had he seen us together last night?*

"Yeah, what was his name? Nicholas?" Luke asked.

I shot Luke a look and shook my head back and forth, wide-eyed to plead for him to shut up.

"I think he's been busy," I stammered.

"Oh," Dad said, suddenly absorbed at something in the news.

Luke looked back with apologetic eyes. I held my breath, hoping the subject would pass. I didn't have a good excuse prepared, and the chances of getting caught in a lie were greater since we just hung out the night before.

"Anyone need anything else?" I asked, as I planned my escape and stood to clear my plate.

"Hmmm?" Dad said while perusing the stock page. "You can clear my plate."

Luke handed me Dad's plate along with his own and gave me a wink.

Normally, I would have told my brother to do his own dishes, but said nothing and moved to the sink, unsure of what he was going to do. To my delight, I heard him ask Dad about the status of some of his favorite stocks. When I turned, I caught his eye and mouthed a thank you. He smiled.

When I took out the trash, I looked around suddenly feeling conspicuous.

What if he's watching me right now?

I tried to see if I could sense his presence, realizing I never felt watched in the past, but the surroundings were void of feeling, so I didn't know. But to think he might be made me a little uncertain. I wondered if I should feel more violated. Was he spying, or just easing his conscience?

This must be how people with bodyguards feel.

I decided I wasn't going to worry about it, or I'd make myself crazy. We'd have to work out all the gritty details later because one thing was for certain; I wasn't going to have some invisible guardian in the shadows my whole life—especially one whom I wanted to spend more time with.

I went back inside and immediately got busy. My insurmountable to-do list consisted of house cleaning, laundry and homework. I'd gotten buried in dust bunnies and dirty clothes since my accident and I had to get most of it done before going to Sam's house tonight.

I didn't have to work, like I'd originally told everyone. My boss had to make cuts in everyone's hours due to declining business. But after Nicholas' and Phil's mysterious disappearances, none of my friends brought up finding me another date. I think they all started to suspect I was cursed.

It was just as well anyway. I only wanted to go with Nicholas, whom I'm sure would have been my date, if his situation wasn't so complicated.

Sam and Todd were doubling with Dena and Morgan, as I'd hoped. Katie was going with Erik, her new boyfriend and lineman on the football team, separately from the group. Cameron was more than happy to skip the dance to play a Magic tournament with the chess club.

"I wish you were coming," Sam said with a sigh while I worked on her hair. "I have an extra dress you could borrow."

Her beautiful brown locks, elegantly piled up on top of her head in a French twist and dangling ringlets, were under assault as I sprayed every last strand with glitter-filled hairspray.

"You'll have a good time with Todd." I tried my best not to sound jealous, because now I wanted to go. "Plus, I'm grounded."

"Oh, I forgot," she said as she wrinkled up her nose. "But you're here . . .?"

"He fudged since he knew you'd kill him if I didn't do your hair and ruined your dance."

"Smart thinking," she said with a wink, while she turned in front of the mirror.

I slumped down on her bed and thumbed through a magazine.

"I wasn't going to say anything, but you seem . . . different . . . happy even. You finally doing better?" she asked, looking at me through the reflection.

I tried to hide my smile. I wanted to tell her I felt a hundred times better now that I knew the truth, but couldn't.

"I am," I said quickly, so I wouldn't say anything more.

Overnight, everything changed and every time I almost said something, I had to bite my tongue. The problem was, I didn't know where to begin. Nicholas' situation forced him to tell the truth after I witnessed his heroic acts, and he was right—you couldn't just blurt it out. I contemplated making up a story, but didn't want to lie to my best friend. I had no choice but to keep it to myself for now.

I checked the time again. The limo was scheduled to pick Sam up last so her mother and I could see everyone and take pictures.

Sam's dress was a lilac strapless, A-line, knee-length number with a sequined bodice and tulle skirt. She wore open-toed heels with sparkly, sequined straps. The whole ensemble with her ringlets trailing down the back of her neck was breathtaking.

She spun around a few times in front of the mirror and I'd never thought she'd looked more radiant. She stopped when her mom knocked at the door. Nervousness hit me from all different directions. Todd must have arrived.

"They're here, Samantha," Sam's mom said.

"Don't worry," I said in response to Sam's newly horrified expression. "I'll go down and talk to him. Come when you're ready."

Sam gulped hard and nodded.

I bounded down the stairs in front of Sam's mom and greeted a petrified Todd in the foyer, wearing a black suit, holding a corsage.

"You look really nice," I said with a smile to give him courage.

He weakly smiled as he rocked back and forth on his heels.

"Mrs. King," he said with a nod.

"Samantha will be down in a minute," Sam's mom said, amused.

I had a feeling he'd already greeted her formally when she opened the door and was stuck for something else to say.

The foyer felt crowded with everyone anxiously waiting for Sam to join us downstairs. I could sense her hesitation, but she finally appeared. We all watched in silence as she sauntered gracefully down the stairs.

"You look so . . . beautiful," Todd said when she touched down on the ground floor.

"Thank you," she said and blushed.

Todd slid the corsage on Sam's wrist just as there was a knock at the door. I left the three of them to see who was knocking, while Sam's mom snapped away on her camera. I opened the door to Dena and Morgan holding hands, with huge smiles on their faces.

"Hey guys," I said feeling smug in my matchmaking abilities.

"Hey, Jules," Dena sang as they stepped inside the house.

I winked at Morgan.

Dena wore an exquisite white chiffon, knee-length gown with an empire bodice and a black ribbon sash that tied around her waist. The dress bounced in slow motion when she walked. Morgan also wore a black suit and I commented on how he cleaned up well.

"Okay, you guys need to hurry up or you're going to be late for dinner," I barked while trying to shoo people out the door.

Sam shot me a wistful glance, but obediently filed outside with everyone else. However, before the group could make it to the limo, Sam's mom insisted on a group photo in front of the rose-covered terrace. Sam's mom primped, preened and positioned everyone for the shots, and the group didn't know who to look at as we both snapped a ton of pictures. Before long everyone got antsy. I watched Sam's mom fuss over Sam and give Todd the lecture about when to bring her home. Sam appeared embarrassed, but I found the gesture very loving. I felt a pang of jealousy. I'd do anything to have a mother who would dote over me.

Watching Sam and her mother, and feeling their unconditional love for one another, brought home the finality of my own mother's life. I could feel tears threatening to break loose. The last thing I wanted to do was ruin their evening, but inside I unraveled. And as if they'd read my emotions, they got into the limo and left.

Sam's mom hugged me goodbye. I held it together until I got into my car, then I let the tears flow. I never realized how much I missed her, counting on the hope she'd return. Thinking of my mom made me want to be with Nicholas again. He was the only one who could understand my pain, could comfort me. Where was he? Would this constitute as an emergency?

On my way home, I decided I needed ice cream—double fudge chocolate ice cream to be precise. I pulled into the Safeway grocery store parking lot. I didn't even need to look in the mirror to know my eyes were red again, so I put on a pair of sunglasses before going inside. I didn't care how silly I looked. I needed chocolate.

I made a beeline to the frozen foods section, pulled out a pint of Ben and Jerry's Chocolate Fudge Brownie and headed to the check out stand. As the checker rang up my purchase I averted my gaze, hoping she wouldn't ask any questions. I was relieved when she gave me my change without giving me a second look.

The sun had descended while I was inside. Without the light, the temperature had dropped and felt noticeably colder. I pocketed the sunglasses, wrapped my arms tightly around myself and headed towards my car. I just wanted to be home, in my jammies, eating my ice cream, watching a good mind-numbing movie.

"Julia."

I turned around, unsure if someone called me. No one was there. I shook my head and continued on towards my car.

"Parker."

This time I knew I wasn't hearing things. I recognized Phil's voice, even though tonight it was raspy and barely more than a murmur. I spun around, but he wasn't there. Weird.

"Phil, where are you?"

I saw movement in the shadows at the corner of the store, just outside the light. That's when I saw him. A gasp escaped from my lips.

He leaned against the wall, with a black sweatshirt hood over his head, shifting his eyes from me to the other patrons who left the store. His skin was no longer tan, but a creamy white and if he hadn't called me by my last name, I wouldn't have recognized him. He appeared agitated and I could feel his extreme hunger—the unmistakable hunger—the hunger of a vampire.

My eyes widened and my pulse increased as I tried to remain composed, frozen in my spot.

"Parker, I need your help," he said soft and slow, sounding like he was hurt.

My mind screamed and told me to run, but my feet stayed firmly rooted.

But how did this happen?

The only thing that crossed my mind was the bites from his attack must have been vampire ones. Is that how vampires are created? I didn't know, but whatever happened, he was one of them now and more than I could handle. I needed Nicholas' help. This was a true emergency.

"Phil," I whispered. It was all that would come out.

"Please come over here for a minute. I want to talk to you in private."

His hunger overwhelmed me and I knew without a doubt what he wanted. I wasn't going to fall into his trap.

"Phil, I know someone who can help you work through this change," I said, talking from complete ignorance, but hoped Nicholas would know what to do.

He gave me a wicked grin.

"Clever girl," he hissed and the leaves at his feet spun up as if caught in a whirlwind and he was gone.

I looked around the parking lot for any evidence of his presence, but he was nowhere to be found.

Phil and his hunger had vanished.

14 – FASCINATION

*U*nsure of whether Phil was still lurking in the shadows waiting for me, I darted back inside the store and took out my phone.

- I'm in trouble. Where are you?

As I clicked *send,* I watched the parking lot with trepidation, waiting for his reply. Nicholas had said I was safer around people, but I would feel better if he were here instead. Someone touched my shoulder and I jumped.

"I'm sorry to startle you. Are you okay, dear?" asked a store employee with a name tag that read "Pam."

"Oh, yes . . . I'm . . . I'm just waiting for my ride," I stammered as I lied, feeling self-conscious about my demeanor and tear-stained cheeks.

"Well, if you need anything, come see me, okay?"

She pointed to the flower shop in the store. I thanked her, plastered a happy grin on my face, and moved to a more secluded area of the store lobby.

My phone vibrated.

- I'm here. What's wrong?

How was I going to tell him in one text message all the details about what's transpired with Phil?

- Long story, but my friend who had an accident, just confronted me in the parking lot. He's a vampire now.

The wait for the reply text seemed to take forever. What would he think? Did he already know?

- Walk out with the next person and go straight to your car. Don't go home. I will follow you. I want to see what he does.

With gritted teeth, I flipped my phone closed and shoved it in my pocket. I didn't like his brilliant idea that I be the bait to lure Phil out of hiding.

I stood at the double-doors pretending to read the labels on the kitty litter and waited for a tough dude to walk out with. When the third old lady exited the store, I gave up and started to head out until I spotted a security guard.

"Um . . . excuse me," I said, as I approached him.

"Yes ma'am?" the gray-haired gentleman said.

I spied his name badge.

"George, I was wondering, would you be so kind as to escort me to my car?"

"Is there something wrong, ma'am?" he said, instantly on guard.

"Oh no . . ." I stammered. "It's my tire. I think it's flat. Can you look at it to see if it might need some air?"

The old man straightened his shoulders and pulled down his jacket. "Why of course young lady."

He motioned for me to lead the way.

The guard made small talk about the importance of car care and how he always had to remind his granddaughter to check her oil as we walked towards my car. I claimed complete ignorance, and promised to have my dad give me some lessons on basics, while I scanned the parking lot.

He examined the tire and made mention that it was a good thing I asked for his help. The tire was low on air and he directed me to go straight over to the Gas-n-Go the next block over.

I gave him the sweetest smile I could, promised to get air immediately, got into my car and hit the lock switch. My heart was pounding so fast it made my hands shake. Luckily, the guard didn't notice.

I drove out of the parking lot as instructed, firmly grasping the steering wheel so my hands would stop trembling. Unsure of where to drive, I headed towards the highway.

I could feel Phil was somewhere nearby because the hunger

feelings were back, but I wasn't sure which car was his. In my side-view mirror, I saw the familiar shape of Nicholas' black Chrysler and watched him pull directly behind me. I felt relieved to know he was nearby.

The crooked road required all of my attention to traverse, my concern staying in well-populated areas. I felt Phil's feelings come and go and my nerves responded accordingly. Then I received another text.

- He's following you. Go ahead and go home now so you'll be safe. I'll deal with him.

I slammed my phone closed in frustration. Go home? Was he insane?

Incensed, I reopened my phone and dialed his number.

"Are you crazy?" I yelled as soon as Nicholas answered.

"It's the only way I can get him away from you where you'll be safe," he said with a tense voice.

"I'm not leading him straight to my house!"

"It won't matter. I plan to deal with him tonight anyway," he said, determined.

"No. Find another way."

Nicholas let out a huge sigh. Through the phone, I couldn't sense anything, so I had to pay attention to his voice inflection to know what he was feeling. I didn't want to anger him, but I wasn't going to let him put my family in jeopardy.

"Why are you being so difficult?"

"I'm worried about my family!" I barked, irritated he didn't consider their safety.

"Fine, let me think." He exhaled sharply and paused. "Do you know where the tunnel is over off of Ravine?"

"Yes."

"Park in the middle of that tunnel, so he'll come to you. Just crack your window when he approaches. But stay in your car and leave it running. I'll only be a minute."

"What are you going to do?" I asked, my heart beating faster.

"I'm going to park above the tunnel and take care of him when he leaves."

Take care of him meant killing him and I hadn't even confirmed he was a vampire yet. I couldn't let Nicholas murder him arbitrarily.

"You aren't going to hurt him, are you?"

"Julia, he's a vampire," he said, his voice laced with annoyance.

"But he's my friend."

"And wants to suck your blood. I need to take care of him."

There was emotional finality in his voice I couldn't argue with. If I was to stop a needless murder, I needed to come at it from a logical angle.

"Well, then answer me this, can a vampire choose to be good and not kill humans?"

Nicholas took longer than I wanted to answer. The silence lingered for ever.

"Yes, but it's rare."

"Okay, so before you *eliminate* him, can we see first? Please?"

Nicholas took a deep breath and I crossed my fingers.

"I'll talk to him," he said reluctantly. "But if he tries to leave, I can't promise anything."

I didn't have to read his emotions to know I frustrated him to no end but knew we needed to at least try. I was sure, with my encouragement, Phil could be good. Becoming a vampire couldn't have changed him that much.

"Okay. How will I know when it's time to drive away?" I asked, feeling high from the adrenaline surging through my veins.

"I'll send you a text message."

"Okay," I said, my breath quickening. "Wait, what type of car is he driving?"

"He's not. He's flying."

"Flying?"

"Yes . . . I'll explain later, just get to the tunnel and be ready to act."

"What if something goes wrong?"

"Honk your horn, but whatever you do, don't open the door," he said, his words giving me courage

I hung up.

Nicholas' Chrysler abruptly turned left, as I continued straight towards the underpass, his car disappearing into the black forest. I figured he'd turned off his headlights to drive stealth again. With white knuckles, I concentrated on the winding mountain road with growing consternation, convinced I'd crash if I attempted to peer into the night sky. The dark tunnel seemed to swallow me whole as I parked inside to wait.

Even though Nicholas told me not to, I shut off my engine. The only excuse I could think up was car trouble. I cautiously looked around and waited for Phil to walk up to my car. Something rapped on the glass of my window and I jumped, letting out a squeal in surprise.

"Sorry to startle you," he whispered. "Having car problems?"

Close up and without a hood over his hair, I got my first good look at Phil's transformation. Every inch of his skin was flawless and translucent and his deep, dark, majestic eyes danced with excitement and power. White perfect teeth glinted in the night, as his smile beckoned me to trust him.

"Um . . . yes," I said, completely mesmerized by his angelic beauty and terrified at the same time. He was taking the bait without hardly any effort on my part.

"Well then, why don't you come out and I'll take a look at it for you?"

He tried the door handle.

"Um . . . that's okay. I've called someone. They're coming to help me. They should be here any minute," I stammered, grateful I'd locked it earlier.

He studied me suspiciously, his dark eyes pulling at me, trying to hypnotize me.

"Parker, please . . . I just want to talk to you."

"No," I said, shaking off the spell. "I can hear you from here. Just tell me what you want to say."

"Fine . . ."

He shifted closer to the front of my car and leaned against the side of my hood. With his head cocked to the side, he watched me, analyzing every angle.

"I'm curious," he finally asked with a soft and golden voice. "How do you know about *us*?"

"I just know," I said, not thinking of a better excuse.

I kicked myself for accidentally revealing I knew his secret earlier.

He shot me another seductive grin but unknown to him, his aching thirst washed over me instead, making me nervous.

"Oh I don't think so," he said with a scandalous smirk, eyes alive. "Because if you did . . ."

His penetrating gaze of desire caused my heart to erupt in a fury. He wanted me and it wasn't just for my blood.

"What do you mean?" I asked. My voice cracked. I struggled to shake off his invisible advances.

"I wish you'd come out of the car, so I could show you." He flashed another mischievous flirty grin, "Stuff that would blow your mind. I'm not all bad, honest."

From nowhere, I felt an overwhelming desire to get out of the car, as if an unseen hand pulled mine to turn the handle. I had to break eye contact in order to regain my senses.

"I'm staying in here," I choked out, unsure how much longer I could spurn his requests. "I don't believe you."

It hurt to resist him, like when all you want to do is sleep, but can't and have to force your eyelids to stay open. I had my hand on the lever ready to pull the door open when he moved away from my car. He turned to scan the front opening of the tunnel and then the back.

"You little sneak . . ." he seethed. He glared at me through squinted eyes, his face instantly stony and cold. "This isn't over."

He disappeared.

Panicked, I picked up my phone, flipped it open to find I had no service. I turned the ignition key and put my car into reverse. Once outside the tunnel, the service returned. The phone vibrated with a message.

- Leave now

Was this message intended for earlier? I didn't care. I threw the car into drive, and headed home. It was the only place truly safe from any vampire, and suddenly where I wanted to be. I forced myself to concentrate in order to keep my car on the road as I drove. Did he find Phil? Were they fighting? I flinched and refused to think the worst.

Phil's amorous feelings lingered and grabbed my inner being as I concentrated on the road. I tried to shake it off, but a part of me couldn't help but enjoy the attention. Any time anyone had feelings like that for me in the past, it left me feeling dirty, but with Phil, it was different, sexy even. I scolded myself for indulging a second thought.

Nicholas is the one for you, not Phil. Are you crazy?

I wondered what Phil actually wanted to show me, if he even intended to show me anything other than how tasty a snack I'd be. But I might never know if he didn't survive tonight for some reason.

I looked at my phone again to ensure I had reception, wishing for an update.

Call me!

As I approached my home, I felt the knot in my stomach tighten. What if Phil had eluded Nicholas and flew above me, just out of the reach of my powers? The thought made me scared and elated all at the same time.

I parked closer to the front of the house than normal. Before shutting off my car, I looked up into the sky. All I saw were stars and a few wispy clouds. My laughter bubbled to the surface and I sat amazed for thinking somehow I was safe in this little tin can. The front door was my beacon of safety.

I quickly grabbed my things and sprinted across the lawn. But just as I was about to reach the porch, my phone rang. The distraction caused my foot to snag on the wooden step and I sprawled forward with both hands, dropping everything on the ground. Ignoring the searing pain in my palms, I scrambled to collect my stuff, threw open the door and went inside. When I spun around to shut it, I glanced back at my car and thought I saw Phil crouched next to it. When I took a double take, no one was there. My phone rang again.

"Is that you, Julia?" Dad called from his office.

"Yes," I said, trying to keep my tone from coming out in a high-pitched breathless frenzy.

I glanced at the phone and flipped it open.

"Hold on," I whispered and held the phone at my side.

"What's all that racket?" he asked, his voice closer than a second ago.

"Sorry," I said and turned towards him, forcing a smile. I tried to act natural as he joined me in the hallway. "I tripped outside and fell. That's all."

My dad furrowed his brow.

"Are you feeling okay? Your head's all sweaty."

"It is?" I reached up and smoothed my damp bangs away from my forehead. "I feel fine. But my ice cream is melting." I moved towards the kitchen and tried not to limp.

"Try to be more careful. You don't want to re-injure your ankle," he said behind me.

I felt his hesitation, so I stuffed the soft ice cream in the freezer and headed for the stairs. Halfway up, I heard the wheels on his office chair squeak as they rolled against the floor.

Whew.

"Sorry about that," I said into the phone and softly closed my door.

"Everything okay?" Nicholas asked.

"You called just as I was coming in the house. My dad wanted to talk to me first," I said nonchalantly. "So what happened?"

"He got away," he said in a low and angry tone. "Why didn't you drive when I texted you?"

"I didn't get it . . . until later. I didn't have reception in the tunnel."

"You didn't get it?" he asked dubiously, letting out a huff. "Well, we have bigger problems now,"

"What do you mean?"

"He saw me, so my cover's blown. And, he knows you know what he is and that we're working together. "

I sensed the danger in his voice, but I didn't feel threatened. Vampire or not, Phil was still my friend. I knew he didn't want to kill me.

"What did he want anyway?"

I fumbled for an answer. I didn't want to tell him Phil *wanted me* and that he almost got me out of my car against my will.

"Well . . ." I laughed nervously. "He's curious how I know about vampires and he's enamored with his new powers. But mostly, he just tried to get me out of the car."

Nicholas inhaled and exhaled sharply. I didn't know if it was a good or bad thing. Then he chuckled.

"Good thing you didn't. He is an interesting one. When you said he was in an accident, what happened?"

I explained everything that went down that night, from the shifty people in the crowd, to the change in Phil's demeanor at the hospital.

"Phil was never meant to be sired," Nicholas said in revelation.

"Maybe he *is* working alone."

"Is this good?"

"I'm not sure yet. Vampires don't let their new sires wander around unsupervised. It's not smart. They cause problems . . .."

"But even still, he's targeted you for some reason and if he goes and tells the others about us, we won't be safe."

I gulped.

"We need to talk privately," he continued.

"We do?"

I gulped again.

"Are you free tomorrow?"

"Yes?" My heart fluttered in anticipation of what he was going to say.

"Be ready at eight tomorrow morning and I'll come pick you up. Don't tell anyone you'll be with me."

"Okay."

"And don't leave your house tonight," he said firmly. "I need to go. Have a good night and don't worry. We'll figure this out tomorrow."

He hung up.

I closed my phone and swooned, holding it with both hands gently to my chest. My heart flittered in elation. Nicholas and I were actually going to spend time together alone. I flung myself on my bed and began to plan what I was going to wear.

15 — COMPLETE

*M*y first order of business for the day was figuring out how to manipulate my dad into un-grounding me. Missing a dance was one thing, a date with Nicholas was entirely another. After playing every possibly scenario in my head, I discovered my safest bet was to ask if I could go and hope he was in a good mood.

My next big problem was figuring out what to wear. Too embarrassed to text for fear I was making a bigger deal of this get-together than I should, I ended up putting on jeans and a tee-shirt—after eighteen outfit changes of course.

Nervous about the outcome, I waited until the last possible minute to come downstairs—the plan being, the least amount of questions from Dad, the better.

"You're up early," he said in surprise over the top of his morning newspaper.

"I am," I said sheepishly, happy he was in another great mood. I helped myself to a cup of coffee, but put it in a travel mug.

"Do you have plans today?"

"That depends," I said while adding cream and sugar.

"On whether or not you're still grounded," he said, putting his paper down on the kitchen table.

I turned to face him and shook my head up and down, trying to keep a straight face. Dad hated it when I gave him doe-eyes or begged in any sort of way. If I could get a flicker of amusement, I knew he'd let me off the hook, but I couldn't smile. I needed to keep looking remorseful.

"Where are you going?" he said, keeping a gruff exterior.

"I don't know, it's a surprise, but I can let you know when I get there," I said quickly, not wanting to cause any alarm.

"And who are you going with?"

"Nicholas, the boy who helped me home the other day," I said with a smile I couldn't help.

"He finally called, huh?"

For some reason, even though they'd never met, I felt approval from my dad when Nicholas' name was mentioned. I think he trusted him since he'd already saved me once. But I didn't want a big interrogation because Nicholas had asked me not say anything.

"Please, Dad. Don't say you want to talk to him. That would be really embarrassing. We are just going as friends."

He took a long drink of his coffee and acted like he was mulling it over. I held still to keep from fidgeting.

"You can go."

"Thank you," I said in a gush, grabbed a banana, kissed his head and ran out the front door.

I heard a faint "You're welcome" resonate from inside. When I turned after shutting the door, I spotted Nicholas' beautiful black car parked out front and savored the moment. When he saw me, he got out of the car and walked up the path just like I'd imagined he would weeks ago—taking long, deep strides full of confidence, the bronze highlights of his hair glinting in the sunlight. I just needed to be patient.

"Hi," he said with an impish grin.

His green eyes danced, and everything inside me wanted to run and hug him, but I stayed calm and walked casually towards him instead. "Hey."

"You ready?"

I nodded and we walked to his car.

"Where are you taking me?" I asked, looking up at his adorable face.

"You'll see," he said with a smile and opened the door to let me in.

We drove down the highway in silence and took the freeway up the coast, flanked with beautiful oceans cliffs on one side and grassy farmland on the other. The day was clear and warm. I tried to keep from fidgeting as I waited in anticipation of our future destination.

Soon he parked in the same gravel parking lot that overlooked the virgin stretch of beach Sam and I always visited. My excitement dwindled.

Why was he taking me here?

I tried to hide my disappointment. Granted, his main concern was privacy, but that could be accomplished with his heavily tinted car windows. I had assumed that he had somewhere more secluded in mind. Somewhere new. Some place I could hold as special. Our place. I felt annoyed he wanted to use the same place I enjoyed with my best friend. I pursed my lips.

Nicholas ignored my expression, wordlessly getting out of the car. I crossed my arms, rooted in my spot. I wasn't going anywhere without an explanation. But his dark hair shimmered in the sunlight as he rounded the front of the car and suddenly my anger melted. I couldn't stand to be away from him another second and eagerly stepped out when he opened the car door for me.

Together, we walked over to the edge of the cliff.

"Wow," I said, peering over the side, feeling a little woozy. "I wonder if anyone ever gets to go down there."

"I wonder . . ." he said, as he pivoted his body towards me, circling me in his arms.

His touch made me hold my breath. I looked at him nervously, but gladly wrapped my arms around his waist in response. The last thing I expected to happen next was for him to jump over the cliff, carrying me with him in the process.

I squealed and grabbed his torso tighter. We soared through the air, out over the cliff and floated towards the sand 1000 feet below. Within seconds we touched down and he made sure I had my balance before letting go.

"Feel familiar?" he asked, emerald eyes twinkling, searching my expression.

"Oh. My. Gosh," I said, remembering the cliff. "Is this how you were able to catch me?"

I would have never believed it if I hadn't seen it in the daylight. Nicholas laughed and nodded his head. I laughed too, marveling how insane that night had been.

"So you can fly too?" I asked in amazement.

"Well . . . not really. Just jump far distances.

" . . .. not all vampires can fly?"

"No," he said and his smile faded from his face.

"I'm confused."

Nicholas looked back at me tenderly.

"Phil's acquired the gift to fly—a very rare ability—something a very powerful vampire wouldn't want to share freely. I suspect *they* never intended for you to come along and take him to the hospital, of all places. The transfusion sustained his life and the venom changed his body. He was never supposed to become a vampire."

His explanation didn't help explain things and I inadvertently reached up and held the base of my neck, wondering if I'd naively just missed a vampire feeding frenzy. What could've happened if I was a little bit sooner? I shuddered even considering it.

Nicholas continued to gaze deeply into my eyes and I lost my train of thought. I looked away and felt my cheeks grow hot.

"Come on," he said in a happier tone and motioned for me to follow.

We walked next to each other towards the water. Every once in a while, I'd watch him. His intrinsic beauty overwhelmed me. I couldn't help it. Today he wore a woolen sweater that showed the contour of his strong rippling arm muscles. I really wanted to reach out and lock my arm in his.

He caught me stealing a glance and gave me an inquisitive look. I looked away embarrassed, but could see his smile from the corner of my eye.

Once we reached the waterline, I discovered hundreds of perfect sea shells and sand dollars on the abandoned beach.

"Wow!" I said while picking up a cantaloupe sized conch shell, putting it up to my ear. "I guess the shells wash up and sit here since nobody can comb the beach."

Nicholas watched in amusement as I started to make little piles of treasures.

I giggled and wondered how I would take the shells home with me.

"I forgot to bring a bag," I said in disappointment.

"Hold on."

Nicholas sprinted across the sand, nimbly climbed up the cliff edge where the car was parked, disappeared for a minute, and then returned with a beach bag, all in a matter of seconds.

My mouth fell open.

"Would this work to hold your shells?" he asked smugly, playing off his immortal talents, holding out the bag.

"Um, sure," I said after closing my mouth, but still staring at him, taking a second before retrieving it. "How did you do that?"

"It comes with the territory," he said quietly. "It's no big deal."

"You can run, jump, climb and see at night. How is that no big deal?"

"Now flying would be something," he said playfully, but I knew he really would like that gift.

"I don't understand the power thing."

"Well . . . it's like with humans. Some people can do things others cannot. Vampires are gifted with special abilities too, passed from the one that creates them."

"Like what?" I asked.

"Well, the ones I know of are the ability to read minds, turn into animals, understand and speak different languages, plant thoughts, invoke feelings, hypnotize, just to name a few. Whatever is helpful for a vampire to lure its prey, besides being stealthy and incredibly beautiful."

Lure its prey?

His comment gave me chills as I remembered all the vampires I'd encountered already—in particular the ones that wanted to bite me.

"Do you have any special abilities?"

"Me?" He grinned widely, flashing his pearly teeth. "Just the ability to walk in the sunlight, something no other vampire can do but I think that's because I'm half-human. I'd be a force to be reckoned with, if I was bent towards evil," he said with a chuckle. "But I don't think I have anything extra special."

Yeah, right.

I hid my smile. It was nice to be with someone so humble.

We headed towards a huge sea cave, worn away by the waves over time.

"Want to check it out?"

I nodded.

We stood at the edge of the cliff in awe as the water ebbed in and out of the immense mouth of the cave down below us.

"Wanna closer look?" he said, with a gleam in his eye.

I started to recognize the twinkle and knew he was going to do some kind of phenomenal act that would blow my mind again.

"Okay?"

"I need you to trust me and climb on my back."

I blinked. "What?"

"Just do it."

"Okay," I said and crawled on.

He held my legs tightly and jumped. I instinctively wrapped my arms around his muscular neck and held on for dear life. For a second we hovered over the water just inside the mouth of the cave. The spray of the waves lightly rained over us and I squealed in delight.

Then like a bird, he gingerly landed on a protruding rock

inside the monstrous cavern. I looked up at the wet walls teaming with sea life, and reeled back, feeling like I was going to lose my balance, when I felt him reach around and carefully lift me off. He placed me so I could stand on the rock in front of him. His strong arms wrapped tightly around me so I wouldn't fall. We stood in astonishment, deafened by the noise of the waves hitting the reef all around us. The warmth of his chest radiated against me. I molded my body up against his, my heart erupting in a flutter that caused my legs to weaken.

"What do you think?" he whispered into my ear. I felt his hot breath against the side of my neck, which caused me to be light-headed as my heart raced even harder.

"Awesome," I whispered, which was all I could get out as I slinked into his chest a little bit more. A seal popped his head out of the water next to us and I nudged Nicholas to alert him.

Its little black eyes gawked at us curiously, then he swam around the rock as if to wonder how we entered his domain. I giggled uncontrollably at the sight.

After a few minutes my teeth started to chatter from the continuous cold, salty sprays. Even though I didn't want to leave, I didn't know how much longer I could stand the wind blowing against my damp skin.

"I think it's time to go. Put your arms around my neck," he instructed as he gently helped me turn around.

I reached up, but feeling shy, kept my head down for fear he'd meet my gaze with a kiss. Within a second, I felt him hug me tight, crouch his legs down and spring off the rock into the air. We were flying again, headed for the sandy beach.

When we landed, I laughed at our dripping attire. He removed his sweater to reveal a white tee-shirt that outlined every muscle of his powerful chest. Again, I saw the emerald medallion around his neck, under his shirt and stared at it. He followed my gaze and fanned the shirt off his skin to release the extra moisture. I looked away still shivering, not willing to take off my sweatshirt, knowing my wet tee-shirt underneath would be too revealing.

"Maybe that wasn't a good idea," he said while looking around. "Come on."

He led me over to a place out of view of the cliff and started a bonfire in the sand. Within minutes, a roaring fire burned and I finally felt warm again. When he broke the driftwood into smaller pieces against his leg, I noticed a tattoo of a cross on the outer side of his bicep. The intricate ornate design was different than anything I'd ever seen. I couldn't stop staring at it.

"Are you feeling warmer now?" he asked as he sat next to me.

His damp, dark hair and his olive skin shimmered in the light from the small droplets of water that clung to him. The sight made it hard for me to concentrate.

"Yes, actually," I said while holding my hands out, feeling the heat on my fingertips. "Thank you."

I wondered how long he'd planned on being here today. From the looks of it, it didn't seem like he was in a hurry to leave, and I didn't mind.

"Um . . . I have a question," I finally asked.

"Okay."

I took a deep breath and held it. I wanted to ask without offending him. Could I just say it? I watched his innocent expression as he patiently waited.

"H-h-how did you know to bring me here? I mean, this isn't . . . um . . . just *any* beach."

I watched his countenance change from curiosity to sheepishness.

"How do I make this sound right?" He hesitated. "I just know you . . . I've been watching you for so long, I know your habits, your likes, your dislikes, your friends, your favorite hang outs and I have exceptional hearing. So I've known ever since you found this place that you've always wanted to come here. I figured it would be fun to give you your wish."

I hadn't realized my life was such an open book. His confession should have bothered me, but I was actually flattered instead.

"Oh," I said while playing with the drawstring on my sweatshirt. "Thank you."

Out of the corner of my eye, I saw his eyes light up as he watched me. It truly was a magical place; far better than I'd imagined. I'd never been anywhere so pure; I felt honored to be one of its only inhabitants. As far as I was concerned, this was the closest to heaven on earth I could imagine. All we needed was lunch. I was starving.

"I was wondering . . ." not really wanting to leave, "do you have plans for lunch today?" I sheepishly asked.

"Why? Are you hungry?"

"No, not yet, I was just thinking . . ." I lied.

"Actually I packed a lunch," he said, matter-of-factly.

"Oh . . . you did?"

"Well, I didn't know how long we'd be out here and it's not like we can go out to eat."

"Why not?" I asked.

"Because you can never be too careful. The less people know about us the better," he said with a very serious tone. "That's why this beach is perfect. There's no way anyone could find us here."

I felt a wave of pain from him. What had happened to make him be so cautious? I could understand not wanting to be seen at night, but why did I matter in the daytime? Vampires were sleeping, or hiding, or whatever they did during the day. But I'd learned my lesson in the past about prying, so I didn't ask. I figured when he wanted to share, he would.

He stretched back on the sand and put his head in his hands while closing his eyes, his thoughts someplace else.

"Yeah, but wouldn't someone see your car parked on the cliff?"

I asked just remembering his car could tip off our location.

"I moved it."

"You what? You did?" I said a little mystified.

"Like I said, I'm careful."

I knew his actions were all tied to what happened with my mother. Feeling his guilt resurface confirmed my suspicion. I searched his face and wondered why he held onto the past so tightly when her death was an accident.

I recalled what he told me. He had no family besides his dad and he never spoke of anyone else. I wondered if he had friends or if he kept everyone at a distance like he did me. Was his secret preventing him from living a normal life?

More than anything I wanted to console him, touch him, run my fingers through his hair and gently caress his face. Make his pain go away. But I knew he didn't want that type of relationship, so I refrained.

"You know, if it wasn't for your super vampire powers, I'd have no idea that you were different. I mean, you've even got a cross tattoo. Isn't that like vampire voodoo or something?" I blurted out and then wished I hadn't said it after I finished.

"Oh, you noticed that," he said looking up at me from the sand.

"Yes," I admitted timidly, not meeting his gaze.

"I got that a long time ago, when I thought I could actually pick a side. I struggle to know where the human in me ends and the evil begins."

He laughed at his own sadistic statement, but I didn't get it. I never felt any evil coming from him.

"I don't think that. You've been nothing but heroic to me."

"I'm honored that you're so understanding, but I have a very dark side to me . . ." he turned and grimaced. " . . .and it doesn't like that I don't appease its wants."

Again, he astounded me. He constantly had to remind me he

had a demon inside, wanting to come out, and he suppressed it.

"My life is complicated," he murmured.

"How so?" I said softly.

"If it was easy, I could just explain it."

"Funny," I said sarcastically. "Try me."

"Actually, it's no big deal really. I guess when I first started my path of vengeance it was exciting and I felt like I'd found my calling. But night after night after night of hunting down the leeches . . ." He stopped and drifted off into thought.

"And?"

"It's just not what I thought it would be. I want something different now."

"And what do you want?" I asked as my heart sped up in anticipation of his response.

He thought hard for a minute, his face pensive and finally said, "I want to be normal."

I looked down and closed my eyes for a second. I couldn't agree with him more, but that's not what I wanted to hear. What I wanted him to say was that he wanted to be with me, but I knew he wouldn't. He'd never allow himself to. He was too noble.

"I'm sorry," I said with a lump in my throat.

"No need for you to be sorry. It's what I am and I've accepted it."

He looked speculatively into the fire and his face became luminous. More than ever I wanted to wrap my arms around his neck and make the loneliness go away.

"That doesn't mean that it's not hard," I said softly.

"You're right. It doesn't."

I watched his jaw flex, as I felt him keep his emotions down to a dull roar. We sat in silence for a minute, with just the fire crackling and the waves crashing for ambiance. I watched him with tender eyes, but he didn't give me eye contact.

"Do you have any other friends?" I asked quietly, still trying to be respectful.

"I can't."

I wanted to ask what had happened, to understand this pain he felt, but I refrained.

"They always end badly," he said, again feeling guilty. "Like I've said, I've tried to have that normal life before. It doesn't work for me. It's not my destiny." He turned to me, his expression pained. "Julia, no one can know about today. It must be kept a secret. I couldn't live with myself if anything happened to you."

"Okay," I said, beginning to feel afraid, hoping we weren't taking unnecessary chances since I'd already mentioned it to my dad.

It was then I realized a normal relationship would be impossible. We'd always have to hide from everyone for fear of retaliation and because of that, there was no chance for a real future for us, and he knew it.

Nicholas closed his eyes again and relaxed in the sand. I needed to change the subject, because if I didn't, I was going to start crying.

"So, what did you do last night?" I asked while gulping down the tears.

"I went looking for Phil and the rest of *them*," he said while letting out a gust of air.

"Having trouble?" I asked, secretly grateful Phil had eluded him.

I felt his disdain and knew he'd have zero tolerance or patience for Phil once he found him again.

"They are harder to track than the vampires I'm used to," he said in frustration "I combed the city all night and came up with nothing."

"You were up all night?" I asked in surprise.

"I normally am. It's fine. I don't require much sleep."

I studied his face and watched him breathe. He looked so perfect next to the fire, almost like he'd been airbrushed. I ached to reach over, touch his hand, but my mind warned me not too. This was someone I could never have, or ever be with, and it made my heart sad.

Nicholas' breathing deepened as he drifted off to sleep. I sat and drank in the peace he finally radiated while the fog rolled in. I didn't want to disturb him after knowing what little serenity he did have and after his busy night. I was content to just be close to him and enjoy the small, simple moment together.

After about an hour, he began to stir. I looked down to see him staring up at me.

"Hi," I said "Sleep well?"

"You let me fall asleep," he said, faking like he was angry.

He sat up and stretched.

"Let you? You told me you weren't tired."

"True. You hungry?"

To answer his question, my stomach growled loudly.

"I'm not taking very good care of you, I'll be right back."

In a flash he was gone.

I suspected he was going to the car again, so I tried to act cool when he returned. But before I could think of a flippant comeback, he'd spread out his picnic lunch in an amazing display. I couldn't help but gawk. Magically, a tray of sandwiches, with grape clusters, cheese, crackers and chips, appeared before me. He handed me a plastic cup filled with sparkling cider.

"Brat," I said, taking the cider. "How could I possibly compete with that?"

"That's the point. You can't."

I turned my head and flipped my hair at him, letting out a loud *humph,* and he laughed. Life with Nicholas was certainly proving itself interesting.

"I was wondering," I began as I popped a grape into my mouth. "Where do vampires come from anyway? I mean, they started somehow, right?"

"I knew this question was coming," he remarked, taking the last bite of his sandwich.

"You don't want to tell me?"

"No, it's not that. It's just . . . involved."

"I've got all day; I think. Well, until sunset, right?"

I laughed generously, but hoped he caught my slip. I wanted to spend at least until then together.

"Very funny," he said with a surly look.

"Please, I want to know."

He took a deep breath. "From what my father told me, it's believed it all started back with Cain. You know, Adam and Eve?"

"Yes." I couldn't believe a vampire was giving me a Sunday school lesson on the Bible, of all things.

"Well, because of Cain's jealousy of his brother Abel, he murdered him. So God put a curse on Cain, marking him to be a wanderer his entire earthly life.

"Legend tells us, the serpent who tempted Eve took advantage of Cain's situation. He offered Cain immortality in exchange for his soul. Cain, who underestimated the value of a soul, agreed readily thinking this deal would put him on the same level as God. When the serpent bit Cain, the venom transformed him into half-man half-snake and he became immortal.

"A vampire's immortality can be perceived to be a pretty gifted life. To come and go as you please, to be incredibly strong and have no limits, to be alluring and beautiful forever, but most importantly to not have a conscience against what you do for sport; killing humans without a thought. It's a downright evil lifestyle, just as the serpent wanted, with a few drawbacks of course; the Achilles' heel being the sun and wooden stakes to the heart.

"The first person he sired was an accident. When Andronicus Vampiro didn't die from Cain's bite, it gave Cain a new weapon in his fight against God. He could make an army of soul stealers all loyal to their Father, their King. But the serpent gave Cain only so much power and after each vampire was sired, Cain found he'd become weaker.

"But after some of the new offspring didn't survive, the power returned. It was easy for Cain to enforce a decree that the coveted vampire life be given only to those chosen because all of them are selfish, little, power-hungry, bloodsucking . . ." Nicholas' nostrils flared and anger tripled. "Sorry, I shouldn't talk like that."

"It's okay," I said with a blush.

"So the Royal families keep tight reigns on all their kin, only allowing the youngest to wander. They also don't kill their own kind because if you killed someone in your lifeline by mistake, it would be over for you as well. Like the thread of their life-force severs.

"So, you can imagine my reputation. Since vampires don't kill each other, they have no natural predators, except me. And I kill indiscriminately and don't leave any witnesses. They don't know who or what I am.

"You'd think, since they know where I'm physically located, they'd send their smartest and strongest after me. But they never do, proving that they're nothing but a bunch of power-hungry cowards who feed off the weak and strive to be important amongst themselves. Funny thing is they don't even need human blood to survive—it's more an addiction than anything.

"But this has created my lifelong dilemma. I know how to stop them permanently, but it would kill my father and possibly me in the process. Maybe one day I will, but all I want to do right now is protect you and not worry about the rest. And *that* has proven to be a challenge, for you're the biggest vampire magnet I've ever encountered in my life."

I forced out a fake chuckle at the remark, but became overwhelmed with the thought of something bad ever happening to Nicholas. I could never bear it. But then the psychic's prediction rang through my head.

The innocent that saves us all from them.

Remembering her words sent a chill down my spine and I felt the blood drain from my cheeks. Nicholas responded to my horror-struck expression and stared back with a face full of concern.

"You okay?" he asked.

My mouth went dry. What could possibly happen that would possess me to go after Cain? Maybe if I were a vampire I'd be able to fight them, but even then I wouldn't want to murder myself, Nicholas' father and Nicholas in the process unless . . .

I closed my eyes and felt the world sway as the worst thought crossed my mind.

I would do it to avenge Nicholas' death.

The terror overwhelmed me and I struggled to stay lucid.

No! Never! She had to be wrong!

"Julia? Answer me!"

I felt warm calming hands grasp my shoulders firmly. The sensation felt like he pulled me up and out of the horror I was drowning in. I forced my eyes open and met his, a piercing effervescent green.

"I'm fine," I choked out.

His eyebrows pressed together. He didn't buy my answer.

"I guess it's good I have a body guard since I'm a magnet, right?" I said hoarsely, lifting the corners of my mouth a twinge, trying to force a smile.

Nicholas' face didn't change, as his gaze flicked from one of my eyes to the other.

"I'm fine, honest," I said, feeling a little bit more in control of myself and my voice. "It just scares me someone has that type of power over your life."

Nicholas relaxed a tiny bit and studied me one last time before drawing me into his chest. My breath became short as his touch sent me into oblivion, and I welcomed the distraction.

"You don't have to worry. I've got it under control," he said softly, gently caressing the back of my hair.

I let out a gust of air in response. His confidence infused my body and I let go of the unknowns of the future. Her prediction couldn't be true. First, she was crazy and I doubted her abilities. Second, I lacked athletic ability and therefore incapable of fighting anything, especially evil. And if I did have some special power, Nicholas would be the first I'd save.

But I didn't care. I didn't want to entertain the thought of being some heroic avenger. I just wanted to be there.

In his arms.

Forever.

16 — FALL OUT

*T*ime flew by. Before I realized it, we'd spent the whole day together—a perfectly glorious day, far better than any dance I could've attended. But as I watched the sun make its way closer to the horizon, a pang of dread filled my stomach. Its light controlled my destiny now and he'd have to take me home. I already started to miss him.

"So what are your plans for tonight?" I asked, trying my best to sound indifferent.

"Finding *their* lair and keeping an eye on you."

He glanced over at me wistfully, his face slightly bronzed from the sun. I couldn't help but smile back.

"Well, if it will help, I promise not to do a repeat of last night," I joked in an effort to cover up my concern. "Actually, I've got a ton of homework to do."

"That would make my job easier."

I turned towards the window and watched the world zoom by. We'd broken the rules today by being together. As we drove, I felt the warmth he had at the beach start to fade into something cold and distant. He was changing back to his serious self.

"We can't do this again, can we?" I finally muttered, still looking out the window, deciding to just get it out in the open.

"No," he said despondently.

I took a deep breath and leaned against the headrest. I didn't need to study his face to know his feelings.

"It doesn't seem fair," I uttered softly in an even tone.

"Nothing we can do about it."

The frequent appearance of his cynical side began to annoy me. I knew there was a way to still see each other and not get caught, like today. Why wasn't he willing to try?

"I don't want to go home," I said in a whisper, secretly hoping he'd change his mind.

He reached over to grab my hand. Excitement and pain flooded directly into my heart and I broke under the strain. The tears spilled down my cheeks.

"Please, don't cry," he said, instantly feeling sorry.

"I'm trying not to. It just hurts, you know?"

I tried to stifle my tears by biting my lip. Secretly, I was glad we hurt together. To know he cared for me on a deeper level comforted my spirit.

"I never meant for this to be difficult for you," he said with remorse.

"It's not your fault. You have no control over this hopeless situation."

"Well, I shouldn't have made it harder on you."

He let go of my hand to take something out of his pocket. I stared down at his palm and recognized the familiar piece of worn journal paper. I looked at his face in shock and then anger.

"How did you get that?" I said, snatching it out of his hand, wiping away my tears.

"I saw you throw it over the cliff," he confessed.

My head swam as I remembered back to that day. I'd poured my heart and soul into that letter never intending for him to read it. And now that he had, I felt violated.

"Well, that's a dirty trick," I said, scowling at him.

I turned away and crumpled up the note in my hand.

"You didn't want me to read it?" he said confused.

"No."

"Then why is it addressed to me?"

Even though he had a point, I hated that he justified his actions. How could he think I wanted him to read it?

"I didn't give it to you. You only got it because you were spying on me." I clenched my jaw, completely mortified.

He sat for a minute, his face hard like ice, insides full of frustration.

"Fine," he growled. "I knew I shouldn't have done this. Today was a mistake."

"Yeah, you shouldn't have after knowing how I felt about you." Hot angry tears flowed over my cheeks. "Why would you want to tease me when you knew that this could never be?"

"Because I'm selfish," he said, raising his voice. "I was hoping it would make things easier."

"Well, I don't know how you figured that!"

"You have no idea what it's been like for me the last ten years, Julia—watching you from afar and never able to even talk to you. It's been a lot worse for me. For you, it's only been a little over a week!"

His angst hit me like a tidal wave causing my anger to subside. His admission left me confused and bewildered. I felt foolish for not seeing that his experience had been far worse than my own.

"Oh," I said, not knowing what else to say.

We sat in silence while Nicholas fumed. I realized I really hurt him badly. I reached over to grab his hand. At first, he didn't respond, but then he interlaced his fingers with mine and the tension between us melted.

"I'm sorry," I said, looking down feeling a little ashamed. "I wasn't being fair."

"It's fine. Like I said, I've accepted it."

He pulled up in front of my house and I felt a pit form in my stomach. As we sat for a minute, I tried to think of a way to prolong my exit when Nicholas spoke.

"Before you go, we need to talk about Phil real quick."

"Oh," I said, remembering Phil *was* the real reason for our tryst.

"Do you have any idea what he's going to do next?"

"He still wants to talk to me." I bit my lip, unsure if I should mention that small detail. "But I don't know what about."

Nicholas kept quiet for a minute, his lips pursed together. I pictured Phil's face the night before when he tried to coax me out of the car and my cheeks blushed in response. I knew partly what he was after, but I wasn't going to mention it.

Even though I longed to be with Nicholas, Phil's attention flattered me. But the tug between the two made me feel like a stretched rubber band. On one side was Nicholas, the most amazing but unavailable guy because he killed a few vampires. And on the other, Phil, the incredibly hot, new, bloodsucking vampire, who wanted me and wasn't afraid to show it. If something didn't stop the tug-of-war with me in the middle, I was going to snap in two.

"I've been thinking about this all day and I think I've got a solution to protect you." Nicholas said, interrupting my thoughts.

I focused on his vibrant eyes. "What?"

"I want you to stay in your house at night."

I furrowed my brow in disbelief. Was he crazy? I just finished a stint of house arrest with my ankle and wasn't about to do it again because some vampire wanted to talk to me. Especially when that vampire was Phil. No. Completely out of the question.

"I can't. What about my job?"

"It's just for now. Make up an excuse, quit, whatever you have to do. I'm serious about how dangerous these vamps are. Especially Phil. Your house is the only place I know he can't penetrate, where you'll be truly safe."

His brilliant solution infuriated me. Not only was he overreacting, but now he acted like a tyrannical parent.

"No," I said with folded arms. "I refuse to be cooped-up in my house."

Nicholas let out a huge frustrated sigh.

"Julia, you need to listen to reason. I'm not doing this to be mean. Phil *will* stalk you."

"You think it's reasonable to lock me up in my house? What are my dad and brother going to say? They'll know something's up."

"You'll have to figure it out. I'm just saying I can't always be there. You have to do this to protect yourself. Aren't you afraid?"

"Well, no actually. "

He eyed me suspiciously. "And why not?"

"Because I don't think Phil wants to kill me."

"And why do you think that?"

"Because he told me so."

He gave me a condescending look and smirked. I glowered back. He wasn't going to win this one.

"You're so naïve Julia. Vampires lie. It's what they do."

"He wasn't lying," I said because I knew it for a fact and didn't need to prove how.

He let out an exasperated groan.

"You're making it very hard for me to protect you," he said slowly through gritted teeth.

"You don't have to worry about it. He's not going to hurt me. Just find out about the others and leave Phil up to me."

"What?"

"He wants to reform, I know it. I just need to talk to him. Encourage him not to go to the dark side."

Nicholas pounded his fist into his steering wheel and cursed. "I can't believe I'm having this conversation."

The rage bowled over me like a suffocating gas. But I didn't care. I was determined to hold my ground. "I'll tell you when I'm leaving, so you'll know."

"Oh thank you," he said sarcastically.

"Just do what you need to do. I'll take care of myself," I said, wanting to antagonize him.

He glared at me and clenched his mouth shut as his emotion grew thick with irritation.

"I should just let you deal with one and we'll see who's able to handle themselves," he seethed.

"Yeah, you should," I said, knowing I was being completely

absurd. We both knew the one behind the alley would have finished me off if I were alone.

"Fine, since you're feeling so brave, do as you want."

"I'm glad you're finally seeing things my way," I said but wondered why the sudden change.

"Well, don't blame me if something happens."

"I won't," I said, with a quiver in my voice. I started to believe he really was going to quit being my guardian.

We both stared each other down.

"I'm going to go," I said coolly.

He turned his face towards the front windshield. "Bye."

My stomach pitched and rolled over. I fought getting sick. All this emotion was more than I could handle and I needed to get out of the car before I lost it on his floorboard. I jerked open the handle, climbed out and closed it before he could say anything else.

My feet practically ran down the cobblestone path, but I listened for his retort that never came. His tires crunched the gravel and spun out instead. That's when I remembered my shells were in the trunk, but he was halfway down the street, turning the corner. It was too late to stop him.

17 – PROTECTION

onfused and heartsick, I walked inside the house. There were two suitcases sitting in the front hall.

"Oh good, you're home," My dad said as he came out of his office with his briefcase. "Have a nice time?"

"It was okay," I said, trying to sound chipper.

I went straight over and wrapped my arms around his chest. His confusion surfaced as I lingered in our hug longer than normal, hoping for some fatherly protective consolation. But it paled in comparison to Nicholas' solace.

"Everything okay?" he asked after I finally let go, his eyes narrowing slightly.

"Everything's fine. I just miss you when you leave," I said fighting back my tears, feeling completely overwhelmed with emotion.

"I'll miss you too." He kissed my forehead but still looked concerned. "I will only be gone for a week this time. I've been to the store and stocked up the fridge so you and your brother will have plenty of food. And I left some cash on the counter in case you need anything."

"Okay," I said and sighed.

"I have to go, though. I don't want to miss my flight. Call me if you need me."

And before I knew it, he was gone.

I slumped down on the couch and pouted. The sun had just set, trapping me until morning. And even though I'd put up a good front to Nicholas, I was scared to leave the house now.

My phone remained quiet in my hand.

More than anything, I wanted him to call. I needed to know he'd always be there even when I acted like a stubborn mule. But I knew he wouldn't. And I couldn't swallow my pride and call him—even if I regretted my actions.

I went upstairs and took out my math book. Algebra would have to occupy my evening. But after solving one problem I found myself lost in thought, the harsh tones of our fight bouncing around in my head. I let out a sigh of exasperation. I needed chocolate.

The double fudge ice cream was still in the freezer, untouched and hard as a rock. I managed to scoop up enough to drown my sorrows, as I caught sight of the morning paper.

The headline read *"Teen death in alley. Authorities asking for help."* I flipped to the story with uneasiness. Apparently a student from Soquel High was found dead downtown. Authorities were asking for eye witnesses. A wave of nausea hit me as I read the gory details.

I wondered if I should report something, but knew that was impossible. Vampires were doing the killings. But I worried if Phil was involved. The whole situation confirmed the danger everyone was in and the validity of Nicholas' concerns. Apprehensively, I looked out the kitchen window, peering into the black night. No one was there, but it still seemed eerie. They were out there somewhere, ready to take anyone who crossed their path. Would I always be afraid of the dark now?

I heard the soft sounds of the TV in the next room and decided to keep Luke company—being with him felt safer than being alone in the kitchen.

"Hey," I said, as I slid into the La-Z-boy.

Luke sat mesmerized with his face glued to the TV. The program he watched showed continuous clips of wild animals in their habitat. I had to turn away when a lion brutally snapped the neck of the gazelle before ripping into its flesh.

"What are you watching?" I asked, while putting down my bowl. I had suddenly lost my appetite.

"When Animals Attack."

I peeked through my fingers to see if it was safe, but re-shielded my eyes when the tiger separated the baby elephant from the pack. I couldn't watch anymore.

"Crazy, isn't it?" he asked with a sick smile on his face.

I started to imagine the same scenario but with the boy from the newspaper article. I could see him minding his own business walking down the street, maybe coming from the local drugstore with cold medicine for his sick grandma, when he hears a noise. Maybe it's an animal whimpering or a baby's cry that lures him into the alley. When he finds nothing he turns back towards the street, but is greeted by three dark figures blocking his way. One cackles an ominous laugh and they jeer and tease him, getting excited as they watch their victim grow anxious with fear. Then one crouches down like a tiger and before the boy knows it, he's thrown against the wall and the vampire sinks his teeth into his neck. I gasped.

"What's wrong with you?" Luke asked with a puzzled look.

I snapped out of my trance and realized my gasp was misplaced. At the moment a commercial played with cuddly koalas promoting Fluffy Soft toilet paper.

"Oh, I remembered I'd forgotten something," I said with a straight face.

He gave me a funny look, shook his head then noticed my ice cream.

"Is there any left?" he asked, pointing at my bowl.

Luke popped up off the couch headed toward the kitchen before I finished nodding my head yes.

During the commercial, I was tempted to change the channel, feeling anxiety from the graphic images in my head. But I couldn't completely blame the show for my state. The events from my real life caused the distress. I wondered how it could be so enjoyable to become basically a cannibal. Then to my horror, I realized, if I were in the same room during a feeding frenzy, I would be able to know. The thought made me shiver.

I decided Nicholas was right. I could never defend myself in an attack. And I wasn't positive what Phil's intentions were, but I didn't want to take any chances. I'd eat crow and beg for Nicholas' forgiveness tomorrow, before my shift started, then quit my job. But just in case, I decided to be prepared.

While Luke was still in the kitchen, I snuck down the hallway towards the garage. The cold rush of damp, dusky air wafted across my face when I quietly opened the door, the darkness a little creepy for my liking. Was this considered part of the house? I figured it had to be.

I felt the wall for the light switch and flicked it just when Aladdin darted between my legs. I yelped as she disappeared into the house.

The light penetrated the room and I felt foolish for being afraid to be in my own garage. Everything looked just as it always had, floor to ceiling cabinets on one side and a work counter on the other. Luke's tools lay on the floor, along with other unknown devices. The space where Dad normally parked was empty; around it was all kinds of junk we'd collected over time, most of it in boxes.

I looked around for something I could use to make into a stake. In the corner was a broken old broom. I ran over and picked it up.

Perfect.

I removed the hacksaw from the wall and after much elbow grease, managed to cut the bristly end off.

"What are you doing?" Luke asked, holding a huge bowl of ice cream.

With a squeal, I dropped the stick. I felt he was close by, but didn't realize he was in the room.

"You scared me! Geez!" I barked, embarrassed I was so jumpy. I nonchalantly retrieved the stick from the floor. "I'm just sharpening this stick."

"What for?"

"Because," I said defensively, struggling for a reason. "It's—it's to garden with."

He paused mid-bite and blinked. I remained composed.

"You aren't going to be able to sharpen it with a hack saw. The sandpaper is in the drawer over there."

He pointed to the workbench.

"Thank you," I said, marched over, found the roughest sheet and went back to the workbench stool. Luke sighed, leaving me alone in the garage.

After a few minutes, I transformed the broom into a vicious weapon and practiced a few jabs in the air against an invisible assailant. An old song my dad listened to came to mind.

I am woman, hear me roar.

There was something very rewarding in being proactive in my protection efforts. I figured since I'd be home a lot, I'd just workout to a Taebo DVD with it. That way, if I ever got into trouble, I'd already have practiced and could just stake the monster in one smooth motion.

I managed to sneak by Luke, while he watched the end of his sickening TV show, and headed upstairs. Nicholas' need for a trench coat suddenly made sense. I didn't own one or anything remotely useful to conceal the stake, so for now, I'd have to store it in my backpack. I just hoped it wouldn't accidentally fall out during school or I'd have some serious explaining to do.

18 – FEAR

$\mathcal{I}$ arrived at school Monday morning feeling numb and annoyed. I hadn't slept soundly because of the recurring nightmares. And sometime during the night, I'd changed my mind about needing Nicholas' help. His behavior still angered me, and I wasn't ready to forgive him yet.

"You didn't call back," Sam said a little perturbed when she caught up with me as I walked alone to first period P.E. class.

Instantly I remembered listening to her voicemail message and felt bad. She called late Saturday night, but I hadn't listened to her request for me to call until early Sunday morning, just before Nicholas came to pick me up to go to the beach. I'd completely forgotten to call back.

"Sorry, how was the dance?" I asked, trying to sound interested.

"It was magical," she said, anger melting, her face suddenly all aglow.

I looked at her happy expression as she continued to fill me in, and softened. I was thrilled she had a good time and decided not to let my "Nicholas woes" interfere. Fight or no fight, my weekend was magical for me as well, but I wasn't allowed to say a word. Yet another unbearable secret to keep. I never felt more alone.

My classmates were also semi-excited and a little depressed, maybe because it was Monday, but I also sensed a general fearfulness. As I half listened to Sam, I scanned the faces around me to see if I could figure out why. Was this vampire thing affecting more people than just me?

"What's wrong with everyone?" I finally asked Sam.

"Huh? I don't know," she said, suddenly paying attention to the people around us. "Everyone seems fine to me."

We changed our clothes and headed towards the basketball court, where I overheard two classmates ahead of us.

"That's so sad about Justin," Mia said to Erika.

"Yeah, isn't it awful?"

I touched Mia's shoulder to stop them.

"What about Justin?" I asked.

"You haven't heard?" Mia gave me a look like I was a complete idiot. "He's missing too."

Her words sent ice down my spine. My last interaction with Justin played through my mind as I continued listlessly into the gym, grieved. He quite possibly could be another victim and I felt responsible.

Why is this happening?

The epidemic was spreading like a disease and I couldn't allow it to continue. Desperate times called for desperate measures. I needed to do something, but what?

The fortune teller's words came to mind, but I pushed away the thought. I didn't care what she'd predicted. I wouldn't go see her. I couldn't go. Darkening her doorstep meant I'd have to accept everything: my true fate, the obliteration of all vampires at my hand and Nicholas' death. The rest of the world wouldn't know the sacrifice. But I'd never do anything that would intentionally kill him. There had to be another way.

I put my face in my hands and searched for a solution.

"Julia, are you okay?" I heard Sam ask, pulling me back towards reality.

I lifted my head and stared into five pairs of inquisitive eyes. Somehow in my concern and denial of what I needed to do, I'd auto-piloted myself all the way to lunch.

"I'm okay," I murmured as I looked down at the table at my uneaten food that I didn't remember getting. "I'm a little tired today."

"Do you know Justin?" Cameron asked me, his eyes moving

slowly to focus on my face.

"Not really," I said, feeling the weight of the responsibility hitting me heavily. "Do you?"

"He's in my Calculus class. He came to the tournament Saturday night," he replied, sort of in a trance. "But never made it home."

My stomach churned at the news. Maybe if I was his date Saturday night, he'd still be here.

"What happened?" Dena asked.

Cameron shifted. All the geeky spunk of his normal demeanor was absent. He looked despondent under his red mop of curls. The heaviness of his heart almost made me well up with tears.

"The chess club met at Clark's house for our tournament. We played until about three in the morning. I decided to just spend the night, but Justin had to be home for Boy Scouts in the morning," he said with a sigh. "We got a frantic call from his mother in the morning because he didn't come home and wasn't answering his phone. So the cops came and interviewed us. He's vanished into thin air."

He looked down at the table and picked at his food. I felt sick thinking about what his parents must be going through, when another wave of conviction hit me.

"That's horrible, Cam," Sam said.

"Well, there's a new curfew now. If you're under eighteen, you're supposed to be home by nine p.m. and rumor has it they might even make it eight," he said without any emotion in his voice.

"Yeah, we know about the curfew," Katie said, her voice laced with annoyance. "They squelched the bonfire with it, but eight? Seriously, that's just lame."

"It's not lame," I piped up, overwrought with newfound terror. "And, actually, I wanted to ask all of you not to go out after dusk until this is over."

"What?" Katie exclaimed. "Are you kidding me?"

I shot her a look. More than anything in the world, I wanted to share what I knew, scare them into submission. This was very serious and I couldn't bear losing any of them to those vicious murderers. I would make them listen.

"Just trust me, okay? I wouldn't ask if I didn't think it was that serious, but my Dad has some friends who are cops, and whoever's doing this is looking for certain kids to prey upon. All I can say is, we fit the type."

Katie let out a groan, contorting her face while she rolled her eyes. "Yeah right," she snipped.

I restrained from reaching across the table, grabbing the collar of her shirt, and shaking some sense into her. But something in my disposition elevated the general fear level from nothing to DEFCON 1 in a matter of seconds. Everyone knew I meant business, and couldn't deny the facts.

"I'll do it," Dena said quickly, watching me with a newfound fearfulness.

I glanced at Sam.

"Me too," she said under the weight of my stare.

"My mom isn't letting me go anywhere, so I'm already grounded," Cam said, still playing with his food. He didn't need any intimidation to agree.

"You will too, won't you Morgan?" Dena asked.

"Yeah," he said, watching me suspiciously.

Everyone's honest commitment eased my conscience. Only Katie remained. One by one, the group's glances rested on her sour expression. She tried to keep a cold front, but eventually caved. Our effort managed to penetrate her childish reasoning.

"Fine," she said with reluctance, while crossing her arms.

I let out a quick exhale.

"You're such a big killjoy sometimes, Julia," she with a sneer and left the table.

Receiving the brunt of Katie's anger didn't bother me when I knew it might possibly save her life. Now, the first part of my plan was in motion—the most important, keeping my friends from harm. My next step was figuring out how to get into my house without needing Nicholas' help after dark.

I bit my pencil and conspired while in Algebra, when I got a brilliant idea. If there was a way to get Phil to follow me home, and I drove into my garage, I could talk to him from the safety of my house. It would take some preparation, but I knew it would work.

With that decision, I just wanted school to be out, so I could put everything into motion. The faster I got through my visit with the dreaded fortune teller, the better.

All the little houses that lined the road next to the theater looked identical, until I settled on the one that looked vaguely familiar. The only problem was the curtains were drawn hiding the fortune teller sign.

I got out of the car and studied the front. The memorable tiny walkway to the porch brought it all back. My senses told me no one was home, but I decided to knock anyway. While waiting, I noticed the pile of newspapers next to the rickety screen door. The mailbox overflowed with mail as well.

Has no one been home since I was here last?

Something rubbed up against my leg and I looked down. A black cat with icy blue eyes sat at my feet—the same one from before. I squatted down and scratched her head, wondering why she was so friendly to me now.

"Where's your mommy?" I whispered, hoping the old woman was just out of town and didn't leave her pet behind.

"She's not here."

The words I heard weren't spoken out loud, but said inside my head—a woman's voice, ethereal in tone with a slight echo. Afraid, I stood up and looked around. I knew for sure no one was there, but someone had spoken to me all the same. Was I losing my mind?

"Who's there?" I asked quietly, thinking that whoever it was hid their feelings from me as well. I didn't like being caught off-guard.

"You're special, aren't you, Julia?" the woman's voice said in my head, like it was a new revelation.

"Show yourself right now," I demanded a little louder, stumbling off the steps, walking backwards down the path so I could scan the bushes alongside me.

"I'm right here."

The voice came from the porch area. I glanced around to see who was there, but only the cat sat perched on the edge of the porch, looking directly at me. I could've sworn the cat smiled at me. I blinked.

I'm officially losing it. I'm talking in my mind to a cat!

I spun around and prepared to sprint to the safety of my car.

"Wait please."

The voice was spoken out loud, followed by her tender, caring feelings of peace and warmth. I turned around to find the source and gaped. On the porch stood a beautiful, angelic, raven haired woman with fair skin and radiant, crystal blue eyes.

"Where did you come from?" I asked in bewilderment.

"I think you know," she said sweetly, a simple smile playing on her lips.

"I am an Enigma," she spoke in my mind.

I was speechless for a second.

"You're the cat?" I choked out.

She didn't say yes or no. She just continued to smile at me and her eyes washed me with such happiness I've not felt in a long time.

"You're looking for Madame," she stated plainly. "She is not here."

"She's not?"

"No," she said, now sending out a little sadness. "She is gone. But it's better this way. It was her time."

I latched onto every word and willed her to speak more. The

melodic quality of her tone was so pleasing to listen to, the absence made everything sound bland. She had to be an angel.

"I'm not an angel," she said, with a slight chuckle.

"You . . . can read my mind?" I asked, instantly feeling vulnerable.

"I can."

I became guarded, unsure if I could trust her. But if she could read my mind, then she would know everything about me. Stepping backwards, I willed my mind to stop, but it rambled through all the things I didn't want her to know.

"Don't worry . . . *I'm your friend.*"

She spoke both externally and internally. But her changing back and forth made my brain feel woozy.

"Who are you? What are you?" I asked, overwhelmed by her presence, suddenly feeling very insignificant and ugly, right down to the repulsive sound of my own voice.

"*Sweet, dear child, I am nothing important, unlike yourself. Don't be so disheartened.*"

"I . . . I'm not doing this," I said in frustration and turned to leave. No one was going to pry around in my head uninvited.

"Don't leave. *I know why you're here. Sense the honesty of my intentions.*"

She finished her sentence in my mind and I stopped mid stride. I could sense her trustworthiness, like she suggested, but I struggled whether or not to stay. If I left prematurely, I could possibly never know the truth behind what Madame said.

I swirled around and frowned.

"*Then tell me what I want to know,*" I forcefully thought.

I heard a gentle purr, though she wasn't in cat form. Her face seemed to look like she was formulating the best explanation, but I knew she was poking around in my head.

"*Well, as you know, the Madame wasn't a psychic. But since I can read minds, I could see what the people wanted to hear and I'd tell her what to say. It made a nice lucrative business for her, and she took good care of me.*

"But sometimes, she'd come up with things on her own. Like her prediction for you for example, so I'm not positive what she meant. But I saw her premonition. It's all true."

Even with confirmation, I resisted the ambiguous vision as my destiny. *"I won't do it. I'm no one important. Why would she tell me that?"*

"Don't underestimate the vision. You're far more powerful than you think and there's nothing you can do to stop fate. But whatever happens, you and your friend will find a way to be together. I have seen it. There are other avenues yet unexplored."

"But how do you know?" I asked.

"I have my ways. But it's time for you to go. I have things to take care of and so do you."

Her eyes twinkled before she turned to leave.

"But wait. When we first met, you hissed at me, why?"

"You, of all people could've revealed the truth about Madame's abilities. I couldn't let you do that. But you didn't betray her and for that I'm truly grateful. I hope I've repaid the favor. Good bye and good luck."

I opened my mouth to ask another question, but she transformed back into a black cat and leapt into the bushes before I could stop her.

The silence left me feeling helpless, with more questions than answers, my deepest secrets ransacked.

While driving home I had to force myself to concentrate on the road. Even though she wasn't in my mind anymore, it didn't feel the same, like she left footprints behind. I just clung to her insight that Nicholas and I would be together: that there was another way. I smiled at the hope until I realized . . . .

Which friend did she mean? Nicholas or Phil?

She didn't specifically say. And she also mentioned that there were other avenues to be explored. What did that mean?

"Ahhh!" I said out loud in frustration. Why does everything have to be so complicated? My life was stuck in the spin cycle.

I looked at the time and pressed the gas pedal harder. If I didn't hurry, I was going to be late for work. I'd checked the lunar calendar online when I went home earlier and sunset was going to be at 6:35 p.m. tonight. My shift started at 6:30. I figured that I'd be safe inside the building once sunset truly happened, but I was cutting it incredibly close.

I drove up into the lot, found a spot close to the front and parked and then I felt him. The sun had barely set a minute and Phil was already here, stalking me. I jumped out of my car, my stomach in my throat, and sprinted for the front of the building. I imagined how silly I looked, but didn't care. Phil was someplace looking to corner me, and I wanted to be safely inside to avoid him.

"You could've just told me you were running late, Julia," Linda said, with a puzzled look, after I'd run through the store doors like the welcome mat was home plate.

"Oh . . . Yeah . . . Sorry," I said breathing heavily, not thinking of a good excuse.

I glanced behind me out the glass windows, glad to be in the store. Phil was nowhere to be seen.

"Actually, Linda, there's something I need to talk to you about."

Either my words or the tone of my voice caused her alarm, which made me start to feel bad. I was still very upset that the situation was so out of control it interfered with something simple like my job. But I had to tell her and this seemed like a good time.

"Okay," she said, as she ushered me into her office.

I sat down and took a deep breath. I'd rehearsed my speech a few times in my head, but now, facing her, I was drawing a blank.

"Everything okay?" she finally asked, after I didn't say anything, obviously looking a little distressed.

"Well, no," I began finally. "I'm just having some challenges in my life right now and my dad doesn't think I'm balancing work and school well. He's asked me to quit, just until I can get a handle on things."

"I see," she said, disappointed.

"I know that you've got me scheduled for the rest of the week and I'll be happy to work my shifts. I know you'll need to hire someone new and I can train them," I said quickly, hoping to lessen the sting.

"That's thoughtful of you, Julia," she said. "But if your father thinks it's best you quit, then I don't want to impose. Plus, with the criminal activity and curfews, I'm going to have to change everyone's schedule anyway. We can handle things in your absence. We managed when you were out after your fall."

"Yeah . . . I guess you did," I said, feeling rejected. "I'm so sorry. Really, I am."

"So am I, but you need to do well in school. You can always come back this summer when business picks up."

I sighed and stood up, prepared to make the best out of my last day. I'd almost completely forgotten about Phil's presence until later in my shift, a wave of his angst hit me. He was still outside, waiting for me. Impatiently. I reached for my cell phone ready to text Nicholas, when I realized it wasn't in my pocket.

It must be in my car.

I took the mistake as a sign. It slipped my mind that I didn't want them to meet until I had a chance to talk to Phil first. Nicholas wasn't going to be patient with Phil and I knew there would be a fight, especially if Phil acted remotely close to the way he did in the tunnel.

But I was already prepared. And I wanted to do this on my own to prove I was right about Phil. The thought made me feel exhilarated and petrified all at the same time.

My shift seemed to take forever as I worked diligently behind the counter. It didn't help make things go faster when Linda made a scene by telling a regular customer that today was my last day. The onslaught of questions from fellow workers afterwards made me kick myself for not waiting until the end of my shift to tell Linda I was quitting. All the questions meant more lies.

"Julia, I'm not going to have you close tonight because I need to take your keys," Linda said sadly when the time came closer for me to leave.

The relinquishing of my keys made leaving feel more permanent, and I got this foreboding feeling that I wasn't going to return.

At the door, I said goodbye and timed my exit so I could walk out with Megan, a bubbly, talkative, fellow co-worker. I appreciated the fact that Megan acted as if we were best friends because she didn't leave my side until I got to my car.

Once I got in, I locked my car door and prayed that tonight I didn't run out of gas while driving home.

19 – TRICKED

*P*hil followed me as planned, and I led him straight to my house. The chase electrified me. As I felt his curiosity grow stronger, I shook my head, amazed I actually enjoyed this game of *cat and mouse.*

So far things were right on course, the last part of my plan being the easiest. The only sketchy part was whether or not Luke would be home. But I just counted on the fact that Phil would not want to be seen, and hoped he'd hide if Luke happened to come outside.

The little tires on the Quantum screeched as I took the last curve on my street a little too quickly. The house, only a few yards away now, would be my safe haven once I entered the garage.

I pressed the magical button on the opener I'd taken earlier and waited for the door to ascend. To my horror nothing happened. Dumbfounded I pressed it again, this time aiming it directly at the garage. Again, nothing happened. I panicked. The opener worked when I tested it earlier. What was wrong?

I pulled into the driveway, continually pressing the button over and over. Then he was there; standing right between my car and the garage door, my headlights illuminating his vibrant skin.

"Hello," he said with a devilish smile. He looked radiantly pleased with himself, as he stood wearing a similar trench coat to Nicholas', apparently the vampire fashion of choice.

I frowned back.

"What's wrong? The door not opening?"

To my horror, he held up a 9-volt battery. I flipped over the remote and opened the cover. The battery was missing. My mouth dropped open.

"How did you know?" I said stunned, instantly afraid. "Can

you read minds?"

"I wish," he said with a cocky grin and looked around inquisitively. I cringed at his overwhelming joy. "Where's your friend?"

I frantically tried to figure out how he knew my plan. He must have seen the remote on my seat and taken the battery out while I was at work. The thought made me feel sick, regretting my decision to do it on my own as my plan fell apart right in front of my eyes.

"I don't know who you're talking about," I lied.

"Julia. Don't play with me," he said with an icy stare. "We can do things your way, or my way, but whatever you choose, you will exit your car, so why don't you just get out so I don't have to break anything."

He placed both hands on the hood of my car while leaning forward with demanding eyes. I could feel his fascination with his power and imagined him rolling the car door back like a sardine can. How would I explain that to my dad? Knowing I needed to survive the encounter first, I decided to test his intentions. If he wasn't going to kill me, I'd willingly get out. If not, it wouldn't matter anyway— the more unexplainable damage to my car, the better.

"You won't hurt me?" I questioned, watching his expression closely.

"I promise," he said with a chuckle and held up three fingers. "Scout's honor."

If I hadn't known for sure he told the truth, I'd have been frozen stiff with fear. Even with his promise, it didn't change how badly he still wanted me. Before opening the door, I reached down nonchalantly and grabbed the stake out of my backpack, hiding it behind my back. With my other hand, I pulled the handle and stepped outside, legs shaking.

"I'm out of the car," I said with a sputter, waiting for his next move.

"See? That wasn't so hard—" he said, his voice suddenly absent from his body, floating in the air. "—was it?" I felt him appear when he whispered in my ear, his breath tickling the back of my neck. My body broke out in a cold sweat.

Startled, I turned, flailing my hand half-heartily forward in an attempted stabbing motion, but found it empty. My stake vanished. I looked up to see Phil, a few feet away from me flipping the stick in the air, mocking me with his smile.

"What's this for?"

My throat went dry and my lips froze partly open.

"As if you could stop me," he said with a tisk.

My face fell, as I watched him snap it in two. I felt totally defeated and knew I couldn't possibly make a break for it now. The front door, just beyond him, seemed impossible to get to. Even with a diversion, I wouldn't be able to move fast enough.

"You're so adorable," he cooed.

He was doing that thing with his eyes; luring me in with his infectious stare, casting a magical spell on me. I looked away.

"I'm out of the car," I said with an indignant tone. "What do you want?"

If he planned to do anything to me, I wanted it over already.

"Oh, where do I begin . . ." he said, slowly advancing, watching me with his nebulous eyes.

I backed up, trying to expand the distance between us, only to be blocked in by my car. I had nowhere to run. He stopped, minding the space between us as if to placate me.

"Well, first, I wanted to say thank you."

"You want to thank me?"

"Yes," he said with a little snicker. "Because of you, I'm now immortal. Little did those silly humans know the transfusion would revive me so I could be transformed." He dramatically tilted his head up towards the night sky, closed his eyes and opened his arms while inhaling deeply. "I do love my new body."

The display made me sick, but his absorption in his exhibition gave me the urge to sneak away. I moved a fraction of an inch in preparation when his arm suddenly appeared at my side, stopping my retreat.

"Where are you going?" he whispered, his lips inches away from mine.

My voice caught in my throat and I stuttered. "You don't have to give in. You can be good."

"Good?" A dark shadow crossed his face. "Why? I'm having too much fun being bad," he said with a wicked cackle.

My countenance fell. I wasn't anticipating this reaction.

"Let me show you," he whispered, using his other arm to encircle me, pinning me to the car.

His body pressed against mine and my heart raced in response. I turned my head away from his face, anticipating a kiss, but realized I'd exposed my neck. My hands flew up to hide my flesh, but instead of biting me, he pulled me close to his chest and shot up into the sky like a bullet.

I screamed and forced my eyes shut. The chilly night air rushed sharply against my face as I clung to his torso, the thrill of his feelings intermixing with my own. My ears popped as we ascended higher, but I didn't dare look down. My body responded and hardened in fear, petrified he'd accidentally drop me at any second.

"Look, Julia," he sang in my ear.

Unable to open my eyes, I shook my head and pressed my face into his shoulder. He tilted me haphazardly over so I lay stomach down, my back against his chest with just his arm around my waist. The sudden movement unnerved my stomach, making me feel sick. I screamed and fought to turn back over, but his arm clutched me tighter.

"LOOK!" he demanded.

I opened one eye for a second to see the miniature world move beneath us. Then flinched and closed them again, turning my head into my shoulder.

"Please," I whimpered. "Take me back down." Hot tears poured out and flew off the sides of my temples.

"Isn't this awesome? We have the world at our fingertips, Julia. Anywhere we want to go!"

"I want to go home!" I cried out, as I started to shake uncontrollably, choking back bile in my throat while my stomach pitched.

"You aren't enjoying this?" he asked, in complete shock, then disappointment.

"No!" I yelled as hard as I could. "Take me down, now!"

He grew discouraged, then annoyed. I feared he'd become disenchanted and felt the need to be more delicate in my approach, or it would be all over. I formulated a new plan.

"Please, Phil. I'm very frightened," I said quieter. "Can you take me down? I think I'm going to get sick."

He let out an exasperated sigh.

"Fine," he snapped and aimed us towards the ground swooping down in front of an abandoned warehouse in the industrial part of the city. I stumbled forward as he let me go, kneeling down to stop my fall. I wanted to kiss the asphalt in thankfulness.

"You didn't like that?" he asked, in confusion.

"No," I said plainly, withholding the barrage of insults I wanted to say, knowing I was still at his mercy. I scanned the area for a familiar landmark. "Where are we?"

"I have some business to take care of," he said, still irritated. I got the feeling the *business* involved me.

"Why aren't you being entirely upfront with me? What are you planning to do with me?"

He looked at me with an expression from his former self, one of compassion and I felt a glimmer of hope. I knew he was in there somewhere and seeing it for a split second inspired me to keep trying to get through to him.

"I just wanted to show you what I can do. I'm not going to hurt you, honest," he said tenderly, without the seduction. I softened.

"I understand you've changed and have this new power. But you *are* frightening me. Please, I just want to go home," I said using the same scared tone he tried to use on me at the grocery store.

"But you hate to fly," he said with a cocky grin.

The reality sank in. That was the only mode of transportation, and unless we walked, the quickest way to take me home. At that moment, I wished for Nicholas. I wanted him to come save me from Phil and his bi-polar behavior. At least with Nicholas, I knew what to expect. I felt in my pocket again for my phone forgetting I'd lost it somewhere.

"Do you have a phone?"

He thought for a second, a flicker of recognition in his eye, and then smiled. Before I knew it, he'd grabbed my hand.

"Come on," he said as he pulled me into the warehouse, his grip tightening down like a vice.

The interior was pitch black inside, and the rusty hinges of the door seemed to creak extra loud when we entered, echoing around the interior. When the door clanged shut, taking away all the light, I clung closer to Phil's side. The possibility of a working phone in the place seemed unrealistic.

"Where are we going?" I asked, feeling uneasy, trying to stop him from pulling me so roughly.

He didn't answer as he continued to drag me behind him like a rag doll through the wide open space, acting as if it was lit up, dodging unseen objects. I squinted and tried to get my eyes to adjust to the darkness as I stumbled, unable to avoid the items littering the floor. But no matter how hard I tugged back, he wouldn't let go, and continued until we reached the other side. Suddenly, I saw a faint glow around a closed door. I felt the feelings on the other side and halted. There were more vampires beyond. Thirsty vampires.

"It's okay. Come on," he whispered, as he bolstered his own

courage.

"No," I whispered, forcefully. "I change my mind; I don't need to make a call."

"Call?" he asked, like my original request completely slipped his mind. His apathy told me he didn't care what I needed.

We barged in on three people hovering over a large map on the table in the middle of the room, vampires. They all stiffened and turned in our direction—the same dark eyes from the beach bore holes into me. I felt the beginnings of a feeding frenzy when they recognized I was human.

"What are you doing bringing *her* in here Phil," the woman seethed, acting like Phil broke some code.

"Didn't you hear me order for take out?" The taller man with platinum white hair cackled, jabbing the other as they both eyed me lustfully, licking their lips. "Good timing, Phil. I'm starved."

Phil shielded me with his body and glared back, full of determination.

"She's mine," he commanded. "I'm looking for Alora, where is she?"

"I don't think you're going to be able to fight off the three of us to protect your little girlfriend, Phil," she said, suddenly advancing closer.

I cowered behind Phil. He stood even taller as she got closer, tucking his arm around my waist to pull me into his back.

"Bettina, I'm serious. She's important. I need Alora," he said with a growl, thick with impatience.

She glowered at him with her pale blue eyes for a minute and then let out an exasperated sigh.

"Fine! Toth, go get her," she ordered, waving her hand in the air at him.

Toth, the one with platinum-white hair, glared at me with his beady black eyes before winking at Bettina and leaving the room. Bettina felt humored, and softened. I breathed a sigh of relief, knowing at least for now they weren't going to feast on me. But I still felt like a tasty steak in the middle of three ravenous tigers, knowing the tables could turn at any moment.

Bettina went back to studying her map, still eyeing me occasionally. She was tall, lean with long black shimmering hair that spilled down over her shoulder and onto the table. Her clothing matched her complexion perfectly and her crimson colored lips puckered while she made notes with her pen. I guessed she was in her early twenties, but couldn't help but feel jealous of her beauty.

The other male vampire was shorter than her, about the same age as me, with brown, bed-head hair and disheveled clothing. He was strikingly attractive like the others, but cagey, his blood lust the strongest as he paced around, barely able to control himself. I recognized his face and almost began to place where I knew him from when the door on the other side of the room opened.

I stood in awe and felt the world around me stop as if to admire the woman who stood before us. Everything quieted in her glorious presence, even the florescent lights. I would have said she was angelic, but even that didn't describe the effect she possessed over her environment. Her auburn hair seemed to dance as it swooped gently across her forehead and shoulders, just barely concealing her big, sapphire doe-eyes adorned with thick black lashes. Her skin glimmered softly like the snow in the sunlight. The thin fabric of her black dress clung to her shapely body, caressing every curve.

Everyone instinctively bowed in her presence, the strength of her intimidation overwhelming. All I could do was stand and gawk as Phil moved aside so she could see me better. I felt helplessly abandoned, nothing between us to prevent instant carnage, if she wanted. She nodded slightly before walking towards me. Phil didn't move from my side while the others left the room.

"Hello, Julia," she said sweetly with a hint of a southern accent, her eyes studying me intently. "I'm, Alora."

She held out her delicate slender hand.

Frozen, I didn't know if I could make my hand reach out to greet hers in return, but like a puppet on a string, my hand obeyed. When we touched, I felt the awesomeness of her power and almost gasped. Whatever she was capable of doing with her small frame, she knew it and oozed confidence. And she had amazing control over her blood lust. More so than all the vampires I'd ever met, with the exception of Nicholas, of course. But then again, he was only half vampire.

"This is the one I was telling you about, Alora," Phil finally said, head bowed, eyes low.

"Phil, you're right. She's so charming and full of potential," she said with a captivating smile, letting go of my hand. "Don't be afraid, we mean you no harm."

Even though her beauty conveyed innocence, she was the epitome of evil. I could feel her empty, shallow heart, and godlike quest for ultimate power. I was appalled Phil trusted her, but I understood why. On the outside, she looked very deceiving. Her name fit her to a tee.

But why did he bring me to her? Was I an offering? My heart leapt in fear as I tried to figure out both of their intentions.

She eyed me for another second and then glanced towards Phil, reaching out her hand to him. He took it and kissed it.

"Well done," she said, her startling blue eyes looking deeply into his eyes.

Phil's pleasure abounded with her words of praise.

I waited uneasily as neither spoke and Phil continued to hold her hand. They stood stiff like statues, eyes interlocked, unmoving for several minutes. I expected at any moment a discussion of their imminent plans for my future, but only eerie silence lingered. The unsettling part was I could sense growing satisfaction and excitement coming from them both. I just didn't understand how they could feel it in unison.

But when the feelings peaked into a euphoria, laced with evil intentions, my skin broke out in goose bumps. I had to get out of here now. My mind willed my feet to run and I subtly shifted my body weight in response, but Phil's other arm shot out and grabbed my hand.

The trance between them was severed when Phil dropped her hand.

"It was nice to meet you, Julia," she finally said, melodic and soft. "Do take care."

Still unable to speak, she moved closer, eyes probing mine. And then unexpectedly she pushed back a lock of my hair behind my ear, took her finger and ran it up the ridge of my jaw, stopping just under my chin. I tried my best to remain calm, my heart pounding so hard I thought I'd start convulsing.

"You'd make a nice little addition to my collection," she said in a whisper, her scent swirling across my face, smelling sweet like honey.

I gulped, wondering when she planned to sink her teeth into me.

Suddenly the pressure of her finger was gone. My legs swayed anticipating my life ending, but we were alone again. Confused, I shot Phil a look, wondering what happened.

"Let's go," he said, with an abrupt tug. I stumbled forward, my legs still locked in response to Alora's touch.

"Where?" I asked, my voice shaking but resurfacing. Somehow I'd survived.

"I'm taking you home."

"You are?" Home sounded like a beautiful, glorious place, but very far away—impossible—a trick. I didn't believe he intended to let me go free.

"Yes. You don't want the others to think I've changed my mind. Do you?"

I was out of the warehouse office door first, but ended up

flailing miserably behind him as he impatiently pulled me out of the building. Outside, I breathed the night air deeply into my lungs, thankful to be alive. All I needed was one minute to recover, but without asking, he drew me into his body and launched up into the sky.

The quick, forceful actions took my breath away. I gasped painfully, struggling to pull air into my lungs. Only after I relaxed did my breathing stabilize. I found it easier to trust Phil this time, having experienced the flight before but he seemed unaware of my distress.

My mind raced. If Phil took me home like he said he would, then I could immediately tell Nicholas the location of the hideout. Nicholas would have to quickly forgive me, considering the magnitude of the find. I felt pleased to be such an instrumental part of foiling the vampires' plans.

But I needed to keep my cool. I had the advantage at the moment, so if I just played my cards right, I knew Phil would think I was on his side.

"Who is that woman?" I asked loudly over the wind that blew against our faces.

"She's the leader of our coven."

"Why did you take me to meet her?"

"Actually, I wanted her to meet you," he said with admiration.

I paused, confounded by the rearranging of the statement. It was almost like I just met his mother.

"But why?"

"To see if she approves of you."

Approves of me?

"How come?"

"Because . . . I want you," he whispered in my ear. I almost fell limp against his arm when he spoke it, but he encircled me tighter, his feelings raw and rapturous. A part of me wanted him too, enjoyed his attention, and craved his company. It alarmed me that I wasn't afraid when he confessed his intentions. Probably only because I was relieved to know it wasn't my blood he wanted.

I started to feel like I wasn't in control of my feelings anymore. That I was losing myself into his wants and desires. His power called to me to try it; conveyed it was safe, fun. And the worst part, my rational thoughts remained apathetic.

I could see we were getting closer to my home, which was good. I needed to get away from him before all was lost. Plus, I started to shiver uncontrollably in my thin blouse, from the thrill and the bitter wind.

He gently set me down in a concealed thicket close to my house. I stood awkwardly for a minute, at a loss for words, trying to encourage myself to at least plan an exit strategy.

"What's happened to me is not a bad thing," he began. "Really, I'm not a monster."

"I know you aren't, I'm just—" I quivered.

He walked over to me and gently held up his index finger to my lips in a motion of silence. I froze as my heart threatened to pound right out of my chest, but he slowly slid his hand and found the small of my back and pulled me into him. I stood there shaking, enjoying his touch.

"You're so beautiful."

His smiling eyes pulled me in and I felt mine slowly close as he tipped up my chin and touched his lips to mine. The iciness of his skin and the sweetness of his breath disoriented me as I gave into his charisma. I parted my lips ever so slightly, as he sucked on my lower lip jerking my body tighter into him. I gasped and my breath became uneven as our lips hungrily caressed one another's. I never would've believed that my first kiss would be so passionate. I almost lost my footing when I felt him ever so gently bite at my bottom lip. His hunger spiked and I threw open my eyes, pushing him away quickly.

"Sorry," he said, chuckling a little.

"That's not funny."

"I just got carried away," he purred." You're just so . . . enticing."

I felt like my legs were going to collapse at any moment, so I locked them in place in a last-ditch effort to stay upright. I didn't know what to say, but I knew I didn't want him to bite me, at least not yet. The fact that I gave in to him so quickly made me question everything about myself. Then the guilt surfaced. How would I explain this to Nicholas? Was I considering giving him up to be with Phil? To be a vampire?

I staggered back to gain my composure. My head swam and I needed to figure out what I was doing, and do it in a place where I didn't have his presence seducing me.

"I need to go," I finally said, as I looked away from his charming, Delphian eyes, secretly not wanting to leave.

"Okay, love. Me too. I have something to take care of." He flashed a big smile and was gone.

"I'll see you later." I heard whispering to me in the wind.

20 – BAIT

*D*izzy, I walked home, proceeded upstairs to my room and closed the door. I flopped on my bed, stared at the ceiling and touched my lips. The weight of what I did began to bear down on my chest and I cringed at the thought of what Nicholas would do if he knew.

How did I let this happen?

I sucked in a deep breath and let the air out slowly. He'd never understand and would probably hate me forever. I'd kissed his mortal enemy. I rolled over, tucking myself into a ball. But the images of Phil's hungry lips locked with mine played behind my closed eyelids. My stomach lurched at the conflict of emotion, elation mixing with remorsefulness.

If only Nicholas and I hadn't fought, then this would never have happened.

"Ahhh!" I groaned as I stuffed a pillow over my head trying to escape reality.

I wanted to hide, forget it ever happened, but I couldn't. For some reason, I enjoyed it. There had to be a reasonable explanation. Phil must have tricked me somehow with a secret vampire spell. I had feelings for Nicholas, strong feelings. We were going to be together in the future; at least that's what I believe the cat predicted.

Maybe Nicholas would never find out. It was Phil's vampirishness that affected my senses. Period. It wasn't real, and once I separated myself from him and thought rationally, I knew it was wrong. Or did I?

But kissing him wasn't my only problem. There was a huge part of me that couldn't give up on Phil. I knew he needed my help, especially after Nicholas finally decimated the rest of his coven. But how was I going to do that when they hated each other? Phil would continue to pursue me, and Nicholas would never allow further interaction, especially if he knew Phil's intentions. I'd be forced to pick between the two of them.

Well, it didn't matter. Neither would make me choose. They'd have to grow up and accept my decision. I'd set stricter boundaries with Phil and not allow his powers to take over my senses. And Nicholas would have to allow me a friendship with another not-so-dangerous vampire, like himself.

But most important, I did need to tell Nicholas about the gang, and quickly, before anyone else turned up missing or dead. I reached in my pocket for my cell phone, then remembered it was still in my car.

Frustrated at my forgetfulness, I jumped off my bed and went back downstairs to fetch it. I opened the front door cautiously before sprinting across the lawn to the car. Only after I slid into the front seat did I feel strangely safe, though I knew I was alone. But the phone wasn't in the console like I thought.

Where is it?

After checking in the door pocket and under the seat, I went back inside to try to call it with the house phone. But the call rolled directly over to voicemail, which meant it was off.

Crap!

Even still, I needed to talk to Nicholas, so I dialed his number instead. The silence before the first ring increased my nervousness. I planned to tell him the pertinent information and deflect the questions until later, but the call went straight to his voicemail greeting too.

"Hey, it's Julia. Call me when you get this," I said quickly after the beep and hung up.

Why is his phone off? Is he still mad at me?

I decided to worry about it after I checked my calling record online. If anyone stole the phone, I'd need to stop the service. From my dad's computer in his office, I discovered all the calls were ones I actually remembered making.

But then my eye caught a recent outgoing text message made just thirty minutes prior. I clicked the details and read to my shock:

- I need your help. I'm in trouble. Please come get me at 223 Front Street.

Nicholas' number appeared as the recipient. A lump formed in my throat. I googled the address. It was only two blocks away from the coven's hideout. Nicholas was being lured into a trap—one I allowed to be set. My indignation towards Phil began to smolder.

When I see Phil, he's going to be so dead.

Moving as quickly as possible, I printed off the map, swiped my keys and headed out the door. I needed to stop them before someone got hurt. And if things couldn't get any worse, the clouds broke open, pouring down buckets of rain. I splashed across the wet ground towards my car when I noticed my broken stake floating in a puddle. Instinct told me to pick up one of the halves and put it in my back pocket just in case.

My heart pounded as I drove like a wild woman through the city, trying to see out my windshield. I hadn't cleared out my latest text messages from Nicholas and frantically tried to remember what they said.

They came during the interaction at the supermarket. Phil would know how we planned to handle his situation just by reading the texts with the date and times. It would confirm his suspicions that Nicholas and I were cohorts.

Why didn't you clear those out, Julia? I chided myself, clutching tightly to my steering wheel.

The rain continued to pummel the desolate streets as I sped to the address, the ink-smeared map in my hand shaking violently from my nerves. I kept a close eye on the road and used my emotional radar for cocky cops who'd love to pull me over. My dad didn't need a long-distance midnight call to bail me out of jail for being out after curfew.

My mind raced as I tried to anticipate what I would find when I got there. What if the other vampires were posted as look-outs or worse? I couldn't bear the thought of anything happening to him. I stomped on the gas, but my car wouldn't move any faster.

I had no idea what I could do to stop the fight, but I had to try. Maybe this was the time when I would use my hidden secret talent. But I wasn't prepared to do real battle. All I wanted was to stop them before something really horrible happened.

My tiny tires lost traction in the rain and screeched as I took the last corner, finally arriving at the address on Front Street. My body shook when I spotted Nicholas' car parked in front of the old building. Frantic, I parked next to him, flung open my door and sprinted across the wet gravel to a nearby door. I tried to pull it open but found it locked. The presence of anger inside told me the fight still ensued, so I decided to try another door. It was locked too. I swore.

If only I was a vampire, I could rip this door open!

Not knowing what to do, I ran around to the back of the dilapidated building and looked for another way to get inside. I spotted a door cracked open, light spilling onto the wet cement. I ran to it and stepped into the vacated lobby at the same time the walls shook, flickering the lights. I heard angry voices coming from somewhere within the heart of the building.

The air was thick with dust and I coughed as I looked around. On the anterior wall was a huge indentation that looked like the aftereffects of a wrecking ball, spilling crushed sheet rock on the floor in huge chunks. Another loud crash sent me scrambling to hide behind the front counter. I anticipated a filing cabinet or something large would come smashing into the room at any second. But all that came down was another spray of ceiling material which filled the air with grime, coating my throat with grit. I slowly stood back up and cautiously walked over the broken pieces on the floor and headed towards the door beyond the counter. My heart started to pound, not sure what I'd find on the other side as I felt wave after wave of incredible revulsion and rage.

At least they're still alive.

"You need to give up! She's mine! She doesn't want you!" I heard Phil say loudly with a hiss.

"There's no way in hell I'm going to let you have her!" Nicholas growled.

Another heavy crack told me something fell and crashed against the floor, breaking into tiny pieces. I cautiously pressed my ear to the door to figure out if I should open it. A string of obscenities followed a thunder clapping boom that shook the wall and dislodged a picture. I ducked as the frame shattered, shooting broken glass everywhere, then froze.

"Not if I kill you first!" Phil retorted apparently not noticing the noise from the neighboring room.

"Be my guest if you can!" Nicholas barked.

Someone groaned after another resounding smash. I imagined the two of them hurling large industrial objects from across the room at each other.

I put my trembling hand on the knob and pushed open the door to witness two interlocked bodies flying across the wide open space. My mouth dropped as they collided into the nearby wall creating another huge body-sized crater to match all the others scattered throughout the vast room. They didn't hear me enter and proceeded to swear while trying to punch at each other. It was hard enough to see them fight with the intent to kill, but to hear they were fighting over me caused something to boil up inside. I refused to be treated like some sort of prize to be won at a carnival. As far as I was concerned, the honor to be my boyfriend was still mine to give.

"Stop!" I ardently cried out.

They froze and turned to look at me in surprise, but Phil took the distraction to his advantage. My mind registering he'd disappeared only after I felt my arms become pinned behind me.

"NO!" I heard Nicholas scream from across the room, but Phil responded with a cackle, way too happy for my liking.

"Ha!" Phil said with smug overtones. "Now you'll do what I want, both of you!"

Phil's muscular body held me tightly as something cold pressed up against my throat. I held back my breath, taking only short gasps and tried to assess the situation. At the moment, I felt he had no intention to hurt me, but I couldn't trust his emotions. One wrong move and the blade would easily slice into my jugular.

"Take that ring and put it on your wrist, or she dies." Phil threatened in a low voice, motioning to what looked like an oversized iron bracelet on the ground, close to our feet.

Confused, I studied the rusty piece of jewelry and tried to understand how it would incapacitate anybody. As I shifted my body to get a better look at Phil's face to judge his next move, he gripped me tighter.

"Don't move," he hissed in my ear.

"We don't need to involve Julia. Let's settle this like men," Nicholas said as he stood motionless, fire burning behind his emerald eyes.

I knew the cuff was a trap and I was the bait. I had to call Phil's bluff.

"Don't listen to him. He won't hurt me, Nicholas," I said calmly, feeling a high as the adrenaline pulsated through my body.

"I'm serious. Put it on now!" Phil interrupted, his voice sounding more ominous, his irritation increasing due to Nicholas' incompliance.

"Nicholas, don't!" I insisted, feeling a little braver, squirming to loosen his grip on me.

"Be quiet," Phil said as he hugged me closer, pressing the blade a little deeper into my skin. I felt my blood pulsating against the serrated edge and struggled to breathe under the pressure, my neck dangerously close to being slit open.

"Please stop," I whispered.

But it was too late. Nicholas had retrieved the cuff, clasped it on and Phil was laughing hysterically, proud he'd won the standoff. Instantly I felt the pressure cease as he released me, and I stumbled forward to catch my fall.

From the ground, I watched in slow motion as Nicholas took advantage of my freedom and pounced in our direction, but Phil had already pulled a small black square from his pocket. A little red light flickered on the cuff and in midair Nicholas was yanked backwards and pulled towards a nearby pole. When the metal of the bracelet collided with the pole, it let out an earth shattering clang that shook the entire building, sending down more debris on our heads. Nicholas struggled, but couldn't get his arm free. He let out a supernatural growl.

"Well, that's much better—" Phil said with an evil smile as he stood just out of reach of Nicholas, who cursed obscenities under his breath. "—and from the looks of it, just like the guy promised. You'd never believe this metal is one of the strongest alloys on the market—just perfect for capturing our kind."

"When I get out of here, you leech, you'll be sorry you ever involved her," Nicholas hissed.

I saw a glimpse of the animal within Nicholas that wanted to rip Phil's head off, his teeth slightly bared, wild-eyed and fists clenched.

"Promises, promises," Phil said with a cluck of the tongue.

"Let him go," I said forcefully, but cringed at how meek my voice sounded in comparison to their powerful ones.

"Why?" Phil sang. "But wait. I thought you two didn't know each other. Parker, I didn't believe you to be such a cunning liar." He winked and shot me his alluring smile. "That will come in handy later."

I looked angrily back at him, annoyed by his gloating.

"What are you planning to do, Phil?" I asked, feeling outraged.

"Let me deal with him, Julia," Nicholas said as he yanked against the cuff again. It moved only a fraction of an inch away from the pole before snapping right back into place.

"Look, our brave hero still thinks he has control of the situation," Phil said full of bravado. "But you're wrong! News flash, Nick! This isn't about you anymore. It's about me. And now that I've got you where I want you, I'm going to get what's rightfully mine and you won't have anything to say about it!"

Nicholas' chest heaved up and down as he seethed quietly, his unblinking eyes never leaving Phil's side.

"What are you talking about?" I asked.

"Just like I told you earlier, Parker, we've got the world at our fingertips. And now, with Nick out of the way, we'll be unstoppable."

He triumphed like he'd just won the lottery.

"I don't understand," I said with a furrowed brow.

Phil shot me a haughty look before laughing uncontrollably, his eerie voice echoing throughout the building.

"I guess I have some explaining to do," he said in a sneer, acting very melodramatic. "So when was it? Oh yes—" He partially turned towards me as if to remember. "—right after the bonfire, I just got finished kissing up to the cops when I spotted this totally hot chick motioning to me just beyond the trees. So, like any idiot would do, I went over to see what she wanted. I think she thought I was a big player at school, so she asked me about you, Nick. And when I didn't know anything, she bit me before I knew it.

"I attempted to fight, but her venom paralyzed me. After a few seconds I didn't care anyway. I closed my eyes and felt my body drift into the night sky. That's when I heard your gentle voice telling me it's okay and to hang on.

"So, you could imagine my shock when I woke up and found myself inside a hospital room, IV's plugged into my arm, and annoying people asking me stupid questions. I had no idea what was happening to me. All I knew was my insides were crawling and I wanted to rip my skin off. Then you came into my room, Parker, so concerned and unsuspecting, my gut instinct told me to run. And I'm really glad I got out of there before anyone found out what was really happening.

"As I ran out of the hospital parking lot, I realized I could run a hundred times faster with very little effort. But my body was burning from the inside out and all I wanted to do was die. So I ran to the cliffs and threw myself over, but I didn't crash on the rocks below. Instead I found myself hovering above them.

"I then took off in the air as fast and as hard as I possibly could—trying to douse the excruciating flames by flying through the waves. It was hell, let me tell you. But that was just the beginning. After it was over, I was so thirsty I couldn't see straight and all I wanted was blood. It kind of freaked me out since I had no clue what was happening to me.

"So, somewhere in Fresno is a pile of truckers I found at a rest stop. Hey, I was looking for some fast food, right?" He let out an obnoxious snort, but never took an eye off Nicholas.

"Anyway, I ended up in L.A. completely out of control and frankly, I couldn't help it. My new body had taken over. She was gone even before I could stop myself."

"Your girlfriend?" I said quietly, nauseous by his excitement and complete disregard for the lives he selfishly took.

"Ex-girlfriend actually. I guess absence didn't make her heart grow fonder. I found her with my best friend. They both deserved what they got," he said with a smirk. "It was their fault I had to move to Scotts Valley anyway."

I turned away in disgust; Phil lied so smoothly in the cafeteria, I didn't even detect it when he said his dad was transferred. No wonder my dad overreacted. Phil must have been in trouble with the law.

"So I stayed in L.A. for a few days, making some wrongs right, and I had fun testing out my new super powers. But I was stopped by another group of *them,* knowing I was a new kid on the block. They tried to capture me, but I escaped and came back here. I decided it might be a good idea to figure out how the heck I ended up this way.

"That's when I found out my *making*—" he said while making air quotes. "—was a mistake and that my coven wasn't too happy to hear about what I'd done in L.A. Since leaving bodies around is a big no-no, they had to teach me the ropes. Mistakes or not, vamps don't kill vamps. Without you, Parker, I wouldn't be here today. Of course I'm not the only *oops.* Have you read the papers lately?" He rolled his eyes. "People disappearing, bodies all over the place, it's a total epidemic.

"Anyway, apparently there are rules and a whole hierarchy in the vampiring world. But my unauthorized killing spree wasn't the most important thing going on at the moment. There were bigger things at *stake*—" He snickered, "—get it? And that's when I found out about you, Nick. It's kind of impressive how big a legend you are and actually a pleasure to meet you. There's a huge price on your head for whoever finds and captures you. I'll be richly rewarded when I turn you in."

His lips curled up auspiciously, his insides bursting with excitement as he stared intently at Nicholas for a response. But Nicholas looked off to the side, watching from his peripheral vision, untouched by the statement.

Annoyed, Phil decided to engage me, the air between us instantly becoming thick with desire. I blushed and hoped that Nicholas didn't notice.

"But you, Julia, I never expected how I would feel about you—" he drew closer to me, teasing me with his infectious stare. His sudden advance made Nicholas agitated and I felt his sudden rage. Phil arrogantly continued.

"When I came to school, I noticed there were a lot of pretty girls, but you did something to me. You were different somehow and I knew after our talk on the beach, I would never be able to leave you alone."

"But after my change, my feelings became more intense and I couldn't stop thinking about you. Finding you became an obsession."

He paused for effect.

My breath grew quick as his words were laced heavily with want. Nicholas stood stiff as a statue next to the pole, but I could feel his hatred increase. Phil was lucky Nicholas couldn't retaliate.

"Finding you wasn't hard to do, it was getting you alone that was the challenge. And that's because Mister Nick here must have tipped you off on how to avoid interactions with curious vampires.

"But that wasn't all you were hiding. From your text messages, I was able to figure out more about your chaperon," Phil said as he turned and glared at Nicholas. "Your little plan in the tunnel might have worked, if I hadn't spot you first. But I still couldn't figure out who or what you were, since I couldn't smell you, hear you or even feel your presence. You can't be human—but after we interrogate you, we'll figure out your secrets."

Nicholas let out a snort. I sensed he wasn't at all worried about being interrogated.

"So, I just needed to stay glued to you, Parker, and Nicholas would show up eventually." He laughed generously again, enjoying his captive audience. After we didn't respond, he made a sour face.

"Justin happened to know where you worked, so as soon as the sun set, I showed up and Nick was nowhere to be seen."

The younger, cagey vampire in the room with Bettina came to mind. His face suddenly clicked. He was Justin transformed, another precious life taken by these snakes. But in spite of the horror now covering my face, Phil continued on.

"I'd planned how I would deal with Nick, unaware he took the evening off. So, with nothing to do but wait, I decided to rifle through your car. And that's when I found your cell phone and your garage door opener and we already know what happened with those.

Your plan almost worked. Too bad Nick wasn't around to stop me. But what I want to know is how you figured out to come here?"

He watched me inquisitively as I stood, shocked at the revelation of how he masterminded this whole plan to find me. Nothing would come out of my mouth in response.

"It's okay, Parker. I'm not mad at you or anything. Actually, you showing up makes this victory all the sweeter," he purred.

"What do you mean?" I said slowly, backing up for an easy escape.

"Well, I turn in the bad guy and we live happily ever after," he said plainly.

"Bad guy?"

"Yeah, Nick here is a wanted vampire murderer. Those idiots are going to be so happy when I turn him in. Can you believe they've been here a month looking for him? And I'm only a vampire for a week and I find him the first day. Morons."

He looked directly at Nicholas to rib him some more.

"And for you, I'm gonna finally get some respect around here, *and* get the girl," Phil said teasingly.

Nicholas lunged towards Phil again, shaking the pole.

My head spun in chaos, trying to process the new information, weighing the fact we had bigger problems now. I needed to escape before Phil could change me, but couldn't leave Nicholas to be turned in like a lamb to the slaughter. Plus, from the sound of it, an angry group of vampires might possibly be showing up any minute. We were trapped.

"I'm not going anywhere with you, Phil," I said, knowing my demand was fleeting.

"Really? How can you say that after the kiss you gave me earlier?"

My mouth fell open and I froze, afraid to look at Nicholas' expression. For a second, I thought he was going to rip the pole in half when his anger boiled over, which flooded my head, making it impossible to concentrate.

"You kissed *me*," I said coolly, hoping Nicholas was still listening.

"Oh, why are you playing so hard to get? I know you want me," he purred again with a chuckle, his eyes sparkling with increased voracity.

"No, I don't," I replied matter-of-factly.

No longer conflicted, I meant what I said. Any confusion I had about how I felt about Phil was cleared up by tonight's events.

Phil started to advance towards me. "You'll change your mind, after—"

"Leave her alone, you parasite!" Nicholas bellowed.

"As if you could do anything," Phil snapped back.

But my mind was spinning. He planned to change me. To make me like him. And it wouldn't be after he delivered Nicholas. It would be now.

"After?" I asked for clarification, my voice cracking.

"Yes, after I change you." His eyes were wild with want and before I knew it, his body was pressing me up against a stack of boxes. Pinning my arms to my sides, his breath brushing against my throat he said, "I've been curious what you taste like."

"No," I pleaded as I hyperventilated, my head starting to feel light, and limbs tingly.

"I'll be quick, I promise," he whispered, his emotions chock-full of excitement.

I needed to do something quick, and trying to reason with him wasn't working. Time was of the essence. I had to think fast. Something sharp pressed against my lower back and I remembered.

"Just imagine. We'll be together . . . perfect . . . unstoppable." His unbridled lust shone in his hungry eyes as he shot me a sly smile just before he leaned in closer, anticipation building.

"Don't I get some last words or something?" I gasped out quickly, hoping to get my hands free for a second.

"Last words?" He curled up the corner of his lip.

"Yeah, I'm going to be dying or whatever. I'd like to have some last words."

"Well, actually, you'll find you'll be living for once, but I don't see why you couldn't say goodbye to your humanity or maybe to him."

He glanced over at Nicholas before releasing me, chuckling as he bowed with a smirk.

My heart surged as I knew this was the moment I'd hoped for. I tried to act calm, my body trembling all over. With shaky fingers, I felt the smooth wood beneath my back. Then I took a deep breath and stepped towards Phil.

"What I would like to say is—" I peered seductively into his tenebrous eyes; flashing him with an evil grin, hoping that I'd be able to distract him long enough to do my dirty deed. "—you can go to hell." I whispered as I quickly plunged my arm forward, aiming directly at his heart.

He caught my arm mid stab, swirled me around and pinned it behind me as he held onto my body, mocking me with a belly laugh.

"This is why I love you," he chimed in my ear. "You're just so spunky, but it's not time for me to go to hell quite yet."

With a tiny forced twist of my hand, I released the stake.

Defeated, I slumped in his arms as I heard it bounce onto the cement floor. I couldn't believe my plan failed yet again.

Phil's appetite was building and I knew it wouldn't be long before he took me. I didn't feel like fighting anymore. Would it really be that bad to become like him? I wondered if my eyes would turn crystal blue too, like the other women's were. And if I'd become eternally beautiful and ageless. That part I wouldn't mind. And maybe, I'd lose my conscience when I became a ruthless killer. If I didn't feel the guilt, then it wouldn't matter what I had to do to survive.

And it felt good to be wanted. He had basically made finding and changing me his mission. That in itself was flattering. And I too, in some weird sick way, enjoyed it and could see myself falling for him as well. I was sure, after I transformed, the bond would grow stronger until we'd never want to be apart. I just hoped when my body died, my feelings for Nicholas would die too.

I was glad Phil blocked my view of Nicholas so I didn't have to see his face when it happened, because at the moment he spewed the most vilest of feelings I'd ever felt from anyone. I just hoped it would be quick and not very painful.

My eyes instinctively closed when Phil turned my head to the side and I could feel his breath on my neck, giving me chills, his excitement unrestrained. I waited and held my breath for what seemed like an eternity.

21- SURRENDER

*W*ith a wanting groan, Phil put his teeth on my skin. Suddenly when I expected pain I felt a gust of wind and my arms became unpinned. Then the pungent acrid odor of smoke filled my lungs. I choked.

I spun around just in time to hear a small clink on the pavement beneath my feet. Through the cloud of ash, I saw Nicholas with his arm awkwardly outstretched; a large grin on his face.

"That's what he gets for turning his back to me," he stated calmly.

My mind slowly processed what my eyes witnessed. Phil wasn't gone, he was dead. Nicholas must have thrown the stake when Phil turned, too preoccupied with biting me. I stared into the ashes feeling numb. I was ready to be transformed and when it didn't happen, I was strangely disappointed.

Something sizzled and I turned to see what it was. The cuff binding Nicholas disappeared in thin air.

"What?" I mumbled in confusion.

"Darn. I wanted that," Nicholas said, but then he was at my side, holding me up. "What were you thinking?" He gently pushed back a lock of my hair studying my face with his charming eyes.

"I . . . I . . . didn't know what to do," I said. My thoughts bouncing around like a broken strand of pearls. I couldn't stop shaking. "You're not mad at me?"

"Mad?"

"Because I kissed him—" I turned away.

Nicholas tensed up and his jealousy surfaced. I closed my eyes, dreading what he'd say next, expecting him to hate me.

"Yes, but you tried to kill him too." He gently lifted my chin up and greeted me with understanding eyes. "It's been a busy day."

I couldn't believe he wasn't angry, and to be so easily forgiven shocked me. And then the jealousy? Could it be that he actually cared deeper for me? His arms enveloped me and I stopped worrying, knowing my feelings were always for Nicholas and never Phil. Though I was tempted, Phil and I could never have what Nicholas and I shared.

"But we don't have much time. I need you to be strong for just a little bit longer," he said earnestly as he gently squared my shoulders to face him. I gulped as I looked into his tender eyes. "Can you do that?"

"What do we need to do?" I asked, my voice quivering.

"Whoever sired Phil knows he's dead and they are going to come after us. I actually want them to come but I don't have time to get you someplace safe, so I want you to wear this—" He unlatched the chain to his beautiful medallion and held it towards me. In the light, the stone shimmered and almost seemed to sing as I watched it change from its vibrant green to a bloody crimson.

"How?" I started to ask but stopped as he put the medallion into my palm. It was feather light and icy to the touch, but then it warmed up turning an electrifying blue.

"Good, it likes you," he said quickly before placing his cell phone in my hand.

I stood confused holding both the necklace and the cell phone wondering what his plan was going to be against the vampires and how these feeble objects could possibly protect me.

"Put on the necklace, Julia," he prompted, noticing my frozen stature.

"I don't understand," I finally said.

"I'll explain everything later. Just put the talisman on and don't take if off for anyone or any reason. And if something happens to me, call my dad. Just press two then send."

I obeyed and put on the necklace. It was hot against my skin. I lightly touched the edge of the stone that now adorned my neck. It sparkled brilliantly as I looked down at it, but now it seemed smaller, more feminine. It was the most exquisite piece of jewelry I'd ever seen.

Before I could say anything more, Nicholas ushered me to a dark corner in the room and hid me behind some boxes.

"Just stay here. Don't move and keep hidden," he said, his voice tense.

"Yes, but won't they know I'm here."

"No. Not anymore, but I'll explain that later."

"Okay," I gulped and then felt the hunger feelings swoop down upon the building like a sudden hail storm.

"They're here," he said, looking up at the roof. He straightened up, flipped a stake off the ground with the toe of his boot and caught it in his hand while he walked to the middle of the room.

My heart started thumping loudly in my ears while I crouched down in the corner, scanning the doorway for their appearance. The chilling quiet sent ice up my spine as we waited, watching. It wouldn't have been that bad if Nicholas was confident like he always had been, but for the first time I sensed fear, real formidable fear.

Instantly they appeared in the room, their black shark-like eyes darting about with Bettina's lone blue eyes shining like beacons in a sea of darkness. She was accompanied by Toth, Justin and four others I didn't know.

A woman with Bettina's likeness stepped away from the crowd, flanking Bettina's right side, same sable hair, high cheek bones, petite nose but with obsidian eyes—an identical twin. My breath caught in my throat. The fact that someone chose to make both girls vampires was disturbing. On her right stood a stocky brunette male with a square face and hard charcoal eyes, locked on Nicholas.

Toth's smirk hid his tension as he puffed his chest out, standing guard at Bettina's right. Behind him stood the dark haired boy from the beach and a waiflike platinum blonde with maroon highlights in the lower half of her hair; deep sultry eyes peered out from within her bangs. Justin hovered behind Toth. They stood tightly together, uneasy.

"Where is he?" Bettina barked out, glaring at Nicholas.

"Jealous you didn't get an invitation?" Nicholas said, sounding very cynical. "You should know, or do I need to spell it out."

"Very funny," she said sarcastically, darting her blue eyes to the others, as if to give secret instructions. One by one they began to fan out in v-formation. "I don't know what kind of secret powers you have, but today will be the last day you'll kill any more of our kind. You've met your match bounty hunter," she said with gritted teeth.

"I prefer Nicholas frankly . . . but you didn't say the magic word."

Before anyone anticipated, the dark haired boy from the beach burned up in a puff of smoke. Nicholas wasted no time, intending to stake the brunette behemoth, but since he moved aside, the unsuspecting dark-haired vampire behind him took the hit instead. Then the blonde cried out as she burned up too.

"Excellent. Two in one." Nicholas said in a jeer, the group stood still in horror.

Bettina's twin erupted in furry, screaming obscenities, calling for Nicholas' death; she crouched down like a tiger, ready to spring, but Bettina restrained her.

"Angelia, get control of yourself. We need him alive," Bettina snapped quietly. The hair on my neck stood up, feeling the woman's scorn.

"But Adrian was wearing his armor . . ." Angelia cried out in confusion, turning towards Nicholas, eyes full of hate. "You'll pay for that."

Nicholas clicked his tongue twice. "Well, they should've been paying attention, now shouldn't they?"

From deep within Angelia's chest came an unearthly growl. But a surge in Justin's courage sent him sprawling forward to strike first, trying to pin Nicholas' arms. Nicholas laughed and flung him to the other side of the room. Justin's body hit the wall head first, shaking the rafters. He amazingly pulled his head out of the wall, stood up unfazed, shook his head and charged at Nicholas again.

Nicholas, without a thought, launched Justin across the room again, but in my direction. I gasped and saw a flash of panic in Nicholas' eye when he noticed he'd disturbed my hiding place, but I just tucked myself in further and no one noticed.

I watched Justin through a crack between the boxes. He sat up, but stayed put, appearing to reassess his plan. I studied the nerdy boy I used to know and marveled at the transformation; no more acne, glasses or goofy grin. It saddened me to think how things could have happened differently if I *was* his date instead. Could it have prevented all of this? Now he was another casualty at our school. But his beady eyes turned and locked on mine. My heart dropped as his upper lip snarled back to reveal his long, pointed teeth. He wasn't angelic, he was a killer

"Is this all you got?" I heard Nicholas cry out from across the room, taunting them further. I wanted to scream and get his attention as Justin watched me quietly, his hunger growing with each second, but Nicholas was busy.

Then I heard a female let out a blood-curdling scream as I caught a glimpse of Toth being consumed in a silent fire, another stake bouncing on the ground. It came from Bettina. Her anger was much more intense than when the others were killed—the apparent death of her man. Both girls, now on a warpath from their losses, took out silver iridescent whips and cracked them at the same time.

I looked around for something to defend myself, as I knew Nicholas needed to spend all of his attention on them.

"Hmmmm . . . kinky," I heard Nicholas say.

They cackled and the whips cracked again followed by the thunderous sound of something heavy colliding, but I couldn't watch. Justin had moved and stood over me now, his teeth bared, appetite ravenous.

"Leave me alone," I whispered quietly.

"Or what? You're going to get your boyfriend to hurt me?" He mocked, looking pleased with my predicament, odds stacked in his favor.

"No," I said while crawling backwards like a crab until I hit the wall behind me, trapped in a corner.

"You know, I've always liked you—," he said with a smile, but his feelings behind his confession made me nauseous. "—and with Phil out of the picture, you could be mine." He reached out and brushed my cheek. I slapped his hand away, giving him a dirty look.

Two in one day? I didn't think I could handle it anymore. What was it about me that made every vampire I met desire me?

"Don't touch me," I said, trying to sound like a ferocious tiger, but my voice came out like a tiny kitten.

He laughed and advanced closer.

Why can't these vampires take no for an answer?

I blindly felt the ground around me, wishing my hands would come in contact with something I could stab him with, but I found nothing but a dirty floor.

"You have no scent to you. I wonder if you'll taste any good," he said in curiosity. But I couldn't worry about his comment as he hovered over me, ready to strike.

"Nicho—" I screamed, but Justin lunged towards me. I threw up my arms to protect myself, closing my eyes hoping it would be quick. But instead he brushed up against my neck and recoiled, howling in pain.

I opened my eyes and gasped. Justin writhed in front of me, screaming out obscenities.

"You witch," he shrieked, holding his arm.

I sat there, dumbfounded when he attacked again. I winced, but he withdrew with smoke coming off his hand. Perplexed, I tried to figure out what happened.

"How are you doing that?" he demanded, overwrought with frustration.

"What?"

"Burning me like that?"

"I'm not doing anything," I said honestly.

"You're doing something."

He sat across from me with fretful eyes. I returned his dirty look just the same, but his frustration suddenly turned to fear and he started to get up.

"Where are you going?"

"Nowhere," he said in a lie.

Courage surged through my veins as I sat up realizing he couldn't hurt me. He was actually terrified of *me*—a feeble human. And as if fate intervened, there was a stake magically placed right at my feet. I grabbed it with confidence, held it firmly in my hand and stood up. It felt very heavy in my palm, heavier than the one I had made.

Justin took one look at me and his eyes grew big as saucers.

"You should have been nicer to me," I said, now feeling invincible.

"What are you going to do?"

Terror spread across his face.

"I'm going to make some wrongs right," I said, but as I spoke, he disappeared in an instant.

Without thinking, I blindly flung the stake forward in his general direction. I held my breath and watched, knowing it was a million to one shot. And as if the stake was a heart-seeking missile, it hit him squarely in the chest. Justin turned with a look of surprise, then pain, and melted in a puff of smoke.

I watched the stake drop to the floor with that familiar clink and the reality of what I'd done hit hard. Justin was the second personal tragedy fulfilling the psychic's prediction that I would *rid the world of them*. Even though this was the only way to stop them, I hated the final outcome. Vampires or not, Phil's and Justin's mothers would hopelessly wait for their sons to come home. And just like my mother, it would never happen.

Suddenly, something rocked the ceiling. The crater-sized hole in the side of the building told me everything. I couldn't believe I didn't notice they'd crashed through, but I was a little bit busy with Justin threatening my life.

I picked up the stake out of Justin's ashes and ran over to the hole to peer out. They were close, but I couldn't see them. I carefully crawled over the broken cement pieces and stepped outside.

My success with Justin proved the talisman was more than just a beautiful piece of jewelry, but I didn't know the extent of its power. My hand grew sweaty under the stake as I gripped it tighter. Something told me Nicholas needed my help, and even if it meant my life, I had to try.

My feet miraculously didn't make a sound when I walked around the building and hid behind a garbage dumpster. I was positive they'd hear me when I accidentally pulled the air into my lungs a little too sharply after I saw Nicholas trapped by the whips just a few feet in front of me. But they didn't.

The twins stood on either side of Nicholas, pulling the glowing silvery strands of rope taunt, a pile of ash at their feet. The two were the only ones left. Nicholas struggled against the restraints while spewing threats.

"Call her," I heard Bettina say in elation to Angelia.

I was pretty sure when Bettina mentioned *her*, she meant Alora. I'd suspected Alora had sent her lackeys to fetch Nicolas after she discovered Phil was unsuccessful. But if Alora came, it would be all over for us. With Nicholas pinned with these unearthly weapons, adding her wickedness to the mix would be all they would need to kill him.

This was my only chance to stop them.

"No!" I screamed.

Startled, Angelia flipped closed her phone and turned towards me.

"Where did you come from?"

With full force, I chucked my stake right at Angelia's heart, hoping to hit her like I did Justin, freeing at least one of Nicholas' wrists. But she caught it in midair and laughed.

"Nice try," she said with a smirk and looked at me like I were a bothersome, buzzing gnat. "Get over here."

Before I knew it, she'd run over, grabbed my wrist and pulled me to her side, still holding Nicholas in place with her whip. The strand magically grew with her movements. In a late response, I tried to jerk away, but found I was trapped in her iron grasp.

"You again," Bettina said with hard, calculating eyes. "I should have killed you earlier."

I shook under her deadly stare, then caught Nicholas' confusion and horror. He didn't know we'd met already. But then he became calm, like he'd discovered a solution to our problem.

"I'll go with you willingly if you let Julia go free," Nicholas interrupted quickly.

Both the girls' focuses went off me to Nicholas' face. I squirmed. The plan could not include him turning himself in and his ultimate demise.

"No," I said firmly. "Nicholas, don't do this."

Everyone ignored me. Bettina's face remained icy, but her emotions told me she was mulling it over.

"What's my guarantee you'll cooperate," she said after a second.

"My word," he said very calmly. I sensed to my horror his intention to keep it.

"No!" I said a little louder.

"Your word?" Bettina said in a sneer. Her lip turned up at the corner and she shot Angelia a look. They both laughed profusely.

"A vampire's word is worthless you fool," she retorted. "I want to know your weakness and then we'll negotiate."

Fear overtook me because I knew without the talisman, everything was his weakness. He was still partly human, after all. My blood began to pound behind my ears in anticipation of what he'd say, even though he still exuded a calm confidence.

"Julia *is* my weakness," Nicholas replied plainly.

I gasped. Why did he tell them that? My mind reeled at the admission and then discovered it to be true. I was. He'd warned me the vampires would use me to get to him. I didn't listen. And my stubborn actions removed the anonymity he used to attack his enemies, and it forced him to give me the necklace. Now the only thing he could do was sacrifice himself through a trade. I would be responsible for his death, as predicted.

"Interesting," Bettina said through squinted eyes, "You'll come peaceably if we let her go?"

"Yes," he said.

Panic welled up and constricted my chest. I struggled to pull the air into my lungs, but pushed it back out with the force of a freight train.

"She lies. She won't let me go," I exclaimed louder than I'd ever yelled in my life.

Bettina's nostrils flared as she yanked down hard on my arm with tremendous force. I yelped out instinctively, expecting my shoulder to be pulled from its socket. Nothing happened.

"Shut up, you little urchin," she spewed.

Her steel grip tightened around my arm and I thought the bones would break under the pressure, but something stayed her hand. I glared back, watching the muscles in her face tense up, her wrist tightening as if she tried to clamp harder but the pressure didn't change. The medallion warmed against my skin and I realized it kept her from harming me. I smirked when her frustration began to swell. I wanted to taunt her, but found I'd lost the ability to speak.

Angelia gave up trying to crush my arm and spoke to Bettina

in a Gaelic tongue. The musical flow of their speech was unlike anything I'd ever heard before. Then I remembered Nicholas telling me vampires had special powers like speaking in foreign languages, but the speed and enchanting sounds they made were musical, completely mesmerizing.

I felt Nicholas stir. I turned to face him. With a grim expression he mouthed to me 'remember what I told you'.

I looked wide-eyed into his beautiful face, shook my head *yes*. He told me to call his dad. But I didn't want to come to the reality he might not survive this. I could never live with myself if he died protecting me and it was my fault.

I started to object, but the only thing that came out of my mouth was air—not even a whisper. I clutched my throat in concern, but his attention was no longer on me. He still remained perfectly calm.

"You have a deal," Bettina finally said. "I'm taking you in and Angelia will stay here with Julia. You cooperate fully, we'll let her go. If not, she dies."

"Fine, but I want to give Julia the keys to my car first so she can leave."

Nicholas turned and gave me a knowing look with imploring eyes. I didn't understand. I didn't need his keys because I drove.

"Take the keys out of my *back pocket*, Julia," he said while edging a little closer to me, as far as the whips would allow.

With my free hand, I reached up under his coat and searched for his keys, but didn't find them. All I felt was a wooden stake within the folds of his coat.

"He wants you to stake Angelia," I heard a familiar voice say in my mind.

I froze. When I discovered the stake, the thought crossed my mind. But I was too afraid Angelia would stop me, lose her patience for sure this time and we'd both die.

What? . . . I can't . . . How? . . . I already tried once. Are you sure?

The chaos in my brain moved a mile a minute, unable to focus on one complete thought to ask what I needed to know.

"Take a deep breath."

I inhaled as instructed.

"You can do this. Our lives depend on it."

Her words miraculously centered me as I focused on channeling her confidence. My heart started to pound, as I visualized my task, the stake firmly in my hand. Then I closed my eyes and in one fluid motion, I swung my arm forward aiming directly for Angelia's chest.

Her sudden surprise caused me to open my eyes and I watched her beautiful snowy face and inky-colored eyes change to an ashy black within seconds. Nicholas was ready once Angelia's whip vanished. He had a stake in his hand, yanking Bettina towards him with her whip. She let out a screech, and morphed into a white cat, darting into the bushes. Nicholas cried out in frustration when the stake bounced on the pavement behind her paws.

Suddenly the sound of a freight train rushed in my ears and the world went topsy-turvy. My body felt weak as my eyes were being pulled into long shadowy tunnels of cold darkness, and something hard whacked my face.

"Julia!"

In the distance, deadly cat screams echoed against the mountains. Then strong, warm hands scooped underneath my body, lifting me upright. My head flopped around on my neck like a puppet, finally finding support in the crook of his arm. The close contact made me feel safe and whole again as he rocked me gently. I felt my trembling subside.

"Is it over?" I whispered, realizing I had my voice back.

My eyes met his tender gaze as he smiled down on me, face full of concern.

"Yes, for now," he said. "Are you sure you're okay?"

I mentally assessed my condition. My cheek felt a little raw from catching my fall, but other than that nothing physically hurt—not even where Angelia tried to crush my arm. For a second I contemplated exaggerating my pains so he'd hold me longer.

"I think so," I said with a sigh, trying to get up.

"I just don't think you should stand yet," he said, "You've taken a nasty fall."

Relief abounded from his body as he drew me into a tighter embrace. I felt him lean over and kiss the top of my head. My joy swelled at the gesture.

I looked up into his wonderful face as he pushed a lock of my hair away from my eyes. He lowered his lips to my forehead—soft and warm. Then he kissed the tip of my nose and my heart quickened. His fingertips wove gently around my chin, tilted my face toward his and he kissed me, deeply.

A small moan escaped my lips as I surrendered to his warm mouth gently caressing mine, his sweet breath filling my nostrils. My hand found its way behind his neck, our lips moving in perfect harmony.

We parted and I felt light headed again. Afraid I'd faint, I slowly opened my eyes to meet his—crystalline, sparkling like a green sea, clear, happy.

"I've wanted to do that since our fight on Sunday."

"Really?" I asked, surprised, trying to catch my breath.

"Please, we can't fight like that again."

I nodded my head and snuggled into his arms afraid my voice might break the heavenly bliss we shared.

*I*t was at that moment, I knew Nicholas was the only one for me. The pull he had on me was stronger than any force I'd known—stronger than hunger, stronger than survival, maybe even stronger than love. And the more time we spent together, the more the intensity of that bond increased. I wondered if it was healthy to be that drawn to someone. I did know one thing for certain; I'd fight heaven and hell to be with him. No crazy prediction would control our happiness. I'd change fate.

I relaxed in his arms and felt his heart beat, steady in his chest, as his hand gently caressed my hair, his mood content and peaceful.

"How did you know?" he asked gently.

"What?"

"To come here?"

"Oh—I realized my cell phone was missing so I checked my calls online. That's when I saw the text message Phil sent you. I knew you'd come to the address thinking it was from me."

My cell phone.

I tried to get up, but he restrained me.

"Where do you think you're going?"

"To get my phone . . ."

His strong arms encircled me tighter making it hard to go on my quest to find it in Phil's ashes.

"It's probably gone."

"What?"

"I'm sure it burned up when I—you know."

I grimaced. Our kiss had temporarily caused me to forget all about the casualties. I snuggled back and stopped fighting his arms.

"I'll get you another one," he said.

The cell phone didn't seem as important any longer. The

burden of my classmates' lives hung heavily in the air.

"I'm sorry about everything," Nicholas said, as if he felt my grief.

"I figured you'd be really upset about how Phil behaved. What he did." I squirmed. "What I did."

"You don't seem to remember I know these filthy beasts inside and out. Of course he'd seduce you. I can see why," he said with warmth.

I looked sheepishly into his eyes. They glimmered back with kind understanding.

"So now what do we do? I don't think I can hold in the secret, with their families thinking they're still alive," I said grimly. "I know firsthand the torture they're experiencing. They need to know the truth."

"Well, I had intended to burn down the building. We can plant the teeth inside if you want."

"Teeth?" I said in shock.

My eyes drifted over to a nearby pile of ash. Hidden inside were white rocks glimmering even when the clouds covered the moonlight.

"I usually take the teeth, to cover up the evidence," he offered.

The weight lifted. This solution solved the nagging problem that pressed on my conscience. A single tear fell down my cheek as my thoughts drifted to my own mother. I finally understood the guilt Nicholas carried this whole time. He'd been there, he'd watched her die. He knew that I'd be motherless like he was; raised by a heartbroken father.

"Nicholas?" I asked, scared to even mention the subject for fear of how both of us would involuntarily act.

"Before you ask me any more questions, I want to get you someplace warm. You're shivering,"

He stood me up and removed his coat. I was so absorbed in both our feelings, I didn't realize my teeth were chattering. When he wrapped his coat around my shoulders, the warmth infused me, though I thought my legs would buckle under the weight.

"What are you carrying in here, rocks?" I said, smiling up at him.

"Just about," he said as he ushered me to his car.

We both sat silently in the car for a minute. I held my hands in front of the heater, unsure if it was a good time to talk about what happened with my mother.

"You were asking?" he said, after a few uncomfortable seconds.

I looked down at the floorboard and bit the side of my lip.

"My mom . . ." I started, but my eyes filled up with tears.

I glanced up into his lush verdigris eyes. The lump in my throat prevented me from speaking further. Nicholas reached over and grabbed my hand.

"Are you ready for me to tell you what happened?" he asked quietly, with compassion in his voice.

My lip quivered and I nodded my head. He looked at me with empathy.

"Julia . . ." he said slowly. "The day I met your mother will always be one of the best days of my life.

"It was another meaningless weekday. For some reason, I decided to stop by the park to get away and think. But while I sat there, I couldn't help but notice the kids and their mothers playing together. It made me imagine what my life would have been like if I'd been normal and my mother was alive. Your mom noticed and just started talking to me.

"For some strange reason, I felt safe opening up to her. So, I came back the next day hoping she'd be there. She was. She invited me to come any day I wanted and visit with her on her lunch break."

He looked out the windshield thoughtfully, reminiscing. I knew the park. I'd been there a lot with my mom before the accident. I saw them talking in my mind's eye.

"I was brave and followed her home after work one day. I

wanted to see what her life was like. I knew she was married and had two kids because she'd always gushed about you two. It was the weekend and your family had plans to go to the zoo. Watching how happy everyone was together stirred up something in me that I wanted so badly. It was the first time I saw you, with your bouncy curls.

"My dad always warned me to stay away from humans, or something would happen to expose my differences. I thought I could avoid it from happening until one day when a large branch almost fell on top of her and I used my vampire powers to catch it. I thought I played it off well, but I could see it in her eyes. She knew I was different and I had to sever our friendship.

"I didn't even tell her, I just stopped coming. But I couldn't stay away. When I finally did come back, she insisted that I come meet her family. I didn't want to. I was afraid I would become attached to you guys too." Nicholas smiled. "But your mother wasn't one to take no for an answer, so after much urging, I finally agreed. We should never have met at the park after dusk. I knew better, but she wanted to pick me up after she got you from preschool.

"I told my dad and he became furious. He couldn't believe that I'd let the relationship go as long as it had. He warned me not to go, and my indecision made me late."

He looked away and clenched his jaw. I remembered what he said about being responsible. My heart ached alongside his, silent tears pouring down my cheeks.

"The events that happened next have haunted me every day since. When I finally arrived, your mom had already been bitten and *he* was fixed on having you for his next meal. It was at that moment I discovered my passion to kill those who mercilessly fed on innocent human lives. I managed to do it quickly, and somewhat away from you, so I wouldn't traumatize you any further.

"But once I came to you and held your hand, you knew I wouldn't hurt you and you stopped crying. I looked into your trusting hazel eyes with your tiny black lashes and golden, bouncy hair and vowed you'd never have to worry again. I'd be there for you forever.

"My Dad helped me push the car into the river to make it look like an accident. And we buried her in a beautiful meadow in the mountains. You never left my side the entire time. A part of me wanted to keep you, but my dad convinced me that you needed to be with your family and you'd be too young to remember, so the secret was still safe.

"So, I took you home. Do you remember what I told you?"

I looked up noticing the viridian flecks glinting in his watery eyes. None of what happened was very clear. My mind circled mostly around her feelings, my mother's face but a blur.

"No," I said with a stutter, somewhat ashamed.

"I asked you not to tell anyone, before knocking on your door. You nodded your head and smiled. I stayed with you until the very last second. You were scooped up by your dad and I faded into the shadows. Every once in a while I'd show myself to you to reassure you that you were okay. But eventually, you stopped recognizing me and once you started talking again, it was as if it never happened."

"I stopped talking?" I asked, surprised.

"Yes, for a while. Your dad was very concerned, so he decided to move the family to Scotts Valley. You needed a mother figure in your life in a new environment to heal. Soon after the move, you started speaking again. Everyone was terribly relieved."

"I don't remember," I said quietly, looking down at my dirtied shoes. "My dad doesn't talk about what happened. I think he's afraid I'll remember and I don't think he wants to know."

"Yeah," he said with a deep breath.

I looked back up into his shimmering eyes. We shared such pain together and it was reassuring he'd understood. But he couldn't keep blaming himself. If he had known, then I'm sure he'd be protecting her today instead of me, or maybe the both of us.

"It wasn't your fault. You were just trying to do the right thing," I said softly. "I know you loved her. You can stop blaming yourself."

Nicholas sat up straight and his face remained blank as he stared out into the wooded trees. I interlaced my hand in his and tried to bring him back to me.

"It's all part of the curse," he said with a familiar disconnected flat tone.

I didn't have the energy to fight him. In time, I knew he'd forgive himself and we could heal together.

"It wasn't all a waste. It brought me you," I said in barely a whisper.

He looked back at me and I swallowed hard as my heart fluttered. I blinked back the fresh tears brimming in my eyes.

"I look into your eyes and see her. It scares me that I'm going to mess it all up again."

The words caught in my throat again. I didn't know what to say, other than I wanted things between us to work out. More than he'd ever know, but I was afraid I'd be the one to mess it up—with my prediction. But he leaned over and kissed me so passionately, I almost melted into the floor. His lips soft yet urgent; his hand finding its way to the nape of my neck, pulling me closer to him; his tongue searching and intertwining with mine. I was gasping for air when he finally released me, whirling with so many feelings I didn't know which one to land on.

Before I could recover, he pulled me into an embrace so hard, that I couldn't breathe and I gasped.

"Sorry," he said, releasing his arms a bit. "I wasn't sure how this would work out and it broke my heart to see you so upset in the car. I should have thought to give you the necklace earlier."

I felt the crystal around my neck grow warm and heard a faint high pitched ringing sound, almost like it agreed.

"This necklace is special, isn't it?" I asked, feeling the heat from it under my fingertips.

"Yes, very."

"Did it save me when I fought and ki—" I gulped and skipped over the word, unable to say it, let alone admit it. "Justin?"

His eyes tightened for a second but his pride swelled.

"Quite possibly."

I had mixed feelings about his approval of what happened. I knew it was a necessary evil, but I felt terribly guilty.

"How?" I asked.

"The necklace provides protection against vampires. When wearing it, you virtually become undetectable meaning they can't smell, hear or feel your presence. If they do manage to capture you, they can't do anything to harm you. They can't steal it from you either. Any vampire that tries to touch it, except the person who gave it, would be burned by it. Same if they tried to bite you."

I thought back to Justin's arm mysteriously burning after he tried to bite me.

"So it's impossible to come into ownership of it by force. It must be given of free-will and the necklace knows. It's said it will turn black and burn any unwanted recipients."

That must have been what he meant when he told me it liked me. I held the stone in my palm and admired the new, rich, deep, sapphire color.

"But it was green before?"

"It changes with each owner."

"Who gave it to you?"

Nicholas frowned. His internal angst punched my stomach— I'd asked another hurtful question.

"It was my mother's. A friend gave it to her so my parents could live together safely without fear. I became the new owner after—well, you know."

"Oh," I said sheepishly.

I decided not to ask any more questions. Somehow I always

managed to pry into painful places that were none of my business. It did shed light on how his parents were able to be married and the answer to how Nicholas and I could be together as well. But with Nicholas being both human and vampire, did it make him virtually invincible?

"I, on the other hand became impossible to kill and track. It's a good thing I was a fighter against evil, because with it, I became the most powerful human and vampire in the world."

I cocked my head to the side and looked into his tender face. How could he ever be evil? His character was the kindest I'd ever felt. Of course he'd be a fighter for good. Would that ever be a question? Then I remembered the prediction and went to unclasp the chain.

"What are you doing?" Nicholas said as he caught my hand.

"Giving it back. I'm safe, threat over. You need this more than I."

"No," he said firmly and he put my hands in my lap. "I gave it to you and I feel better with you wearing it."

"But you need it," I said in earnest.

"I'm still immortal and equally as strong. Of course they'll smell my human scent which I can use to my advantage, but I have other means to protect myself. I need you to wear it."

I grimaced and looked hard into his eyes. One way or another, I'd get him to see things my way.

"No," I said more forcefully.

"Julia, why are you so worried?"

I gulped back the tears, hating that I always got so emotional at the wrong times.

"You're going to think I'm nuts," I said as I looked away, trying to gain some sort of composure.

"You can tell me," he said softly.

I took a deep breath.

"On the night we ran into each other at the theater, I was given a prediction by a fortune teller that you were going to die and I should avoid any interaction with you," I said quickly, suddenly embarrassed.

"Hmmm . . . I see," he said, a smile forming on his lips. "I hope you didn't pay her."

"You think this is funny?"

"Oh, no. Very serious. Sorry."

"I believe her," I said while squinting my eyes. I reached up to unfasten the chain.

Nicholas was disappointed in my statement. I'm sure because my actions showed my lack of faith in his abilities.

"Well, you can't give it back," he said plainly.

"What? Why?"

"I willed you to have it," he said solemnly. "Only after your death would I be able to retrieve it. Fortunately, your death will be virtually impossible while you wear it."

I gasped at the confession, my hands falling limp into my lap. There had to be another way. But his determined face told me I'd not win this fight today, plus I didn't have the energy to try anyway.

"If it's impossible for me to be injured, then why does my cheek hurt?"

"Okay, let me clarify. You can't die from a vampire's hand, though you could still be under their influences. But it doesn't save you from yourself."

"That's good to know," I said.

I thought back to when I'd lost my voice. I knew Angelia had somehow silenced me but that's as far as her power went. No matter how hard she tried, she wasn't able to crush my arm.

Suddenly, I felt very tired. I slunk into his side and he wrapped his arm around my shoulders. With a yawn, I looked at the time. It was after one in the morning, much later than I thought. I sighed because I didn't want to go home, but I didn't know if anyone worried I was missing. Without a cell phone they wouldn't be able to reach me.

"I should be getting home. It's getting late," I said, as I started to reach for the door.

I felt his disappointment was just as strong as mine.

"I'm sorry to ask you this, but before you go, I need your help with one last thing."

"Really?" I was confused.

"Bettina said that she should've killed you earlier. What did she mean by that?"

"Oh," I said looking down.

Even though Phil was dead, I didn't want Nicholas to think I willingly went with him when he kidnapped me. I kind of hoped the whole sordid thing would have gone away when the others died. But Alora was still alive and she knew who I was.

"Well . . ." I took a deep breath. " . . . Phil kidnapped me and took me to meet the others. He wanted their blessing before changing me."

"Everyone's blessing or just one?" he asked.

"Don't tell him about Alora' I heard in my mind.

My eyes shot outside. Enigma was nearby again.

"It's not time for Nicholas to know about her yet. I promise it will be detrimental to tell him.'

My heart started to beat a little faster as I felt time passing while he waited and I struggled to give him an answer.

"Be-Bettina," I finally said.

"She was the head vampire?"

"Tell him there was another, but she's not here locally, but was planning to visit.'

"There was another . . . but she's not here. She was going to be coming," I said quickly, amazed at how easily the lie came with the cat's help.

"We need to go there. Where did he take you?" he said, while starting his engine.

"What about my car?" I asked, as he pulled out of his spot.

"We'll worry about that later."

I looked down the street when he got to the corner, to get my bearings.

"That way," I pointed.

The hideout was closer than I realized. I worried Alora was still there and in the confrontation I'd get caught in the lie. I didn't want anything else to ruin our budding relationship, especially after I had the chance to come clean and didn't. The closer we got, the more I resented the cat and saw our relationship unravel in front of my eyes. He'd never forgive me for keeping this from him.

"What are you planning on doing?" I asked, feeling my fear heighten.

"I'd like to take care of this before they can replace their numbers. If you invite me inside, then I can hopefully surprise them."

"Invite you?"

"It works both ways for vampires. If they live there, I can't come in uninvited either, neither can you."

"Oh."

My mind raced. I didn't know how to get out of this and the cat was back at the other building.

"I wouldn't allow you to do this without the talisman though," Nicholas said, full of new ambition. "Just come back to the car once you invite me inside. You'll be safe until I'm finished."

"How's that?" I asked, still not understanding the significance—like the car provided some unseen protection.

"Because I've never invited anyone in here but you."

"Oh."

I gave a weak smile and thought back to the tunnel and my driveway. If I only had stayed in my car that night, then Phil wouldn't have taken me to meet Alora. I was safe all along. The revelation hit hard. I closed my eyes as my insides crawled in alarm.

"Won't they feel you coming?"

"Maybe. It was a lot easier when I had the talisman. Don't worry. I'm good at ambushing. They won't understand my power and by then, it'll be too late," he chuckled, excited. I felt the beginnings of a panic attack.

What do I do? What do I do?

I sat on my hands to keep from biting my nails; the building was in sight now. He pulled up across the street and parked. This could be the moment the prediction came true, and he died.

"Ready?"

I nodded sheepishly.

He was out of the car before I finished nodding, opening my door.

I looked at the ominous building, remembering back to the events just a few hours ago. Nicholas grabbed my hand and walked me swiftly towards the door. Nicholas was far gentler than Phil, but déjà vu grabbed me, unsettling my stomach.

Once we got to the door and I stopped, my body started to tremble.

"I'll be okay. Just invite me in and then you can wait in the car," he said, noticing my petrified expression.

"Please don't do this," I said, knowing Alora was ruthlessly powerful.

"Don't worry about me. Just hurry. They're going to know I'm coming."

Against my better judgment, I quickly lugged the squeaky door open and whispered "Come in".

He was by me in a flash, dusty swirls the only evidence of his flight into the darkness. I stood wide-eyed trying to adjust to the dark, reaching out to see if I could find Alora's presence. Nothing registered beyond Nicholas. I wondered if I was close enough.

"She's not here."

I jumped and looked down, withholding a yelp. A familiar black cat wove around my ankles. I hated that she could sneak up on me like that, not being able to feel her in her cat form.

"Geesh. You again. What are you doing here?"

"Talk in your mind. I don't want Nicholas to hear you."

I glared at her, miffed at all the demands placed on me.

"Happy?" I thought in a distempered tone.

"Don't be upset. I'm only here to let you know Alora is gone."

I waited for her to pry around in my mind and come up with some wild retort. I didn't get why she needed internal conversation when she knew everything I thought anyway. It seemed juvenile to go through the pretenses.

"And?" I thought, feeling impatient.

"What do you mean 'and'?"

"Don't pretend you aren't rifling through my thoughts."

"I can't read you anymore. You've figured out how to block me."

My anger subsided. I wasn't sure if I entirely believed her, since she was in cat form and I couldn't read her back. I thought some vile insulting things about her as a test and waited. Nothing.

She didn't hear me unless I spoke directly to her.

"So where'd Alora go?" I said in my mind.

"Since her coven was annihilated today, she left to recruit more followers, since she doesn't sire people. Phil was a mistake."

I'd wanted to know who'd originally made him, since Phil didn't name names.

"And Bettina?"

She purred loudly in my head. *"Gone."*

I looked at her little, sweet, kitty face and swore I saw a smile.

"Will Alora come back?"

"Yes. I'm sure in the near future. She didn't get what she was looking for."

The necklace suddenly turned icy cold against my skin and I fought to reach up to touch it, not wanting to bring attention to my medallion. I sensed it knew who Alora was. How would she know about the talisman if it stayed in Nicholas' family? I convinced myself the cat meant Alora's purpose was to capture Nicholas.

"He's coming. I'll warn you when she returns, until then keep the secret little one."

And she was gone.

"No one's here," he said, his face crestfallen

"And you're frustrated?"

"Well, I do enjoy a good fight," he said with a wink.

I'd never seen this side of him. I liked it. But before I could do or say anything else, he'd swooped me up in his arms and kissed me again. My mind went dizzy as my body fell limp; yet another part of him that I was powerless against.

"What a day," I said, breathless as he gently pulled himself away, brushing my hair out of my eyes again.

"Yes and I should get you home, now that it's over."

The guilt of pushing the limits overpowered everything now. I was sure everyone was looking for me by now. And before I knew it, we were back in the car driving stealth in the direction of my home.

"But my car?" I said, realizing we weren't going back to retrieve it.

"If you give me your keys, I'll bring it to your home for you. I have business there later, anyway."

I remembered he was going to burn the building.

"Okay," I said with a yawn.

I guessed his plan was to park at my house, do his fancy vampire sprinting back to the building, burn it, then drive my Quantum home. The details weren't of consequence to me anymore, anyway. We were both alive and everything worked out, the only things that truly mattered. I leaned my head on his shoulder suddenly feeling very tired.

I felt the car stop; I groggily opened my eyes.

"We're here," he said sweetly, kissing my forehead.

I was home.

I felt the atmosphere inside my house and it was peaceful. No panic, no worries. I was glad, considering it was now 2:20 AM. I smiled, thinking of all the times I'd awakened at this time to the aftermath of frightening dreams. I never imagined one day I'd be living the nightmare for real, but have it end like a dream. Just like the cat had promised.

"I'm going to be toast tomorrow, look at how late it is," I said, yawning again.

"Late? Nah. It's prime vampire hunting time."

I caught the twinkle in his eyes, the misty flecks in his eyes glowing.

We walked hand and hand up to my door. Peace surrounded us like tiny petals fluttering in the wind. Nicholas would never run away again out of fear of what some retaliating vampire could do to me now. Every cell in my body wanted to sing for joy.

"I'll call you tomorrow," he said when we got to the door.

"On what? My cell phone burnt up tonight, remember?"

"Oh, well . . . Then I'll be seeing you tomorrow, I guess."

He gave me a surly look. I jabbed him in the ribs, knowing he was joking.

And the day after and the day after.

But before I could object, he kissed me again, deeply and I swooned.

"Good night, Julia. Pleasant dreams."

23 — ROLLER COASTER

We waited together, a little nervous as the repeated clicks filled the air, followed by the chilling screams. The smell of grease and oil mixed with the sweetness of baking waffle cones and cotton candy. In the distance, the ocean waves could be heard intermixing with the sounds of people milling about, enjoying the evening. Nicholas and I stood in line, waiting our fate, his arms wrapped around me and his head resting gently on the top of mine. Gawking onlookers exuded annoyance for our blatant displays of affection.

"I can't believe I'm at an amusement park," he whispered into my ear, while attempting to nibble on it just to annoy me. I shook him off, feeling the disdain change to disgust as we shuffled slowly closer to the front of the line. I tried to ignore inquisitive eyes focused on us.

"Well, I can't believe you've never been. It's all the rage for humans you know," I teased quietly, knowing my use of the word *human* would confuse eavesdroppers, but I didn't care. Being daring seemed to be the theme of the evening.

I felt a little awestruck as I recognized how closely my life mirrored the roller coaster ride we waited in line for. For a first timer, you hear the clicks and the screams unsure if they signify something good or bad. Once you take your seat, your heart races in anticipation as the bar is securely fastened across your lap, pinning you in place. The time to retreat suddenly becomes a point of no return when the conductor waves goodbye and the car moves forward plunging everyone into darkness.

"You scared?" I teased as the ride started, jealous that it wasn't my first experience riding a roller coaster.

"Only if you are," he chided back, putting his arm around me, transmitting excitement but playing it cool. I'm sure if I could see him, he'd be smiling, the malachite streaks of his eyes vibrant.

I used to live my life in the dark not so long ago, the track invisible with unseen horrors lurking around dark corners. I was naïve to what happened right under my nose, every little twist exciting. But then I surfaced into the light, exposed to a whole world of deadly creatures. The fear building as I crept closer and closer up to the top finally reaching acceptance. And then the clicking stopped and the car paused for an instant before spiraling downward, the real thrill just ahead. That's the precipice we stood on. I could see things were going to drop out from under us soon, I just didn't know when.

I knew choosing a life with Nicholas wasn't going to be ordinary. And actually, I'd never been more alive or happy in my entire life, dating the most eligible and only half-vampire in the world. But, a relationship with Nicholas meant an uneven path ahead filled with twists and turns. Possibly life threatening. Was I ready for it? Would I scream through it? Or white knuckle it quietly? Or would I smile, raise my hands up, enjoying the wind in my hair?

I guess the choice was up to me.

Inside, I really wanted to throw caution to the wind, tempt fate and just see what would happen, secretly feeling invincible because I wore the talisman now. But I had this awful feeling that what we'd encountered a few months back wasn't anything compared to what the future would bring. Things would get worse when Alora returned, determined to capture Nicholas, to take him as her prize. I worried about his vulnerability and the prediction, but trusted that the cat would warn us upon Alora's return. I still battled telling him, thinking maybe we should do something to prepare. He'd already insisted though, after my continuous nagging, that he was prepared and to stop worrying.

Why wasn't that easing my fears?

With the necklace, I felt totally safe. It had become a permanent part of me. I was worried people would take notice, questioning why I wore such an expensive piece daily, but no one ever did. Nicholas said it had a way of making itself look unattractive to others, its beauty only shown to the beholder. I found that strange, since every time I saw Nicholas wear it before, it sparkled brilliantly as if to call attention to itself. Maybe I was always supposed to be its owner.

Nothing really happened after we got rid of the gang and ran Alora out of the city. Because of that, Nicholas actually let his guard down, relaxing a bit, even allowing this evening date to take place. For a fleeting moment it felt as if vampires didn't even exist and we had a normal relationship for once. But I didn't want to hold my breath because, like the ride, the ground was going to plummet beneath us at any minute. But I was going to be where Nicholas went and help with my unknown ability.

Other things had changed too.

I could finally tell Sam that Nicholas had returned and I wasn't cursed after all. But Nicholas warned me to be careful how much I shared. The necklace kept me safe, but others could be placed in harm's way knowing too much. I decided to keep things between us a secret.

Dad broke down out of frustration from being my chauffer when he was home and purchased me an Acura—complete with OnStar for emergencies. I wasn't sure how to handle such a luxury until I found out I had to pay half. Thankfully, Linda took me back at the deli with open arms. Business had picked up after the hysteria subsided and she was in dire need of a trained cashier.

My home-life improved too. Both Dad and Luke appreciated the change in my demeanor, no longer brooding about.

Most importantly, after the authorities investigated the fire, Phil and Justin were laid to rest. But I had a very hard time being around their mothers still feeling somewhat responsible for what happened. Nicholas was there in the distance the whole time. His support, even from far away, helped me keep it together in a way that no one else's could. I had many haunting dreams afterward, my mind trying to sift through the past. I just hoped there wouldn't be anymore vampire changing sprees in my town because I didn't think I could handle going through the grief and drama again.

I also worried about the cat delivering bad news. All her secrets wore on me, and I wanted to come clean before Alora came back. Daily, I contemplated telling Nicholas the truth, but worried the cat might not warn us if I betrayed her.

So, to sum it all up, we were basically just waiting, unable to plan when the car would come plunging down either freaking us out or giving us the time of our lives—our reaction unknown. Whichever way it went, I knew I didn't want to do it without Nicholas. I couldn't.

"So what do you think?" I asked, my hair blown askew, a huge smile plastered across my face as the ride ended.

He looked a little stunned, but exclaimed, "Excellent!"

I wanted it to be just that.

We left the ride and made our way down to the beach. All I wanted to do was find a vacant spot and snuggle by a bonfire, but fires weren't allowed on this beach. Nicholas led me down to the end where the cliff met the shoreline instead. Typically, beach-combers had to turn around at that point, but Nicholas had a different idea. I giggled when he swooped me up into his arms and carried me from rock to rock around this little blockade (in his eyes) towards our beach that was only a few miles down the coast. Of course, since it was dark, no one would see his extraordinary feat of strength.

"What are you worried about?" Nicholas asked, after making me a fire in our usual spot, getting comfortable by me in the sand, gently caressing my hand.

I took a deep breath. It was useless to try to hide my feelings from him. The collapse of our perfect world terrified me and I didn't want to tell him. But I found it insightful that he had started to pick up on my emotions as if he'd acquired a tiny bit of my gift.

"I just feel like something is going to happen to ruin this," I whispered, looking away and focusing on the surf in the distance while leaning over into his shoulder.

He pulled me closer, wrapping his arms tightly around me, beckoning me to lean against his muscular chest.

"I won't leave you like I did in the past. I wish you'd trust me."

"Oh, Nicholas." I turned to face him. He'd misunderstood. "No, it isn't that. I know you aren't going to leave me. It's just, I'm enjoying seeing you relaxed and acting human for once. I just don't want it to end. Has this ever happened before? Where the vampires left and you had a period of reprieve?"

"Never this long," he said, a twinge of worry now appearing. "I've never thought to look at the pattern in the past, but now that none have returned, I'm beginning to think what happened before wasn't a coincidence."

Nicholas had explained in the past that he believed that I'd been some sort of magnet to them, and when they came to town, he'd been able to exterminate them before any havoc broke out because they were always attracted to me. It made finding them super easy. But with Alora's clan, there had been so many that he hadn't been able to stop them as fast. It was as if they'd been alerted to his special abilities which led him to think they came for another reason.

"When fighting some of them, they'd tell me that they'd heard of me, but it didn't click until Phil had told us of my legend," he said with a grimace. I could tell he didn't want that type of fame in the vampire world. "Really, I just hunted them to protect you, since you attract them. It never occurred to me they came for any other reason than that. But I never let anyone survive to speak of my abilities. I'm still wondering how they figured it out."

I knew Alora knew. And because of that, they all knew. How she knew exactly, I wasn't sure and for one brief second I felt the urge to tell him, but clamped my mouth shut. Again, reminded of what the cat had said. I wanted to protect him more than anything.

Maybe I worried for nothing.

"Well, Phil had said he knew you were different and not part of their coven. Maybe they guessed? I mean, didn't you say, after killing Phil that they'd know and come looking?"

"True," he said and was quiet for a moment. "They'd feel the power shift back up the lineage."

That fact confirmed why Alora didn't like to make other vampires. I felt her greed and knew she preferred to hoard her power. She must have really thought Phil special to keep him around after discovering her mistake.

"How do you track vampires anyway?" I asked, probing to see if he was indeed still on the look-out.

"I have what would best be described as vampire radar. We can sense when another is close. We also have a particular scent. I do run the perimeter of the city every night and check to see if anyone has entered by foot or not."

"In the past, only lower lineage vampires would come into town and were easily tracked. Most of them were generally weak with no special abilities, making easy targets.

"If they made a home here, I would have to wait until they came out at night to feed to attack them. I always wondered if the parent of the vampire kept tabs on where their children went and if they got upset when they were exterminated. Maybe that's how my legend started."

"And Alo . . ." I caught myself. I'd been thinking about her so much, I almost said her name out loud. "Um . . . Bettina's clan? How come they were so hard to catch?"

"They flew into the city, so the scent has nothing to cling to, like following foot prints in the sand washed away by the sea. Plus, they were very careful about where they went and hid in multiple locations. All of them must have been close to the royal family to have so much power. That's why I've been concerned about a potential backlash. It's odd no one has come to avenge their deaths.

We wiped out a whole coven."

He looked down at me, waiting for my reaction, and I looked away, trying to appear somber. I knew too much and didn't want him to notice how uncomfortable this deception was for me.

"Yeah, I guess we did," I mumbled, biting my lip.

"You don't have to be afraid, Julia. Honestly, I've been in worse situations and I've had a lot of practice. I can handle this." He pulled me tighter to his body and kissed the top of my head. He'd misinterpreted my reaction for fear, but that didn't ease my conscience any.

What a tangled web we weave . . .

I sighed.

"Are you okay?" he asked while petting my hair.

"Yes. It's just . . ." I fumbled for the right word. " . . .scary I guess. Not knowing, waiting for the other shoe to drop so to speak."

"Well, you have me and the talisman, so you'll be okay."

I reached up and felt the necklace resting in the hollow of my throat. It comforted me knowing that if anything ever did happen, apart from Nicholas, I'd be safe. But I did live in fear of how the truth would play out.

"Have you ever thought to ask your Dad for help?"

Nicholas instantly stiffened and grew cold inside.

"Only as a last resort—" he mumbled.

I worried about this. Something must have happened to strain their relationship. I knew they talked occasionally, but doubted any true sentiments were ever exchanged. I was starting to believe that maybe Nicholas blamed his dad for his half-breed issues, but I didn't feel comfortable asking him about it.

"It's fine, Julia. Really. I can handle it."

I decided to trust his judgment and not to push any further. He seemed confident enough.

We sat in silence, but with each passing minute, his confidence slowly flickered to worry; I'm sure because I wasn't talking. But I didn't know what else to say. I hated the impending doom.

I let my mind wander through all the events of our earlier interactions instead, like I did everyday. In order to never forget, I'd run through the details—unable to journal about it. Nicholas strictly forbade me to write down anything that would reveal the true nature of his identity. And then I remembered.

"Um . . . I was wondering. Do you still have that note I wrote?" I uttered a little embarrassed.

"I do," he said, taking a worn piece of paper out of his pocket.

"You carry this with you?" I said surprised, looking into his enchanting eyes with astonishment.

"Yes," he said, feeling nostalgic. "For a while, it was my only connection to you even though you were mad at me in it. But that was because you felt the same way about me as I did you."

I blushed and looked away, feeling a little ridiculous and then gently took the note from him and unfolded it.

Dear Nicholas,

I'm writing to say goodbye . . .

I don't know what happened to me after I met you, but something inside me changed and I can't stop thinking about you or what happened. Why did you promise to come see me when you never intended to? I thought you were different. And when you didn't show, I thought maybe there was a good reason for you not to come. But after the way you treated me in front of the theater, I knew I was wrong. You had no right to be rude to me. You're just like all the other boys who like to flirt and make promises they NEVER INTEND TO KEEP! But the worst of it is that I can't seem to get you out of my mind, and something inside keeps pushing me to care for you. But I refuse to give in to your fake charm and I will learn to shut it off.

So, for what it's worth, I'm done with you. I will be forever thankful you saved me. But that's it. I won't let you hurt me anymore and from this point forward, I will stop missing you and wishing you'll

come back into my life!
     GOODBYE and good riddance.
     ~ Julia

I folded it back up, studying the wrinkled corners. The note looked like it had been reopened many times. A large part of me wanted to rip it into tiny pieces, erasing how silly I'd been. Instead, I played with the paper.

"I was tempted the next morning to leave a note on your car to say sorry, but I chickened out," he said while putting his hand over my fidgety fingers, holding them still, taking the note back.

The day after came to mind. I'd forgotten about the anonymous note I found on the ground, left by mistake. Deep down inside, I'd hoped he'd left that note for me. Maybe the gesture kept me holding on until I could discover the truth.

Within my own pocket, I took out the piece of wood I'd carried around ever since that day and held it in my palm, reminiscing. Suddenly, he cupped his hand under mine and placed the other half in my palm, fitting them together.

"I wondered what this was," he said sweetly, taking the newly formed wooden token closer to read the inscription.

"I needed a memento," I said with a chuckle. "I guess that seems funny, since I was trying to say goodbye."

"Well, I'm glad you couldn't."

"Me too." I blushed.

"Well, then I'll keep your half and you can keep mine for a while—" He handed me his half, forming our hands into a ball. "—and make a promise."

I looked again into his lustrous eyes.

"A promise?"

"That no matter what, we'll always trust each other, even when it seems unexplainable. No matter what I have to do or say, I'll always be loyal to you. From now until the end of time."

Relief flooded my heart while I turned over his half in my hand. I could finally let go of my worries and trust that one day he'd understand. The time would come when the timing would be right. He'd promised not to jump to conclusions.

"Good, because I don't think I could ever let you go."

Suddenly, his lips were tight on mine, gentle yet fierce, a kiss that launched an unquenchable yearning with an intensity of force I could never have dreamed of. My trembling fingers reached for his face to pull him closer, his arm drawing me in at the small of my back. I swooned, because for the first time I felt just one emotion shared between us.

Love.

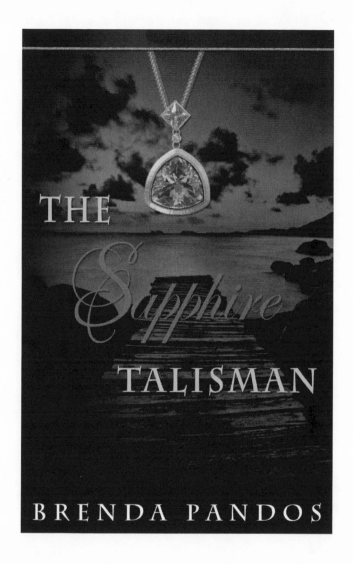

The Sapphire Talisman, the second novel in Brenda Pandos' addictive TALISMAN series, where destiny rules over desires, is on sale now.

Read on for a special excerpt.

Chapter One

I sat in the waiting room together with my older brother Luke, my dad, and Erin, my uncle's sister, in upholstered chairs with wooden arms, my internal experience vastly different from anyone else's. Our scenery consisted of four white walls adorned with pastel flower paintings, and a TV hung in the corner, playing a late night talk show. My eyes kept drifting to the large red "NO SMOKING" and "NO CELL PHONE USE" signs, reading them over and over, wishing I didn't have the ability to read other people's emotions, especially in a maternity ward. When another wave of pain would arrive, I'd close my eyes and place my hands under my legs to grip the edge of the chair where no one could see, desperately trying to ignore the stifling agony. Relief only came when invisible explosions of incredible elation burst forth, sweetly followed by Brahms lullaby tinkling throughout the corridors.

With each passing episode though, I hoped the next birth announcement would be for us. Suddenly, my uncle John appeared in the hallway, dressed in a blue smock and booties, overflowing with love.

"It's a girl!" he exclaimed.

We all jumped to our feet simultaneously. The wait was finally over.

"A girl," Dad said in jubilation while putting his arm around my shoulder.

"Yes." John's eyes were moist. "Our little Emma Mae is finally here. Come. Jo would like to see everyone."

When John turned, motioning for everyone to follow, I nudged Luke in the ribs. We'd had a bet whether it was a boy or girl. Luke's wrong guess meant he'd be doing dishes for a week.

Josephine, my aunt and somewhat adoptive mom, had invited

me to be a part of the birth and initially I had agreed until I found out she was going to give birth in the hospital without drugs. There was no way, with that much pain, I'd be able to compose myself and not let everyone in the room know my talent—the secret ability I'd acquired at age five, right after my mother's mysterious disappearance. Though I didn't actually feel the pain itself, it seemed real enough to overwhelm me. Pain, of all the emotions, was very distracting. Later, after watching a documentary of a real birth in Health Class, I had to gently tell Jo I didn't think I could handle it. She was disappointed, but understood.

I figured, *if* I ever had kids of my own in the future, I'd definitely get drugs just in case someone in the room next to me decided to go without like Jo did. I wanted to avoid that kind of pain at all costs. But with a half-vampire as a boyfriend, even if we did get married someday, I didn't know if having children would be a possibility.

"Jo did so well . . . without any drugs . . . her nurse kept saying she was a natural at it," John said breathlessly, as he padded down the hallway in his slippered feet.

Part of me was glad to hear everything went well, but another was annoyed he kept telling the details—her story. I just wanted him to lead us and keep his mouth shut.

We arrived at her door and walked in. Jo looked slightly tired but gushed a beautiful sea of love while holding a little pink bundle in her arms. Her eyes were glistening as she invited us to come in.

I got to Jo's side first, wringing my hands awkwardly, unsure if she'd let me hold Emma. Without a word, Jo passed me the baby. I smiled down at my new cousin.

Emma's peace surrounded me instantly while she slept, taking me to a utopia I'd craved all night sitting in the waiting room. Faintly, in the background, I heard Jo fill her sister-in-law, Erin and Dad in on what happened. Luke stood by John, slightly grossed out at the details.

A little tuft of black hair stuck out from under Emma's hat, framing a wrinkled forehead. Tiny lashes rimmed closed eyes, rosy cheeks surrounded a button nose and little puckered lips,—she looked like a cherub. I remembered back to the first time I'd felt Emma's emotions. Sometime during Jo's second trimester, Emma's contentedness began to compete with Jo's general motherly woes. Emma loved her sanctuary within the protection of Jo's womb. Only yesterday did I sense something new—a growing disquiet. I wasn't surprised to hear after I left, Jo's water had broken.

"Five more minutes," a heavy-set brunette nurse called through the open doorway. "Then you'll all have to leave."

Erin's agitation increased and I sighed, gently passing Emma to her. She'd been anxiously awaiting her turn. Without Emma's sweet aura to hide within, I suddenly wanted to go. Hospitals drained me.

As if sensing my discomfort, Jo's hand caught mine and she pulled me into a hug. The embrace comforted my spirit.

"How are you?" she asked quietly.

"Me?" I laughed while shaking my head. "Uh, you just gave birth. How are you?"

Jo squeezed my hand a little tighter. "If only I could share how wonderful I feel."

I glanced away and grinned. I already knew.

"—but I want you to remember, while Emma is my real child, she's not going to replace you or your brother. I still consider you both my children too, you know."

"I know," I whispered, leaning into her shoulder.

She'd become our mother when Dad moved us from L.A. to Scotts Valley after our real Mom disappeared, shortly before my sixth birthday. But, unbeknownst to any of us at the time, she hadn't disappeared; she was murdered. I'd just learned the truth a few months ago, when Nicholas saved me a second time from an unseen stalker—a vampire. The first time, I was lucky while my mother was not. Nicholas, too late to help her, prevented the bloodsucking vampire from taking my life as well. In his guilt, he vowed to secretly protect me always.

But with my second encounter, Nicholas was no longer able to keep his presence or his identity a secret after I learned the truth. We'd been dating ever since.

Jo kissed the top of my head. Her loving tenderness covered a multitude of longing and sadness for my mother.

"So proud of you, Jo," Dad called across the room. "Emma is beautiful."

A general murmur of consensus rang through the group. Being between two ecstatic parents and a contented baby put me in the perfect Bermuda triangle of love. Everything seemed perfect until *Attila the Hun* came back.

"Visiting hours are now over," Atilla said in a gruff voice. "My patients need their rest."

I rolled my eyes, said a quick goodbye, and waited for my family in the hall. I wanted to text Nicholas and tell him the good news anyway. I'd been keeping our relationship a secret from my family. Nicholas believed, even though I wore a vampire-thwarting talisman, anyone I loved could still be in danger of retribution since Nicholas was a hated vampire slayer. Luckily, and completely puzzling to us, none of the leaches had returned after the last attack. Whether Nicholas' reputation preceded him or they were off wreaking havoc on easier targets, we didn't know. Even still, he wanted to be extra careful.

Within two seconds his reply text came back.

- **Congrats. Leaving soon?** <
- **Yes. 30 mins. 3**
- **Great. Sleep tight.**

I bit my lip to stop the huge grin from forming upon my lips. Sleep tight didn't mean good night; it was code for us to meet outside my bedroom window on the roof ledge later, something we did almost every night. The < from his text and the 3 from mine represented a heart when put together, reminding us of the one I'd carved into a piece of symbolic wood that brought us together, but broke when I carved it, both of us keeping a half. For sometime, I'd suspected my dad frequently checked my text messages online, so we'd resorted to code.

I read his messages several times before deleting them—another precaution I decided to take after the last attack. If another vampire ever stole my phone again, they'd never know who I consorted with.

I rested my head on the back of the seat during the drive home, relieved to finally be free from the birthing tormentors. Dad and Luke wordlessly sat in the front, all of us emanating a tired peace. I held the talisman that hung around my neck, anxious to get home for my good-night kiss. Our nightly roof-top meetings were risky, but I was confident that I would feel if someone had awakened, and was close enough to catch us.

Dad parked in the garage and I feigned needing something out of my car so I could see if Nicholas was here yet. The crisp night air refreshed my tired senses as I walked across the dewy grass. Once I rounded the corner, I felt a tiny bit disappointed when I discovered he hadn't arrived. I wondered what might be taking him so long when my phone vibrated.

-Give me 20. <

-3

I grinned as my heart beat a little faster, knowing the wait was only 20 minutes more. Maybe he had a surprise for me.

Just before I opened the front door to go inside, I noticed movement in the shrubs next to the porch swing. I knew it had to be an animal, since I couldn't sense any human emotion.

"Aladdin, is that you?" I whispered, keeping my distance, worried to get too close in case it was a raccoon. I squinted to see evidence of our tuxedo cat, Aladdin, when another cat appeared—pure black with icy blue eyes.

One I knew. One that wasn't really a cat.

I froze.

"She's back."

ACKNOWLEDGEMENTS

First and foremost, I give thanks to God for giving me the talent to express my imagination on paper and people like you to share it with. Secondly, I want to thank my husband, Mike, for his love and patience. You always encourage me to dream big dreams and have given me the priceless gift of time to create, design and imagine. I owe you everything. Thirdly, to Mom and Dad, Jana, and my mother-in-law, for your encouragement to keep going and being kind to my ego after reading bad manuscripts. Nate, my trailer kicks booty! Ryan, thanks for the use of your couch during the day to get away and write.

Pookie, I <3 hot vampires too. Pam, if it weren't for your kindness after reading the first horrific chapter and seeing potential, I'm not sure if I would have continued on. To S.M., for your inspiration. To the girls at PSP-Paradise, specifically Tracy, Mingo, Adry, Kelly and Nancy who have stuck with me through thick and thin, you all rock! To my first readers, Grandma Helen, Savannah, Robin, Katie, Dee Dee, Marla, Joanne, Renata and others who read early manuscripts; your enthusiasm kept me going. Dori, I will forever be in your debt. Thank you for plucking me out of the sea at *Authonomy* and giving me endless encouragement and wonderful feedback—your edits made my story so much better. I can't wait for the world to read your legal thriller. Lori, for painstakingly proofreading my final copy, offering valuable feedback and lending moral support in MOPS. I thank you. And to all my other friends at MOPS, your support has been priceless! Abra, thank you for becoming my friend, mentoring me and being a fabulous encourager in the fantasy young adult genre. May we continue to enrich the world with wonderful stories and empower new authors to reach for the stars. To everyone else, who've given me words of praise along the way, become a Facebook fan and maybe even purchased a book; without you all, I'd not be here today! I wrote this book for you.

To my special supporters: My mom, Renee Henry; Mom #2, Patty Radford; Brittany McCarthy; Ann Carrillo; Karylle Allick; Eric Linden; Pamela King; Mike Leibovich; Marilyn Airozo; Sarah Ramsden; Joanne Gray; Willy Kesseler; Abra Ebner; Adriana Angilella; Cindy Anderson; Helen Godsall; Colleen Lawson; Grandma Betty. Thank you for believing enough in me to invest in my book. I hope I make you proud!

You can find more information about the author and future installments at:

www.theemeraldtalisman.com **&** *brendapandos.blogspot.com*